Kay gazed at the key in bewilderment

She made no move to pick it up. Though she couldn't have explained why, she didn't want to touch it. "What's it *to*?"

Startled, Alan demanded, "Don't you know?"

She shook her head. "No."

Alan hesitated, dumbfounded. "I was sure..."

Kay wrested her gaze away from the key and looked straight at him. Her eyes were too bright, he noted—a sign that she was perhaps not as self-contained, as much in control of her emotions, as she appeared to be.

"I suppose we must talk about it. About the way Randy gave the key to you. About what happened..."

Alan saw Kay swallow hard. And suddenly he envied the late Randolph Dillard. What would it be like to be loved by a woman like Kay? Alan had considered this visit to Dillard's widow an unpleasant task to be accomplished. Now he realized he was having trouble concentrating on the situation, the key. He was entranced by the woman herself....

ABOUT THE AUTHOR

Meg Hudson often uses her travels as the basis for her novels. A recent trip to Savannah so captivated the author that she made it the setting for *Until April*, her seventeenth Superromance. To balance the antebellum charm of Georgia, she added an exciting edge of intrigue to the story. But even a New Englander like Ms Hudson would have to admit, the South can't be beaten for romance!

Books by Meg Hudson

HARLEQUIN SUPERROMANCE

174–A GIFT FROM THE SEA
188–MORE THAN A MEMORY
234–THE FOREVER PROMISE
250–A WAY TO REMEMBER
274–CHANCE MEETING
295–THE DAY BEFORE DAWN

HARLEQUIN AMERICAN ROMANCE

25–TO LOVE A STRANGER

Until April

MEG HUDSON

Harlequin Books

TORONTO • NEW YORK • LONDON
AMSTERDAM • PARIS • SYDNEY • HAMBURG
STOCKHOLM • ATHENS • TOKYO • MILAN

FORTY YEARS OF
Romance

Published May 1989

First printing March 1989

ISBN 0-373-70357-0

To my very wonderful family...
Chuck and Steve and Dick
and Kathleen and Ali and Alex...
and, perhaps most especially,
to Russ who, I suspect,
has more than a little of Alan in him

CHAPTER ONE

HE STOOD at the third-floor window of the inn, looking out over Bay Street. The dogwoods and magnolias were budding in the park across the way, the magnolias lacing the sultry April air with a fragrance evocative of the old South. Earlier, driving around the quaint squares in Savannah's historic downtown district, he'd seen white and pink and cherry-red azaleas blooming gloriously.

Alan felt as though he'd stumbled through a time warp. It had been snowing in Burlington yesterday afternoon as his plane waited at the end of the runway for takeoff clearance. He'd more than half expected the pilot to come on the intercom and announce they were heading back to the terminal. At the last moment, he'd actually prayed the flight *would* be canceled. Then they were airborne, and he knew he was committed to making a trip he dreaded.

Now he turned from the window and scanned his surroundings, well aware that he was stalling, still trying to delay making the gesture that would put him past a point of no return. Nevertheless, those surroundings were very attractive. The Randolph House was one of Savannah's many impressive renovations. The building—a nineteenth-century cotton warehouse—had been converted into an inn, with charming results. An enormous four-poster bed took center stage in his comfortable room, its cotton canopy reminiscent of bygone days. The rich cherry wood chifforobe—or was the correct term *armoire*?—stood at least eight feet high, its numerous cubbyholes, a center mirror and side closets with folding doors as intriguing as they were functional.

Alan sat down wearily in an overstuffed armchair, thought about unpacking his single suitcase and decided to defer that task till later. He was beginning to wish he'd handled this entire unpleasant matter by mail. But the problem with going that route was his conscience, which had persisted in blocking him every time he put a piece of paper in his typewriter and began to compose a letter.

At the least . . . he should have called her first. He should have had the guts to pick up the phone and say, "Mrs. Dillard? I'm Alan Johnston."

The man who lived . . . when your husband died.

That fact, always haunting his subconscious, thrust itself to the surface. Simultaneously, Alan felt the beginning of a throbbing headache.

"Tension headaches," the neurologist who'd examined him had diagnosed. "Time's the only real cure. Time, adjustment and learning to come to terms with your memories."

Those memories he was supposed to learn to live with pushed forward now, as they always did when a new headache started. Alan got to his feet, angry with himself, determined not to give in, not to let himself relive that blazingly hot, early July time of horror on the other side of the world, almost nine months ago to the day.

Pulling himself together with an effort, he headed for the small elevator off the third-floor foyer. Downstairs in the main lobby, he took a deep breath, donned that shield of hard-won composure that was like invisible armor and approached the registration desk.

KATHERINE DILLARD'S private apartment occupied a rear quarter of the Randolph House's third floor. At ten-thirty, sunlight was streaking through her partially drawn window shades, the golden motes freckling the pages of the accounts book she was working on. The effect was distracting in a rather pleasant way. The sun sprinkles made her want to push her ledgers to one side and play hooky. She could drive over to Tybee Island and wander barefoot along the beach. Or...

The phone at her elbow jangled. She picked up the receiver, heard Francey's soft voice ask, "Aunt Kay?"

Kay fought back a surge of irritation. How many times, since Francey had come to work as a front-desk clerk at the Randolph House, had she told her niece by marriage that during business hours she was to be referred to as Mrs. Dillard?

For that matter, she reflected wryly, how many times had she wished she'd given her brother-in-law, Gerard Dillard, a firm negative when a desk-clerk position had become vacant and he'd asked her to let Francey have a chance at it.

"Aunt Kay?" Francey queried again.

As owner and manager of the Randolph House, Kay Dillard had been up since seven. She had coped with her temperamental, but excellent, chef, listened to her housekeeper present her with a list of problems to be remedied, set straight an electrician who was attempting to overcharge her, heard the pitches of two salesmen from whom she'd decided not to buy anything and talked on the phone with a close friend, who like most of her friends was always asking her for lunch or bridge or dinner, and simply couldn't understand her almost constant refusals.

She'd dealt with more than enough in three and a half hours. This wasn't the moment to give Francey another lesson in proper business etiquette.

"What is it, Francey?" Kay asked, summoning an elusive patience.

"There's a gentleman here who wants to see you," Francey said. "One of our guests. He says it's important."

Kay lowered her voice in case the "gentleman" in question might be near enough the front desk to overhear her part of this conversation. "Do you think it's really important, Francey?" she asked. "Don't you think it's something you can handle yourself?" So often the matters Francey called her about were things the girl was perfectly capable of dealing with by herself. And part of the reason for allowing Francey to work at the inn was to try to teach her to stand on her own feet.

"Just a sec," Francey said, and briefly went off the line. She returned to say, "His name is Alan Johnston, Aunt Kay, and he says he really has to see you personally."

Alan Johnston. Not an especially unusual name, yet...

Kay had the odd feeling the name should mean something to her. Something significant. But the significance escaped her.

She sighed. "Tell Mr. Johnston I'll be right down," she instructed.

Reluctantly Kay went out into the foyer and pressed the button for the elevator. As she waited, she studied the effect of this gathering point from which corridors radiated out to the other rooms and suites on the third floor. The furnishings were not entirely antique, but the reproductions interspersed among the genuine articles were so good that they would fool all but the most astute expert. A huge rose medallion bowl filled with potpourri centered on a copy of a Duncan Phyfe table to the right of the elevator. Kay stirred the mixture with a long slender finger. A spicy aroma wafted upward, pungent, sweet and nostalgic.

The elevator slowly cranked downstairs. Kay stepped into the main lobby, which was furnished like a drawing room in an antebellum mansion, then stopped short as she saw the man who must be Alan Johnston standing next to the front desk, talking to Francey. Staring at him in profile, she felt a sudden sense of panic. She still didn't know who he was, yet there definitely was something familiar about him. He was tall, broad shouldered but too thin. The jacket of his gray suit hung on him as if it had been cut to fit a larger man. The cloth sagged. He sagged, too...in a way. She saw him straighten his shoulders as Francey said, "Oh, there's Mrs. Dillard."

Suddenly they were face-to-face.

Kay could have sworn that he flinched, and that puzzled her. She found herself focusing on his eyes, light gray eyes, weary eyes, eyes that at the moment were astonishingly pain filled as he gazed down at her.

Why was this man hurting? And why did she have this crazy feeling she knew him or, at least should know him? He seemed to be waiting for her to recog-

nize him. Yet she sensed his apprehension, his dread
of that recognition, and was all the more mystified.

"Mrs. Dillard?" he asked.

Kay nodded.

"I'm Alan Johnston," he offered. And waited.

When, after a long second, she didn't speak, he
asked, "Is there somewhere we could talk?"

Kay didn't attempt to hide her perplexity. She said,
"Francey told me you're a guest. Is there a problem
with your accommodations, Mr. Johnston?"

"No, no," he said hastily. "I'm delighted with my
room."

"Then what is it?"

"It's a private matter, Mrs. Dillard," he answered,
then asked again, "Could we find a quiet place to talk,
please?"

Kay hesitated. There was a tiny office behind the
reception desk, but they might be interrupted there.
She considered her own apartment, but she had absolutely no intention of taking him *there*. She made a
quick decision. "Let's use the lounge," she suggested. "It's not open to the public at this hour."

He nodded. "Fine."

She led the way across the lobby to the Buccaneer
Lounge, which was tucked into a corner of the Randolph House. Kay had deliberately kept it small,
wanting to create an intimate setting where people
could relax. At the end of the room, a curving flight
of steps descended to the Buccaneer Restaurant, already one of the most popular restaurants in a city
famed for fine eating places.

Kay closed the door behind them, selected the first
in a series of circular booths in the deserted cocktail

lounge, then asked, before sitting down, "Would you care for some coffee, Mr. Johnston?"

"No, not just now, thank you," he said politely. "Maybe later."

"As you wish," she agreed.

She sat at one edge of the circular booth. Alan Johnston sat opposite her. She waited for him to speak, but he didn't. Instead, he clasped his hands on the table and stared at them. He had good hands, she noticed—long strong fingers, their nails neatly filed. His hands, in fact, were the best-groomed things about him. For the rest . . . he came close to being shabby.

His thick, sandy-brown hair was graying at the temples and was at the shaggy stage—not by design, Kay suspected, but from neglect. He had a nice face. More than nice, actually. If he spruced up a bit, gained a few pounds, got some rest and didn't look even more tense than she felt, he'd be downright attractive, she conceded—then had to smile at her off-the-cuff evaluation.

Alan saw her smile and was startled. He'd already been floored by her appearance. He'd had no preconceived ideas about what Katherine Dillard would be like, so it was pointless to say that she was entirely different than he'd expected. Still . . . she was.

She was younger, for one thing. Despite the strain he saw etched on her face—and he was an expert on strain—Mrs. Dillard was both youthful and beautiful. That mass of dark hair. Cameo features. A camellia skin. Eyes as blue as the Savannah sky. She looked to Alan as if she might have just stepped from the pages of *Gone with the Wind*. Even her swirly-skirted blue dress had a Southern-belle appearance about it.

He was forty-two. He guessed that Randolph Dillard had been about his age. But Katherine looked several years younger.

He knew she was waiting for him to say something, and he couldn't blame her for the edge of impatience he heard in her voice when she finally asked, "What is it you wish to see me about, Mr. Johnston?"

Alan looked at her, started to speak and lost his voice. The loss, he knew from experience, was psychosomatic. Physically, he could speak. Mentally, he was blocked. A very real, very frustrating situation.

He managed with difficulty to say, "If you don't mind, could we have that coffee you spoke about?"

Her annoyance showed briefly, and he couldn't blame her for that, either. Then she nodded, made a graceful exit and returned after a minute. "The coffee will be here directly. Look, Mr. Johnston..."

"Yes?" Alan croaked.

"Are you all right? That's to say, is it laryngitis you're suffering from? If so, perhaps a soothing lozenge..."

He shook his head. He wished he were able to come out and state the simple truth, but he couldn't. He still cringed away from actually saying to anyone, "It's nerves, that's all." But that, of course, was exactly what it was. Like the tension headaches, the frequent bouts of insomnia, the horrible, recurring nightmares when he *was* able to sleep.

"It'll pass," he rasped.

A young black woman wearing a becoming red-and-white uniform brought the coffee. Katherine Dillard poured, asked Alan if he wanted cream and sugar. He shook his head and accepted a steaming cup from her.

The coffee nearly scorched his throat, which was exactly what he needed.

After a moment he managed huskily, "Mrs. Dillard...you don't recognize my name, do you?"

Kay hesitated, then admitted, "No. Not really. Yet...I keep feeling I've heard it before."

"I'm sure you have," Alan said gravely. He mustered his courage, took the plunge. "Mrs. Dillard," he began again, "last July I was on the same plane on which your husband was taken hostage."

Kay was picking up the sugar bowl as he spoke, and involuntarily her fingers tensed. She clutched the fragile porcelain handle and it took all her effort to maintain her composure. Inwardly, she was shaking as if she were in the grip of a terrible fever. She wondered if her teeth weren't chattering audibly. She kept hearing, again and again, what this man had just said to her. At the same time, she tried to pretend she hadn't heard him at all.

It was the quality of his silence that eventually made her look across at him. What he *wasn't* saying was drawing her toward him like an invisible strand of fine steel wire.

She met his eyes and had a sudden preview of hell. She heard him mumble brokenly, "My God, I'm so sorry!"

"Please, Mr. Johnston," she protested. Tried to think of what to say next. Managed, "Were you also taken hostage?"

"Yes, I was."

She met his eyes again, and the torture in their depths was something hard to witness. She suddenly found herself wanting to comfort him, even though he was a total stranger, even though she couldn't imagine why he'd come here today. Certainly he must have gone through enough last July not to want to invoke the past. Certainly *she* had.

She tried very hard to keep her voice level as she said, "Then you must have been with Randy when..."

"Yes."

"Is that why you've come here? To...to tell me about it, to say you're sorry? What I mean, I suppose, is that...nine months have passed. And I see no reason why you should need to tell me you're sorry. After all, you were not responsible for what happened to Randy."

"Responsible, no," he conceded.

"You and he and a number of other people were in the hands of fanatics," Kay continued steadily. "It's a miracle any of you came out of it alive."

Rather indistinctly, Alan Johnston mumbled, "It was...a toss of the coin."

She stared at him. "What are you saying?"

"Not an actual toss of the coin," he amended, "but it amounted to the same thing. I was sitting next to your husband in the plane. I was on the aisle. The window seat was unoccupied. We were on the ground for hours. Overnight, as it turned out, while the hijackers negotiated their demands, including fuel, so they could take off again. Anyway, I was sitting on the aisle and your husband was next to me," he repeated.

"Yes?" The question was forced out of Kay. What she wished was that she could tell him she didn't want to hear this. But those words wouldn't come.

"It was...an incredibly tense situation," Alan Johnston went on. "There was not a single moment when we were without a gun pointing at us." He paused, then continued heavily, "Come daybreak, they threatened to shoot one hostage each hour on the hour if their demands were not met. We were all bone tired, exhausted. I asked to use a bathroom, and one of the hijackers accompanied me."

"And?"

"The hour apparently struck while I was in the bathroom. So...they chose your husband. If I had been there, in the seat on the aisle, they probably would have taken me. So you see..."

Kay's throat had gone dry. She rose suddenly and went behind the bar. She found a bottle of brandy and two small glasses and poured out two shots.

Alan Johnston accepted the brandy, swallowed it and said, "Thanks." But his voice was still husky as he commented, "When your receptionist called you earlier I was afraid you might recognize my name and refuse to meet with me."

Kay was shivering inwardly, yet at the same time she felt as if she were burning up. She said, "I suppose I should have recognized your name. Maybe I did, sub-consciously." She was beginning to realize how many memories she'd been blocking out. She asked, "How many hostages were there?"

"Forty-eight." It was a number Alan would never forget. Forty-eight, and forty-six had come out alive. Only Katherine Dillard's husband and an elderly man—a funny little man from Dayton, Ohio, who said he'd been a circus clown—had paid the terrible, final price.

"Forty-eight," Kay mused. She shuddered, then admitted, "As I've said, your name did...nag at me. When I saw you standing by the front desk there was something vaguely familiar about you...."

"I had a beard by the time I was released," Alan said. He fingered his chin. "We were locked up for twenty-six days after we reached the island. Kept in a shed near the airfield." He looked up and added quickly, "I'm sorry, Mrs. Dillard. I didn't mean to get into details." He nearly added that the part about the island wasn't of any real importance to her, anyway. Her husband had been dead long before they reached the island....

Kay listened to what he was saying and nearly snapped, Then why did you start this? But she held back the words even though she resented what he'd been telling her. For nine months, she'd been trying to put the pieces of her life back together. She'd gone ahead with her plans to finish renovating the Randolph House and managed to open the inn on schedule six months ago. She'd put all her energies into the inn, the cocktail lounge, the restaurant. People said she was brave. Sometimes she wanted to tell them it wasn't bravery she was acting from but desperation.

Now, nine months later, she was just beginning to make a new life for herself outside the inn. She was starting to accept an occasional invitation to a small dinner with close friends. She was thinking that maybe after a time she'd begin to entertain a bit herself— maybe a cocktail party here at the inn, for a few special people. She knew she was too young to be alone forever. She needed companionship, though she thought only of group companionship. She had no desire to become seriously involved with a man again. In fact, she shrank away from the thought of ever again concentrating her considerable emotional energy on any one man.

Slowly she'd been coming out of a very dark cocoon. But now Alan Johnston was making her feel as if she were about to plunge back into blackness. He was forcing her to remember things she didn't want to remember. Telling her about things she didn't want to know about.

Her resentment was evident in her voice as she asked coldly, "Why did you come here, Mr. Johnston?"

To Alan, her tone penetrated in a way that reminded him of the barbed wire around the airfield where they had been imprisoned in an old canteen after the plane reached the island. Once he had tried to escape, only to be recaptured very quickly. But a piece of rusty barbed wire had torn across his hand and he'd had a nasty infection afterward. Fortunately he healed well. There was only a slight scar left. Still, it was a reminder. As was Katherine Dillard's tone of voice.

He said quietly. "I didn't want to come here, Mrs. Dillard."

She'd been staring at nothing in particular. Now she focused on him, her deep blue eyes wide and questioning. She was lovely... beautiful, Alan thought. Strangely, her beauty hurt.

He said, "Nine months have gone by...."

"I'm well aware of that."

"Yes, I know you are. I mention the time lapse because...there's a significance to it you don't yet know about."

Watching him closely, Kay saw that Alan Johnston seemed to be getting a new grip on himself. Maybe the brandy had helped. More likely, she suspected, it was an innate fortitude, a strength that had enabled him to endure the ordeal.

When the plane had first been hijacked, she'd watched every television newscast she could. The story was headline news, and the networks had covered the ongoing crisis accordingly. But then, once she knew Randy was dead, she'd shut out the news—until she heard that the hostages who'd been spared had been released and were coming home. A few days later—perhaps it was a week—she'd not been able to resist turning on the *Today* show to watch an interview with several of the hostages.

That was it, Kay realized. That was where she'd heard Alan Johnston's name and seen his face. Except then it had been a bearded and far more haggard face.

She said slowly, "It has been painful for me to have you ... rake this up. But I can see I've been thinking entirely of myself. It must be even more painful for you...."

"Well," he admitted, "it's something I usually try not to think about ... at least consciously. Subconsciously I'm afraid the memory still lives with me. And will, I fear, for a long time to come. But that's neither here nor there. During the time we were together in the plane, your husband and I—" Alan broke off abruptly.

"Please go on," Kay prompted.

"Well, your husband and I managed to talk a fair bit. Under circumstances like that, people tend to talk about things they'd never get into ordinarily on such short acquaintance. We both knew what we were up against. There was no rationality to the hijackers. Nothing human about them that could be appealed to. So we were very conscious of the fact there was a strong possibility we'd never leave the plane alive."

Kay could feel her pulse throbbing again. She pressed her fingers against the hollow in her throat. "Please," she implored, despite herself.

"I'm sorry," Alan said softly. "I'm sorry, but I have to do what he asked me to."

"What?" Kay's eyes were glazed as she spoke; she felt slightly nauseated.

"Just before I left my seat that day, your husband managed to give me something," Alan said. "It's a miracle the hijacker guarding us didn't see him do it. Actually, he—your husband, that is—slipped the object in my pocket. I started to speak, but his eyes warned me to remain silent. Then after a moment he managed to say in a very low voice—without looking at me—'My wife's name is Katherine. She lives in Savannah. If I don't make it, in the name of God take this to her, will you? But not until next April. Early next April...'"

Kay sat stock-still as Alan Johnston finished, "You don't refuse requests at moments like that. I couldn't refuse his. So, now it's April. And I've brought you this."

He fumbled in his coat pocket, found what he was searching for and clenched it in his fist. Then he opened his fist and let the object fall to the table.

Kay found herself staring at a dull, bronze key.

CHAPTER TWO

Kay gazed down at the key in bewilderment. She made no move to pick it up. Though she could not have explained why, she didn't want to touch it.

"What is it?" she asked numbly.

Alan's lips twisted. "A key," he said.

"Oh, please! What I meant was ... what's it *to*?"

Startled, Alan demanded, "Don't you know?"

She shook her head. "No."

Alan, hesitated, dumbfounded. "I was sure ..." he murmured.

Kay wrested her gaze away from the key and looked straight at him. Her eyes were too bright, he noted— a sign that she was perhaps not as self-contained, as much in control of her emotions, as she appeared to be.

She had gorgeous eyes. Their color reminded him of the deep blue hydrangeas that had bloomed every night in the yard of his grandmother's house in Vermont. The house had been sold a long time back. Recently it had come up for sale again and he'd nearly bought it. But he had fought the impulse, asking himself wryly what a confirmed bachelor in his position would do with an old Victorian structure that looked like something out of a Gothic novel.

He forced his attention back to the matter at hand. He said, "Your husband was adamant about entrusting the key to me and getting my promise to deliver it to you, Mrs. Dillard. It's hard to believe you don't recognize it. I don't mean to imply I'm doubting you," he added hastily. "It's just that I assumed it was something that would..."

"Ring bells for me?" Kay suggested.

"Yes, I suppose so."

"It doesn't," she said flatly.

Alan saw her lips tremble, a small, telltale sign that made her seem very vulnerable. He had a sudden, crazy impulse to move around to the other side of the circular booth and take her in his arms so he could comfort her. He could imagine nestling his chin against her soft dark hair as he held her and murmured consoling little phrases in her ear. The idea of her softness, her warmth, in addition to the wafting floral scent she wore, was an aphrodisiac.

He sat up straight, astonished by his reaction to her, and asked in a voice gone hoarse again, "Do you suppose I could have another brandy?"

"Of course," Kay agreed, instinctively becoming the hospitable Southern hostess. She brought the bottle from the bar and refilled his glass, but left her own empty.

She was grace in motion, Alan thought, as she set the brandy bottle on the table and resumed her seat opposite him. She moved like a dancer. He wondered if she'd ever been a dancer. He wondered what she was like, really like. He knew he'd principally seen a facade thus far, and that made the occasional glimpses he was getting of a vibrant, sensual yet sensitive woman all the more provocative.

Kay finally punctured the silence between them by saying reluctantly, "I suppose we must talk about this."

"About the key?"

"About the way Randy gave it to you. About what happened...then. I suppose I need to know about that if I'm to make any sense of this," she said, her eyes sweeping over the key again.

Alan saw her swallow hard. And suddenly he envied the late Randolph Dillard. What would it be like to be loved by a woman like Katherine Dillard? To have her as your wife, your partner?

It was an effort to concentrate on the situation between them, rather than solely on Mrs. Randolph Dillard herself. But unpleasant though it was going to be for both of them, they needed to explore the circumstances leading to her husband's death. Alan needed to retrace what had happened and to search his memory in the hope that something Dillard had said to him in those last moments might contain a clue he'd temporarily forgotten. A clue that would open a door. Or a locker. Or a car, or trunk, or...something. As he looked at the key, it appeared more and more anonymous.

He'd had the key in his possession for nine months, but he'd never really studied it and had never wanted to. He'd kept it in a box at the back of a desk drawer, where it could not be mislaid but where it would be out of his mind most of the time. It represented an unpleasant task to be accomplished—this visit to Randolph Dillard's widow.

Now, on an impulse, he picked it up and scrutinized it. It was ordinary looking. Dull brass. Medium size. Nothing engraved on it, no letters, no numbers.

Nothing at all distinctive. It looked neither brand-new nor antique.

He glanced at Katherine, saw she was eyeing him curiously. He put the key back down, then said, "As I mentioned earlier, your husband and I were sitting next to each other when the plane was hijacked. When we landed the first time, because we were low on fuel..."

He could feel his voice getting hoarse again.

"Yes, go on," Kay encouraged him.

Alan reached for the brandy. Then he said, "Well, it was incredibly hot that day. It was stifling in the plane. We were ordered to pull down all the window shades. Remember, we had no idea exactly where we were...either then, or later on the island." Guesses, of course, but that was all.

"Anyway, as I said, it was terribly hot. They shut off the air-conditioning. The hijackers, that is." He paused, but Kay didn't say anything, so he continued. "We were sweltering. Your husband and I were both wearing suits. We soon took off our jackets. Our shirts were soaked through, and the material clung to our skin. We tried to joke about it. I told your husband he should be used to such heat, being a Southerner. Whereas I was a Yankee, used to the cold."

Alan was remembering Randolph Dillard as he spoke. Tall, terrific physique, smooth dark hair, dark eyes. Good-looking, charismatic personality. He and Katherine must have made a striking couple.

"We were there through the day, through the night, while the hijackers negotiated their demands. At one point they released twenty passengers in exchange for fuel. Those of us who were left knew we were the—

how shall I say it—the *chosen* ones," Alan decided, deliberately mocking the word.

"Even after they got the fuel," he continued, "we stayed on the ground. I guess the hijackers were hoping their other demands would be met. It was a long night. The hijackers themselves blew hot and cold. Sometimes we'd be told to shut up, told we'd be shot if we spoke a word. Other times they seemed to become immersed in their own problems and didn't pay much attention to us. At those moments, when we had the chance to talk, we began to confide the way people do under, well . . . life-threatening circumstances. I found out your husband was in the textile business."

"He was, yes."

"And that he'd been in Egypt buying a special kind of cotton fabric."

"Yes."

"He started talking about Savannah. He was very proud of this city. I gathered his roots here went back a long way."

"Yes, they did."

"He spoke about his home here, about you." Alan reached again for the brandy. Just now, the fiery liquid was medicinal, keeping his voice. He doubted he could have talked without it.

Mustering determination, he went on. "Finally it started to get light outside. The terrorist who seemed to be in charge told us the negotiations weren't proceeding well. He said they were going to have to shoot one hostage each hour in order to make their intentions clear. At that, your husband leaned over to me and whispered, 'If that happens, I expect I will be among the first.' I tried to get him off that track. I asked him, 'Why you? Why not me?' He shook his head, and said, 'The tall one, the one with the reddish hair. Every now and then he eyes me, and there's something malevolent about his expression.' "

Alan paused. He'd emptied his brandy glass, but knew he couldn't risk refilling it again. Any more alcohol would go straight to his head.

"Your husband," he continued, "remained convinced about his feeling he'd been selected for execution by that particular hijacker. I have to admit it's true that in extraordinary situations one's senses go into an overdrive of sorts. You become receptive to vibes that normally would pass right by you. Maybe that's the way it was with your husband. Anyway, there was a long interval during which we were forbidden to speak. In the meantime, your husband had slipped a key ring out of his coat pocket without being noticed, and he'd been fooling with it, not jangling the keys or anything like that, which would have attracted attention. Just moving them around. I thought at the time it was just a ... kind of tension release.

"Then I felt him slip something into my pants pocket. As I told you, I started to speak but he gave me a warning look. Then..."

Katherine stirred restlessly, and again Alan couldn't bring himself to look at her directly. He said, "I'm trying to remember his exact words. It's not easy because, frankly, afterward I tried to block them and a lot of other things from my memory. But I think what he actually said to me was, 'I don't want to sound maudlin, but I'm going to ask you to do something for me, assuming you make it out of this and I don't.'

"I still hadn't dared touch the object in my pocket. His eyes warned me not to. And then he gave me his instructions."

Alan slumped back, feeling exhausted. "I didn't know it was a key he'd put in my pocket until much later," he said. "If I had, I might have had the chance to ask him what it opened. As it was, at that point I saw the redheaded hijacker approaching. So I told your husband I'd do as he asked. He started to say, 'Tell her...' but that's as far as he got. The hijacker brandished his weapon in our faces and told us to shut up.

"Shortly after that, another hijacker accompanied me to the bathroom. When I returned, your husband was gone. A second or two later I heard a shot. They'd taken him into the first-class section. The rest of us were herded toward the rear of the plane. I... never saw him again, Mrs. Dillard."

For a second, Kay felt icy cold. Then she broke out in a sweat. She touched her forehead and felt moisture. Her hands were clammy and her throat parched. She became saturated with an odd mixture of numbness and sorrow. She'd felt worse when she first heard of Randy's death, she supposed. But the reaction then had been shock as much as misery. Shock combined later with agony, because their situation had been finalized by something entirely beyond her control. Death. You couldn't quibble with death....

Kay forced her thoughts away and surveyed the man sitting across from her. He looked terrible. Pale. His gray eyes shadowed not only by memories but also by pain. She was certain he was hurting physically as well as emotionally. She asked anxiously, "Is there something I can get you, Mr. Johnston?"

Alan managed a slight but very appealing smile. The smile softened his tired, rather stern face and carried to his eyes so that they seemed softened, too. Kay drew in her breath, suddenly and sharply aware of the appeal of this man. That, plus a strength of character that transcended his pain and fatigue.

"My problem's a headache, that's all," he said.

"That's all?" she echoed. "I'd say that's more than enough. Can I get you something for it?"

"Thanks, no. Before I came downstairs I took a couple of the tablets I keep for the purpose. They don't seem to be working as effectively as they usually do, though."

Kay nodded understandingly. Alan Johnston was indicating that frequent headaches were no stranger to him. She didn't wonder at that. She'd read about the aftereffects of captivity on former hostages. Headaches were probably among the least of them.

"How about some food?" she suggested. She glanced at her watch. "The Buccaneer doesn't open officially for lunch until noon. But I'm sure we can come up with something for you."

"Thanks again, but I'd rather wait till the headache subsides a bit," Alan told her. The smile returned, and now there was a surprisingly boyish quality to it. "I probably shouldn't have had that brandy on a near-empty stomach," he confessed.

"Then please...let me give you an early lunch."

"I'd rather take a rain check for a later lunch, if you'd join me."

The suggestion surprised Kay. This meeting had been so traumatic for both of them that she'd assumed Alan Johnston wanted it over, wanted to see the last of her as quickly as possible. She noted that he looked surprised himself, and she sensed the suggestion was one he hadn't intended to make. That meant she could let him off the hook, say a graceful good-bye and that would be that. Except . . .

This man was a guest at her inn. She didn't know how long a stay he'd booked. That, she'd find out as soon as she had a chance to speak to Francey at the front desk. But while he was around she couldn't simply avoid him. Not when he'd come here specifically on a mission for Randy.

That was another thing. The mission. The key.

She still hadn't touched it, still didn't want to.

Alan suddenly stood and, looking a little wobbly, said, "I think I'd better go outside and get some fresh air and exercise. Maybe walk awhile."

To Kay, he didn't seem in any shape to cover more than a few steps. She suggested gently, "Why don't you go back up to your room instead? The air-conditioning is individually controlled. I'd suggest you set it on the cool side, then lie down and get some rest. I'll send up some lunch on a tray a bit later."

"There's no need for you to do that, Mrs. Dillard."

"I'd like to," Kay said simply. She hesitated, then added, "I appreciate how difficult this must be for you, Mr. Johnston. But . . . we do need to talk some more about . . . that." She nodded toward the key, then asked impetuously, "Would you mind keeping it for the present?"

"Why . . . no," Alan said, "if you wish." He picked up the key and slipped it into his coat pocket.

"If you're free tonight," Kay persisted, "perhaps we could have dinner together? I don't want you to . . . well, I don't want you to agonize over details again. My thought is that if we just talk, maybe some things will surface by themselves."

"Perhaps," he conceded.

He was swaying slightly, and Kay wanted to reach out and steady him. She even started to extend her arm, but Alan said quickly, "I'm okay, really I am. Sometimes my sense of balance gets a bit out of whack in the midst of one of these headaches. In a couple of hours, though, I'll be good as new."

Hearing that, Kay wondered what he'd been like before last July. Before the hijacking and subsequent captivity had taken their toll and left their scars. He'd piqued her curiosity. She was discovering she wanted to know more about him. She wondered where he lived, what he did. She wondered if he was married, maybe had children.

Her curiosity surprised her. It was a long time since she'd wanted to learn more about a man she'd just met, even longer since she'd felt a tantalizing spark of something that could be defined only as attraction. Yet now, at the unlikeliest of moments, that was exactly what she was feeling.

ALAN WENT TO HIS ROOM, turned on the air-conditioning, then took off his shoes. The room was quiet, peaceful. A songbird was singing just outside his window. As he stretched out on the big four-poster bed and covered himself with a handmade quilt of heirloom quality, it occurred to him that he was behaving like a dutiful child. His friends and colleagues back in Vermont would find that amusing. Out of character, at the least.

At the front desk, Kay checked the guest register and found that Alan Johnston had booked a room for three nights. Further, he was on the third floor, her floor. He'd signed in at ten this morning—unusual, she thought, until she discovered a notation on the previous day's register that read, "Mr. Johnston called from New York. Flight delayed. Will stay the night in Jacksonville, and arrive midmorning. Would like to check in then if possible."

Next, she sought out Ernest, the porter. From him, she learned that Mr. Johnston had arrived in a rental car. The inn had a private parking lot to one side of the building. Ernest had assigned him a space. There'd been no baggage to take up, Ernest remembered. "Only one small suitcase. He handled it himself."

It was nearly two o'clock when Kay went down to the restaurant's kitchen and ordered lunch sent up to her weary guest. A cup of crab bisque—a specialty of the house—and a delicate shrimp omelet. Coastal Georgia prided itself on its shrimp, and the Buccaneer featured a variety of shrimp dishes. For his dessert, she chose angel cake with fresh strawberries, plus a carafe of piping hot coffee.

She ate a hasty late lunch herself, then headed back to her apartment. She was poring over her records again when the phone rang.

"Thank you for a delicious lunch," Alan Johnston said, in response to her hello.

"You're more than welcome. Did you get some sleep?"

"Both before I ate, and after. I just woke up, as a matter of fact."

"How's your headache?"

"A thing of the past."

"Good."

He sounded stronger, Kay noted. He had a pleasant voice, with only the slightest of Yankee accents.

"About our dinner engagement," he said. "I don't want to impose on you, Mrs. Dillard. That's to say, maybe you've had enough of me, and the key, for one day."

"Not at all," Kay told him, almost too quickly. "I can't let it go. This question of the key, that is. If it meant so much to Randy for you to get it to me, I should know what it unlocks. Since I don't, finding out has become a priority."

"Are you sure you really want to find out?" Alan asked quietly.

The question took Kay by surprise. Since returning to her apartment, she'd tried not to think about the key, or about Randy, and had succeeded—at least partially—by plunging herself into work. Math and music—those were her escapes. Bookkeeping with Bach in the background. For the past couple of hours they'd kept this other concern at bay. Now...

She felt a disconcerting chill, and managed honestly, "I don't think it's up to me. That's to say, what I might personally want really isn't relevant. You felt an obligation to bring the key to me. Certainly my obligation to find out what it unlocks is even greater."

"You still can't think of any possibilities?"

"No, I can't."

Saying that, Kay could appreciate that Alan must have hoped she'd come up with something, some memory, since their meeting in the lounge. At the same time, she began to feel slightly guilty. He'd asked her if she hadn't had enough of him for one day. The truth was, he'd probably had more than enough of *her* for one day. She'd caused him to relive traumatic memories to the point of developing an excruciating headache.

"Would you rather we didn't meet for dinner?" she asked bluntly.

"No," he answered without hesitation. "I was thinking of you when I mentioned that. I know this morning was difficult for you."

"Equally so for you, I'd say."

That was true. But Katherine Dillard's saying so surprised Alan. He'd been so sure this meeting with Randolph's widow could be nothing other than a disaster. He'd geared himself up to cope with her resentment of him because he was alive and her husband was dead, when it could so easily have been the other way around. But instead . . . she seemed not to blame him. It was the situation she appeared to be uncomfortable with, not him.

That was ironic, in a way. For nine months, Alan had suffered endless guilt trips over Dillard's death. Fate's whims were incredibly fickle, so totally beyond one's control. He'd felt sure that if he hadn't had to use the bathroom when he did it would have been him instead of Dillard who would have served as a target for an executioner.

During many a sleepless night, while his head throbbed, Alan had thought about that narrow, narrow margin between Dillard's death and his life. He'd been especially unable to justify Dillard's dying and his living because Dillard had a wife waiting for him, while he had no one. But he'd never expressed to anyone his guilt over what had happened—not to his friends nor to the psychiatrists who'd counseled the hostages after their release. It was something he'd kept strictly to himself, even though at times it was like having a hole burning deep inside.

Now Katherine Dillard's attitude made him feel— almost—reprieved. But he warned himself not to grasp that feeling too tightly. It could easily prove fleeting, might fade away entirely once Dillard's widow had more time to think things through. Then, perhaps, her resentment would begin to build, her hatred would begin to brew...

Kay said, "I'd suggest we dine in the Buccaneer, where," she added with a chuckle, "I highly recommend the cuisine. But too many people would want to speak with me there." She paused, then asked, "Are there any restaurants in Savannah you've heard about? A place you might want to try?"

"I have to confess my ignorance about Savannah's restaurants," Alan admitted. "I've heard that this city is famous for great food. But as for a specific place..."

"There's a rather pleasant seafood restaurant out along the river," Kay suggested. "It's a few miles out of town. Just a small place, nothing fancy... and not especially famous. Still, you can try the Old Pink House and the Pirates' House and some of the others another time. Would that be agreeable to you?"

It was more than agreeable to him. Alan found he was looking forward very much to having dinner with Kay Dillard. He hoped there would be flickering candlelight at their table, soft music in the background.

An inner voice warned him that Kay Dillard was the last person in the world he should permit himself to become attracted to. They had a powerful ghost between them. How could either of them ever exorcise the memory of Randolph Dillard? Kay had even named her inn after him.

Alan was usually guided by his considerable common sense. But as he told Kay he'd meet her in the lobby at seven-thirty, he recklessly switched off that inner voice.

CHAPTER THREE

KAY CHOSE a full-skirted, rose silk dress for her dinner date with Alan Johnston. The dress almost exactly matched the color of the azaleas blooming around the inn, and only after she slipped it on did she consider that her outfit was anything but widowlike.

But then, she thought with a slight grimace, she was hardly a traditional widow.

Primarily the color was cheerful, and she wanted to start this evening on a more cheerful note for both their sakes. Their first encounter had been mutually traumatic. Alan Johnston, she thought, deserved a better memory of his stay in Savannah. She was beginning to fully appreciate how difficult it must have been for him to make this trip. And how frustrating it must have been for him when she'd failed to recognize the key.

She arrived in the lobby a few minutes after seven-thirty to find Alan seated in an armchair, scanning the local paper. As she approached him, Homer Telfair, the night desk clerk, intercepted her.

"May I have a word with you, Mrs. Dillard?" Homer asked softly.

Kay slanted a smile of apology at Alan. Alan smiled back, and his smile was so charming that it made her catch her breath. When she'd met Alan this morning she wouldn't have said that his was a charismatic personality, but she was changing her mind. Now that he'd gotten some rest, shaved and combed his hair more carefully, he was looking not only quite handsome but . . . sexy.

Kay became aware she was staring at him. Flustered, she quickly turned toward the desk clerk. "What is it, Homer?" she asked.

"It's about Francey," Homer said.

Kay had long suspected that Homer Telfair had a crush on her niece by marriage. She was equally certain Francey didn't return the infatuation. Homer was a slight young man, tall but skinny. His poor eyesight required him to wear thick glasses—unfortunate, because he had really beautiful dark eyes. Kay had seen those eyes revealed once when she'd come upon Homer cleaning his glasses.

Despite Homer's nondescript looks, he had a very engaging personality. That was why Kay considered him nominally in charge of the front desk. She knew he wanted to carve out a career in the hotel field, and he took his responsibilities seriously.

Kay had hoped Francey would learn a few things from Homer. The guests, young and old, took to him, and he went out of his way to oblige them. He was a native of Savannah and a knowledgeable student of the area's history. Kay knew he occasionally moonlighted as a tour guide, but she didn't object to those extracurricular activities. In fact, it pleased her to think about the lucky tourists who were fortunate enough to hire him.

Francey was a native of Savannah, as Homer was, but the only time she'd been allowed to step out of the rather narrow and rigid confines of the social stratum into which she'd been born was to go to business school. Tracy—Francey's mother—had hinted to Kay that Francey's having been sent to business school was in the nature of a form of punishment. Evidently she'd "fooled around" so much in the girls' school she'd been attending that, according to Tracy, Gerard had exercised his parental rights and determined she was going to "buckle down." Business school had seemed the solution.

The ploy hadn't worked. Francey had flunked out early in the second semester, at which point Gerard had prevailed upon Kay to give her a chance at the front-desk job.

It had been folly to listen to him, Kay thought now. But then, it always had been folly to listen to Gerard.

She bit back impatience as she asked Homer, "What's going on with Francey? Has she been coming in late or—" She was stopped by a negative shake of Homer's dark head.

"It's nothing like that, Mrs. Dillard," he said. "I've been hoping maybe she'd confided in you about her problem. I can't get her to tell me anything."

"What problem?" Kay couldn't imagine Francey having a serious problem. That was a problem in itself. She couldn't imagine Francey being really serious about anything. She suspected that Francey took after her mother . . . and she doubted if a truly serious thought had ever passed through Tracy Dillard's pretty blond head.

"I don't know," Homer admitted, "I just feel sure she has one, that's all. She's been out back crying three times this past week when I've come on duty. Luckily there weren't any guests around. Look, please, I'm not telling tales out of school about Francey. . . ."

"Of course not."

"Mrs. Dillard, I'm worried about her," Homer confessed. "Something really must be wrong."

Kay frowned. Though she saw Francey on a daily basis, she could not recall the last time they'd had a bona fide conversation. She'd been determined not to show any favoritism toward Francey that might be resented by others on the staff. Consequently she supposed she'd actually gone the other way, almost ignored Francey a fair bit of the time.

She said carefully, "Homer, don't you think you may be blowing this up? Girls Francey's age can become emotionally unstrung rather easily. Maybe you just happened on her at a bad moment."

"Three bad moments in one week?" Homer asked skeptically. "Believe me, Mrs. Dillard, I'm not blowing anything up. Maybe you haven't noticed but...well, Francey just hasn't been Francey for quite a while. You know the way she usually is. Bubbly. Full of fun."

That was true enough, Kay conceded. Francey, in her opinion, was usually too bubbly, too full of fun. Thinking that, Kay suddenly remembered a cocktail party a while back at Gerard Dillard's house, when Tracy had murmured something about dealing with daughters in this day and age.

Tracy had complained that she'd thought once Francey was through high school she would have latched on to some purpose in life. *Purpose* was the very word Tracy had used, Kay recalled. She'd been amused, because Tracy appeared to be so purposeless herself.

"All Francey wants to do is sleep late and watch soap operas," Tracy had complained. "When you talk to her, she just says she plans someday to get her a rich, handsome husband, who'll give her gorgeous clothes and jewels and fancy cars.''

As you did. Kay now remembered that was the silent thought that had passed through her mind.

She said to Homer, "I'll talk with Francey tomorrow."

"I hope she'll talk to you," Homer said morosely.

Kay gave him a calculatedly cheerful smile, then moved across the room to Alan. As she neared him, he stood. She was wearing shoes with slender high heels, but he was still considerably taller than she was. He'd changed the crumpled suit he'd had on earlier for a lightweight beige jacket and brown slacks. He still wasn't a fashion plate, he still needed a haircut, but regardless, he was a very attractive man.

Kay felt a sudden intensely sensual reaction toward him that was so foreign to her she was thrown off base by it. Desire's strange sweetness twisted deep inside her, coiling and lingering. Impatient with her lack of inner self-control, she suggested a shade too sharply, "Shall we go?"

"Sure," Alan responded, but he was frowning slightly, and she knew her sharpness had registered.

This was verified when, once they were outside the inn, he said quietly, "Kay, if you'd rather skip this dinner date I'll understand."

"I don't want to skip it," she assured him quickly. "Why would you suggest that?"

"I had the feeling there in the lobby that you were upset about something. I thought maybe it had to do with whatever that young man at the reception desk told you." He paused, then admitted, "I also had to consider that it could have to do with me."

Kay smiled. "You were right the first time," she told him. "Homer presented a slight problem, which can wait until tomorrow."

"Good."

Kay gave him directions and they started out of the city, driving along its namesake river. The night was warm, the moon nearly full, the soft black sky star-sprinkled. Alan switched on the radio, and sweet music filtered around them. Kay felt herself relaxing. More than relaxing. Melting.

She forcefully reminded herself that for all she knew this man at her side was married and had a dozen kids. Also, there was no reason why he should have a personal interest in her...in fact, a number of reasons why he probably didn't have. Also, he'd allotted only three days of his life to Savannah. After that, he'd be going home—wherever home was.

Keep remembering that, she warned herself.

The restaurant she had chosen was built close to the river's edge. She and Alan were given a window table. Outside, shafts of moonlight spread silver over the dark water. A candle burned at every table, and the mellow background music was like a soft satin cushion. Distracted by the obviously romantic ambience, Kay tried to take logical stock of the situation.

She wasn't a child. She knew Alan Johnston was not unaware of her. His eyes—in the occasional glances she intercepted—told her that. She knew, too, that he was an intelligent, perceptive man and probably just as sensitive to vibes as she was. But she had few illusions about men, perceptive or otherwise. Especially since she'd become a widow, she'd discovered how many men were ready for casual, brief affairs, even when given little or no encouragement. Affairs that would leave no lasting damage on the resilient male psyche.

She'd become adroit about keeping men at arm's length these past nine months, and until now attachment had been easy enough to sidestep because she'd felt no corresponding emotion when sexuality entered the picture. But being with Alan Johnston shifted matters into a potentially different dimension, and she was shocked at her responsiveness. She couldn't afford to be so vulnerable.

She was taken aback when Alan urged gently, "Please . . . try to take it a little easier, will you? I was afraid this was going to be too difficult for you."

Kay's eyes opened wide. "Am I that transparent?"

"Not transparent, Kay. It's just that I've become something of an expert on tension." He paused, then said, "I don't mean to repeat myself, but once again, if you'd feel more comfortable we can leave after we've finished our drinks."

"Aren't you hungry?" Kay queried.

"Yes, but that's beside the point."

"Alan, do *you* want to leave?"

"No, but that's also beside the point. I don't want you to feel uncomfortable. That's the most important thing to me right now."

Kay didn't know how to answer him. She'd initiated this dinner date, motivated by their need to speak more about the key. But her reasoning had changed. If the truth were to be known, she didn't want to talk about either Randy or the key. She was only beginning to realize that she both wanted and needed a pleasant evening with someone like Alan Johnston. Suddenly she wished she and Alan could declare a moratorium for tonight on talking about the past and just enjoy the present.

Alan said softly, "It's up to you, Kay. Shall we stay or leave?"

Kay opted for honesty. "I'd like to stay."

Until she said that, she didn't realize that Alan had been pretty tense himself as he waited for her answer. He expelled a long breath and said simply, "Good."

With that single word there was a subtle switch in atmosphere between them, like a sudden wind change. Kay could feel at least some of her constraint slipping away, and she saw that Alan was also looking more relaxed as he studied the menu.

They ordered, Kay suggesting some of the local specialties she thought he'd like. While they ate, Alan kept the conversation light. At his urging, Kay told him a bit about Savannah, starting with how the city had been settled more than forty years before the American Revolution by General James Edward Oglethorpe, whose plans had been so innovative that Savannah still stood as an urban model.

"Are you a native of Savannah?" Alan asked.

"Almost. I was born in Atlanta, but I lost my parents when I was only seven and after that I came here to live with my Grandfather Randolph, my mother's father. By then, he was a widower himself. It was he who owned the cotton warehouse on Bay Street that I've now converted into the Randolph House."

So she'd named the inn after her grandfather, not after her late husband. Alan didn't know why that should please him so much . . . but it did.

"I finished high school in Savannah," Kay continued, "then went on to Savannah Junior College." She paused, then continued rather hesitantly, "I met

Randy at a cotillion in town. I was twenty when I married him, and that was fourteen years ago. So," she finished with a smile, "now you know my age."

"Thirty-four," Alan said, "which makes you eight years younger than I am." As he looked at her, lovely in her rose dress, her beauty enhanced by the candlelight, he felt at least a thousand years older than she was.

"Randy was forty-one," Kay volunteered, then abruptly switched the subject. "Are you married, Alan?"

Alan, momentarily taken aback, rallied and shook his head. "No."

"But . . . you have been?"

"Yes." He hesitated, hating to get into this. "Twice," he conceded, then felt a sudden need to explain.

"I was a product of the Vietnam era," he said slowly. "The Army drafted me just out of high school, so I ended up volunteering for a special job. Anyway, with that misguided romantic zeal that's part of youth, my high school sweetheart and I eloped shortly before I was sent to Nam. I was gone a year, the first time."

"The first time?"

"I volunteered for a second tour of duty. Crazy, eh?"

"I don't know," Kay decided. "I mean, offhand, I'd say yes. What did you do in the service?"

"I was a helicopter pilot. Dropped soldiers into hot spots, retrieved them later, transported wounded...."

Kay stared at him, genuinely surprised. She would not have pictured him doing anything like that . . . yet, perhaps that was where he'd acquired that subtle but steely reserve. She said, "With all due respect, Alan—and I mean that—you *must* have been a little crazy to go back."

"I was mad, stupid, immature, bitter. You see... after a time, on the first tour, I was given a leave. An R and R in Hawaii. I wrote Valerie—my bride—to meet me in Honolulu. I even sent her the money, which, needless to say, was never returned to me. Instead of accepting my invitation, I got a letter from Valerie's lawyer requesting a divorce."

Though he seldom thought about it anymore, the memory of receiving that document on the other side of the world, far away from home and under the most terrible conditions possible, still stung.

He heard Kay's sympathetic murmur and, without looking at her, went on, "I agreed to the divorce, and it went through quickly, as far as the legal aspects were concerned. But...it tore me apart. I was pretty young, remember, and... well, I guess I did go slightly berserk for a while. Combat flying, as incredibly scary as it was, was my way of retaliating against my hurt feelings. Things over there just *happened*. Maybe you can imagine that. I mean, hardly a day went by when I didn't wonder if it might be my last. Anyway, I got involved with a Vietnamese girl—a very lovely and innocent girl, I want to say. There were many of them, as well as many of the other kind. Then, when I found out she was pregnant, I married her."

His gray eyes were shadowed as he said, "I was ordered, at that point, to go to Saigon for a special assignment. Nothing to do with helicopters. This was something else. A one-time intelligence project I was suited for, actually. I wanted Meiling to go with me. She wanted to have our child in her own village. I've felt, ever since, that I should have been a lot more insistent than I was because..."

Kay found she was holding her breath. "Yes?" she urged.

"Before the baby was born, there was an air raid. She was killed."

Kay impulsively reached across the table and took Alan's hand in hers. Her touch was so electric that it jolted him. But he didn't let go.

"How terrible for you," Kay managed. She struggled with emotions already frazzled by everything that had gone down today. Wanting almost desperately to move away from sorrow and pain, she tried for a wide switch in subject and asked, "What did you do after you returned from Vietnam?"

"I went back to school," Alan said. "History has always fascinated me, especially ancient history. In due course I became an Egyptologist. That's my forte, and what I went for in my doctoral dissertation."

"You mean, it's Dr. Johnston?"

"Academically, yes. I prefer to use the title only in the classroom."

"You teach?"

"Yes. I teach at Mansfield College. It's a relatively small school in Mansfield, Vermont. I was born not far from there. You might say I returned to my roots. The town's small, tranquil, out of the mainstream. I like it there. Also, by a strange quirk of fate, the college was heavily endowed by a man who was even more of an Egypt freak than I am. Instead of the usual gazebo or war-hero statue on the village green, there's an obelisk that's a miniature version of the Cleopatra's Needle in Central Park in New York."

"Given by the man you speak of?"

"Yes. It was his first gift to the town, as a matter of fact. His name was Horace Coolidge Eastman. He was born in Mansfield. He went away as a young man to make his fortune and actually spent a major part of his life in Chicago. But his allegiance to his hometown and his interest in things Egyptian never wavered. Which, as it turned out, was lucky for me. By the time I was ready for such a job they were looking for someone just like me."

Kay said with a smile, "You're full of surprises, Alan."

He *was* full of surprises. And she wanted to know a hundred, a thousand, more things about him. She started by asking, "Do you live on campus, at your college?"

"No, I have an apartment in town. Second floor of an old home converted into rental units."

"You keep house for yourself?"

"Well, I have a woman who comes in and cleans, or tries to. Like most bachelors, I'm not as neat as I could be. Other than that, I do for myself, yes."

"Your own cooking?"

"Such as it is."

"You sound very self-sufficient."

"Do I?" he countered, amused. "I have an aunt living in Montpelier who'd love to hear you say that. She's my mother's older sister, eighty-five years old and quite a character. She would completely disagree about my being self-sufficient. I think she feels the only time I ever get a decent meal is when I visit her."

"What about your parents?"

"They both passed away some time ago."

"Brothers or sisters?"

"I was an only child."

"So was I," Kay said softly.

"Lonely?"

"No. I can't say I ever was especially lonely. Were you?"

"No. Funny, isn't it? People always assume that only children must be lonely. But I've found that's seldom the case."

They finished their entrée as they reached this point in their conversation. Then their plates were cleared away and the waiter proffered a dessert menu.

"The rum cake's terrific," Kay told Alan. "A house specialty."

"Then I'll try it. You too?"

"I couldn't," she confessed. "Just coffee for me, please."

As he stirred sugar into his coffee, Alan asked, "What made you decide to go into the hotel business, Kay?"

"Well," she said, "I inherited the cotton warehouse from my grandfather a few years ago. And enough money as well, so that I had a base to start working with. I loved the things that were being done to Savannah . . . the restorations, that is. The city has been so transformed, in a relatively few years. I wanted to contribute to that transformation, but I also wanted to do something functional with the warehouse. An inn seemed to be the logical solution."

"And so you simply started out by converting the warehouse into an inn, with no previous experience?"

"Not quite. Gary Madison, my lawyer, and an old family friend as well, is married to a lovely lady named Lucinda who has operated an inn in a former old family homestead for the past several years. Lucinda and Gary became my guiding lights. You'll probably laugh at this, but I signed up for correspondence courses in hotel management and I still study like mad, trying to learn, learn, all the time."

"I find that anything but funny," Alan said sincerely. "On the contrary, I find it admirable. But it's difficult to see how you managed to accomplish so much in such a short time."

Kay looked puzzled. "What do you mean?"

"I was thinking," Alan said, faltering somewhat, "that it's only been nine months since..."

"I started the inn project long before Randy's death," Kay told him after a moment of intense silence. "I started my planning four years ago. I'd long since set a target opening date of last October."

"And so you kept to it?"

Kay nodded. "In fact...I worked all the harder to accomplish it. I needed to fill in the hours..."

Her voice trailed away. And she asked herself dismally how she could ever have hoped she and Alan Johnston could get through this evening without Randy Dillard's ghost coming between them.

"Would you like a liqueur?" Alan asked, trying to break through the small impasse.

Kay sensed he also was trying to prolong their time together. Which was exactly what she wanted to do. So she said, "Yes. Perhaps some Benedictine."

Alan ordered Benedictine for both of them, then he said slowly, "Kay, I hate to get into it again as much as I sense you do. But we can't avoid the damned key."

"No," she agreed, and was unable to repress a small sigh. "I realize that."

"I've been wondering...the inn wasn't ready for occupancy until October, did you say?"

"That's right."

"You moved in yourself, then?"

"Yes. I have my own apartment."

"Where were you living last July?"

"At our house on Oglethorpe Square," Kay answered. "Why?"

"Do you still own that house?"

"Yes. But it's rented to a writer and his wife. His name is Clark Creighton. You may have heard of him. He's writing a book based in Savannah, so decided he wanted to live here for a year."

"I wonder if the key might be to something in that house," Alan speculated, "or maybe to something in your inn. It's about the size of an average house key, maybe a shade or so smaller. Actually, house keys vary quite a bit. I know that I, for one, sometimes try to open the door to my apartment with my car key, and sometimes I try to start the car with my house key. And sometimes I get the key to the trunk mixed up with both of them." His grin was lopsided as he added, "What I'm trying to say is...a great many keys are a lot alike at first glance."

Kay laughed. "There are so many keys involved with the inn that at times I wonder I don't have nightmares about them," she confessed. "But I can't imagine the one you've given me matches any of them. Randy had very little connection with the inn. Still, it would be a starter to go through the keys I have around, including the inn keys, to make sure this isn't a duplicate."

"Yes, you could do that. But . . ."

"But what, Alan?"

"Why would your husband have been so insistent about getting a duplicate key back to you?"

"I have no idea," Kay admitted.

"I suppose," Alan conceded, "there's a chance he didn't know it's a duplicate, didn't realize you had the original." He frowned. "I guess the logical course *would* be to check all the keys in your possession before coming to any conclusions."

"I'll start hunting as soon as I get home," she promised.

"No," Alan protested softly. "There's not that much need to rush, Kay. It makes more sense for you to get a good night's sleep, once we're back at the inn. The key will still be there in the morning."

There was such an appealing tenderness to Alan's smile that Kay had to forcibly remind herself he'd probably look at anyone like that, under similar circumstances. He added, emphasizing his point, "The key's waited this long. It can wait a day longer."

"Mmm, you're right," she agreed. As she spoke, her emotions were zigzagging around like Fourth of July firecrackers let loose. Those kinds of emotions had not merely been suppressed in her, they'd been totally buried. But under the spell of this beautiful spring night and the candlelight setting and this intriguing man sitting opposite her, she was beginning to feel more of a woman than she had for far too long.

She could sense Alan's eyes on her and knew he was watching her intently. Searching, almost desperately, for a safe conversation subject she said, "One hears so much about New England winters. Tell me, what do you do on all those long, snowy winter evenings?"

"Correct papers," Alan said with a grin. "I seem to have endless papers to correct, probably because I give out so many assignments. You should hear my students groan."

Kay, finally veering back toward even keel, smiled. "You must have a social life," she suggested, letting her curiosity about Alan Johnston override her innate politeness.

"Some," he agreed. "Though I guess I have the reputation of being something of a loner."

"Nevertheless," Kay persisted, and was surprised at her persistence, "I would think you'd be in high demand as a guest."

"The extra man?" he asked wryly. "Well, I suppose that's true to an extent. Mostly, though, it's faculty get-togethers I'm asked to. And..."

"And?"

"During the holidays I get deluged with invitations from faculty wives who pity my single state. I try to avoid those occasions as much as possible. It's not that I'm ungrateful, but..."

Kay chuckled. "I think I get the picture." She paused, then asked, "Do you take advantage of all that New England snow? Do you ski or go in for other winter sports?"

"I do some skiing. I'm not the world's greatest, but I can hold my own on the slopes. We also have a lot of lakes in Vermont and most of them freeze solid in winter. So there's skating sometimes, and ice fishing.

"I should think you'd freeze to death."

"No, you light little fires to keep you warm. And you bring along a supply of other warming agents, like bourbon." He smiled. "You sound as if you've never been to New England."

"I haven't," Kay admitted. "I got as far as New York, once, on a trip with Randy. Way back, we took a couple of Caribbean cruises. Aside from that, I haven't traveled much."

The waiter was hovering. Though Kay knew they couldn't prolong staying in this lulling atmosphere much longer, she fought back disappointment when Alan asked for the check.

Not often did she want something to last forever. But now she wished it were in her power to halt time... if only for a little while.

CHAPTER FOUR

KAY PAUSED outside the door of the restaurant and said impulsively, "Let me show you something."

She reached for Alan's hand as she spoke. He gave it to her willingly, but the touch of her smooth palm nicked the edge of the self-control he'd been trying very hard to maintain. He felt as if he were being washed by a warm tide that was sweeping over the flatlands of a heart that had been pretty barren.

Kay tugged, and he followed her. She led him around the far side of the restaurant to a wide gallery that ran along the top of the bluffs edging the river. Moonlight silvered boats rocking gently at anchor and sprinkled shining celestial confetti across the dark water. The fragrance of magnolias sweetened the warm night air, and there was an exotic sultriness to the warm, gentle breeze.

"I've stepped backward into *Gone with the Wind*," Alan murmured.

"I hope not," Kay said. "That march across Georgia you Yankees executed back then still isn't exactly a favorite topic in these parts."

"You're giving me a guilt complex," he protested.

He saw her mouth curve into a smile. "Well," she said, "I'll say one thing for your General Sherman. He recognized beauty when he saw it. He was so impressed by Savannah that instead of razing the city he wired Lincoln that he was giving it to him as a Christmas present.''

Alan said softly, "I recognize beauty when I see it, too, Kay."

He suspected she had been about to continue her history lesson, but his quiet tone stilled her. She turned toward him, her silk skirt rustling, her eyes wide and questioning. He was shocked by the intensity of the longing, the *wanting* that possessed him. True, it was quite a while since he'd been with a woman, but that in itself wasn't reason enough for this. He was thankful that night—even a moonlit night—acted as a camouflage. He wasn't ready for Kay to see the evidence of the effect she was having on him.

She had released his hand once she'd gone to stand at the stone balustrade that edged the gallery. But she was close to him, so close that her scent vied with the magnolias, and the combination was incredibly heady.

She said slowly, "I suppose we'd better get back to the inn."

He heard the regret in her voice, a tone that matched what he was feeling. He doubted he'd ever wanted anything more than he wanted to take her in his arms and to personally blot out the moon and the stars with his kiss. Further, though it seemed incredible, he suspected Kay Dillard wanted the very same thing. Yet he had a strong, gut feeling that if he yielded to impulse they would both later regret it. There were too many shadows between them. Too many ghosts.

Alan had a sharp, sharp vision of Randolph Dillard, and he flinched.

Kay turned away, and Alan found himself looking down at the back of her beautifully shaped head. She was so close that he easily could have reached out, clasped her waist, drawn her to him. He actually went so far as to raise both hands, then forced his mind to assume control of his actions and at the same time wished he were not so disciplined.

Perhaps he'd already been a fairly controlled person before going to Vietnam. Even so, his experiences in that strange and terrible war had taught him added habits of self-containment and alertness and the ability to keep a clear and logical mind under the most trying of circumstances. His training as a helicopter pilot, involved with a rescue unit, helped him make full use of all the wits he possessed. Being able to function efficiently under conditions he sometimes still had nightmares about was a main reason why he'd survived and brought many others to safety with him.

He'd thought many times that he should have been able to put his training into play the day the plane had been hijacked. But that had been an entirely different situation. To act as he'd wanted to act would have meant bringing a further risk to the lives of the other hostages. Nevertheless, he had been totally on the alert, waiting every second for a chance to take advantage of even the slightest opportunity. But the chance had never come. Otherwise, maybe he would have been able to prevent Randolph Dillard's execution. In which case he wouldn't be here now, staring at Randolph Dillard's beautiful widow as she slowly walked away from him, heading for the restaurant parking lot and his rented car.

As he drove back into the city with Kay at his side, Alan tried a couple of times to make casual conversation, but his attempts fell flat. Each time Kay answered him politely but monosyllabically, and it was plain that she was preoccupied, her thoughts far away.

Alan wondered what she was thinking about, wished he knew, then decided it was probably as well he didn't know because he feared maybe she was regretting having come out to dinner with him tonight, after all.

She was gracious, she was lovely, she was charming, she was inherently polite. Was it that inherent politeness that had been motivating her ever since his arrival on the scene? Underneath it all, did she resent him?

No. He nearly spoke the sharp negative aloud. There had been no resentment as they dined together in the restaurant. And, as they'd stood on the gallery looking out over the river, there had been a strong and wonderful chemistry flowing between them. Regardless of anything else, he was absolutely certain of that.

As they entered the inn, Kay said, "Excuse me a minute, will you, please?"

Alan nodded and watched her walk over to the registration desk, where she engaged in a brief conversation with the dark-haired young man to whom she'd spoken earlier.

She rejoined Alan to say, "Won't you come into the parlor for a liqueur?"

Before he could answer, she elaborated, "We offer liqueurs to the guests every evening, courtesy of the house, in that little parlor near the elevator. It gives people a nice chance to mingle, and I always stop in when I can, just to say hello."

Alan had never felt less like mingling with strangers. "Thanks," he said, "but I think I'll call it a day."

As he spoke, he reached in his pocket and pulled out the bronze key. "You'll want this," he said, "so you can compare it with the keys you have here in the inn."

"Yes," Kay agreed, but she made no move to immediately take the key from him. He saw her lips
tighten slightly, and knew that the key was somehow
distasteful to her and wondered why.

Didn't she want to find out what it unlocked?

Finally she accepted the key, their fingers touching
only briefly in passing. But the touch was enough to
make Alan aware that her hand was trembling slightly,
and he was all the more mystified. He would have
thought she might be eager to discover what it was her
husband had considered so urgent just minutes before he faced death. Alan tried to put himself in her
place. If he were to receive a message from beyond the
grave like this from someone he'd loved, how would
he feel about it?

One could never be sure about anything without
having lived through a parallel experience; the things
that had happened to him had vividly demonstrated
that truth. Nevertheless, it seemed to him that if he
were Kay, he would have viewed the key as a kind of
legacy from someone beloved, and probably he would
have dropped everything else he was doing in the effort to find out what it unlocked.

Certainly that was not the way Kay was responding.

He became aware that she'd said something to him
and just then he'd been the one who was a million
miles away.

"I'm sorry," he said with a contrite smile.

"I was only about to say good-night," she said,
"and to thank you for dinner. I enjoyed being with
you."

She spoke simply, artlessly. She meant exactly what
she was saying; Alan was sure of that. And he felt as

if a great weight suddenly had been lifted from his shoulders.

She had enjoyed being with him.

For once, the ghost of Randolph Dillard stayed in the shadows.

KAY'S DOCTOR HAD GIVEN her some sleeping pills after Randy's death, because the sheer horror of what had happened had caused bouts of insomnia, night after night.

Once she left her guests still sipping liqueurs in the parlor and went up to her apartment, she thought about taking a pill because she was afraid the insomnia was going to return to plague her tonight. But she disliked drugs—even when prescribed—and decided she'd rather risk the sleeplessness.

She bathed, slipped on a lace-trimmed yellow nightgown and then, on her way to bed, paused by her dresser, atop which she'd placed the bronze key.

She had such mixed feelings about this key. She had to find out what it unlocked. She dreaded finding out what it unlocked. For nine months, she'd been closing the prior chapters in her life and starting a new book. Now it seemed to her that all her effort had been wasted. Randy was back, almost larger in death than he'd been in life.

She shivered as she slipped under the covers, though it was a warm night, and she didn't immediately switch off her bedside lamp. A combination of this day she'd just lived through, Alan Johnston and the key was forcing her to go back in memory to last July, something she didn't want to do.

Randy's body had been recovered once the plane had moved on to the island where it finally was captured. The body had been sent back to the States, and there had been a funeral here in Savannah in the church the Dillards always had attended, then burial in the family plot.

Kay still marveled that she had survived the funeral and the subsequent burial ceremony without giving way completely, and she winced as she recalled the American flag that had draped Randy's coffin being handed to her. The day had been blazingly hot, even for Savannah in mid-July. It would have been understandable if she had fainted from the combination of heat, grief and guilt, and she nearly had. But not quite. She had wished fervently for that final jab of unconsciousness, wanted desperately to sink to the ground and, even for a few minutes, blot out the sights and the sounds and the sympathetic people thronging around her.

Gerard Dillard, evidently noting her pallor, had gripped her arm and said, "Steady there, my dear." She'd tried to wrench her arm away without being obvious about it. She'd never been able to bear having Gerard touch her—not since the first week after her marriage when she and Randy had just returned from a honeymoon in the Bahamas and gone to Gerard and Tracy's for dinner.

She fought away that memory because what Gerard did or didn't do really was no longer of any consequence, as long as she could avoid him for the most part. But she still shrank from the vision of herself at Randy's funeral, garbed in proper black, dry-eyed. People said she was so brave, holding up so well.

Fraud, she thought, branding herself viciously as she had so many times. *Fraud!*

She switched out the lamp. Moonlight filtered through the filmy curtains at the high, narrow windows, striping the bed sheets and slanting silver ribbons across her pillow. The moonlight made her think of Alan. The scent of magnolias wafting through the air made her think of him even more. It would have taken only a single gesture on his part—the hint of an invitation—to have made her go into his arms as they were standing out on the gallery this evening.

Experiencing that kind of an impulse toward a man she'd just met made her feel strangely unsure of herself. Maybe she'd been working too hard, maybe she was alone too much—or had been alone too long. Maybe that was the problem. And it was a long time since a man had made love to her. Way, way, before Randy Dillard left Savannah on that ill-fated trip.

She became suddenly, acutely aware that only a single wall separated her from the room in which Alan Johnston was sleeping. She knew exactly which room he'd been given.

Kay thought about the fabled walls of Jericho and decided she'd have to read up on them. Hadn't those walls tumbled down? Not, she added quickly, that she'd want history to repeat itself.

Smiling slightly, she turned on her side, plumped up the pillow under her head, and after a time in which she fought valiantly to concentrate only on the darkness, she finally drifted off to sleep.

KAY BECAME SO BUSY the next morning with routine matters involved in running an inn that she had no chance to do any key comparisons.

Before leaving her apartment, she put the key in her desk drawer, and then on an impulse, she locked the drawer. She chided herself for the gesture, as she went down to the lobby. Who, after all, would want to steal a dull bronze key? She quickly answered her own question. The value of the key obviously depended on what it was a key to.

Nevertheless, she was in danger of becoming paranoid about the blasted object, she thought with a frown. For one thing, knowing Randy as she had, she couldn't understand this gesture on his part. Why had he been so concerned about getting the key to her when he felt himself to be at the moment of death? Why had he been so sure he was the next one scheduled for execution? Alan had spoken of vibes that come on strong under the kind of pressure the hostages were experiencing on the airplane. Even so, the Randy she remembered had not been an especially intuitive man. Rather he had been inclined to live each day for itself . . . and for himself.

Kay approached the registration desk, hoping that diplomacy would work with her niece by marriage.

Francey was speaking to a guest, so Kay had the chance to observe her for a moment. She came to the quick conclusion that Homer Telfair probably hadn't been suffering from an overactive imagination, after all.

Francey was pale, there were dark circles under her eyes, and though she was smiling as she chatted with the guest, she lacked her usual effervescence. Homer had mentioned that Francey was "bubbly," which was true. Today Francey was not bubbling, and once the guest moved away, her smile faded and strain took over.

Kay moved in before Francey had a chance to recover the smile.

"Hey, there," Kay said lightly.

Francey looked up, her pretty face still reflecting the strain as she said, "Oh, Aunt Kay."

Francey was nearly as tall as Kay, but had always been slightly on the plump side. Kay noted now that she looked as if she'd lost some weight.

Maybe that was it. Maybe Francey had embarked on a crash diet that was wearing her down.

Usually Francey was meticulous about her hair— arranging it in a variety of styles—and equally careful about her makeup. She had studied makeup and often offered to make Kay up, insisting that Kay did nothing about "bringing out" her features or the deep-blue color of her eyes.

Francey's eyes were a lighter blue, and today they looked naked, because Francey had left off her customary shadow, mascara and liner. Her blond hair was combed carelessly, and looked as if it could do with a washing. Her fingernail polish was chipped.

Homer was right. This was not the usual Francey.

"Been very busy?" Kay asked.

"Not too," Francey said. "Most of the guests went out early. It's such a beautiful day, I guess they want to do some sight-seeing."

"Probably." She said carefully, "You and I don't get to see much of each other, do we, though we both work in the same place?" She delivered the words with a smile. The last thing she wanted to do was put Francey on edge.

"Well, no, I guess not," Francey said uncertainly.

Francey picked up a stack of mail and started inserting the letters into the room boxes. Kay, given this opportunity to observe her again, noticed a nervousness about Francey that was also unlike her.

She wondered if either Gerard or Tracy was aware that their daughter was not running entirely true to form, and decided they probably weren't. Gerard appeared to notice Francey primarily when she annoyed him, and just about the same could be said of Tracy, even though Gerard and Tracy were as different as two individuals possibly could be.

Physically Francey took after Tracy, at least in her coloring. Kay did see, though, a Dillard family resemblance in her features: her rather high forehead, straight nose, full sensuous mouth and firm chin. The combination was an effective one. But then the Dillard men were handsome, Kay had to admit. Randy had been very good-looking. Gerard was even more so.

"What time is Homer coming in today?" she asked Francey.

"Four," Francey said rather listlessly.

"Why don't you come on up to my apartment after he gets here and we'll have some tea together?" Kay suggested.

"Why..." Francey began.

Kay didn't give her a chance to think up an excuse. "Four o'clock?" she asked.

"Well...all right," Francey answered.

Kay might have chuckled inwardly at Francey's reluctance under other circumstances. But there seemed nothing funny about it now. Francey was certainly not eager for a teatime chat—that was clear enough. And she probably was not going to be very communicative once the two of them were alone together.

All I can do is try, Kay told herself. She gave Francey another smile and turned away from the desk just in time to see Alan Johnston striding through the entrance.

He was wearing snug-fitting jeans, which showed off his nicely developed hips and muscular thighs, and the open-necked silver-gray sport shirt stretched across his broad chest brought out the color of his eyes. Somewhere along the line he'd paused for a haircut, and this small transformation made him look very unlike the rather shabby, slightly stooped man who'd presented himself only yesterday.

This Alan was standing tall and straight, and there was confidence in the set of his wide shoulders and a heady dose of charisma in the smile he directed at her.

Kay moved toward him as if their meeting had been planned.

They met in the middle of the lobby. Kay returned his smile and said, "You look as if you slept well last night."

"Like a baby," Alan assured her. "I think I'll have to take that big four-poster bed of yours home with me. There's something about it that makes me feel as if I'm snug in a cradle again."

She laughed. "Good. I was just thinking about redoing our brochure one of these days. Maybe I'll use that in our advertising."

"Be my guest," he invited.

"What have you been doing with yourself?"

He touched long, slim fingers to the top of his head. "Well," he said, "as you can see I got rid of some of the excess. I hadn't realized I'd gotten so shaggy. Trouble is, a good cut shows up more of this gray at the temples."

"Distinguished," she said. "Becoming."

His smile flashed. "I'm glad you think so. Anyway, after the haircut I took a sight-seeing tour around Savannah. Incidentally, my guide was that young man who was working on the desk here yesterday."

She nodded. "Homer Telfair. I'm glad you drew him. He's the best."

"I agree. I was very impressed, both by your beautiful city and its environs and by Homer. Which brings me to something Homer said."

"Oh?"

"He said you have to explore the waterfront district on foot to really get the feel of it. He said the waterfront area's one of Savannah's major restorations."

"True."

"I suppose you've browsed around there a thousand times."

She smiled. "Not quite. Would you believe, the waterfront's literally across the street from here but I seldom get the chance to go near it since I've been running the inn."

"I think," Alan diagnosed, "that you're so committed to the Randolph House you don't take time off for yourself, even when you might be able to."

"You could be right."

"How about today?" he suggested.

"What?"

"Right now. Could you snatch an hour or so and go over to the waterfront with me?"

"Alan, that's not fair," she protested. "You're tempting me."

She would have sworn his eyes darkened slightly. He said, "I'd love to tempt you, Kay," a slight but disturbingly husky note in his voice. Then he laughed and added lightly, "And that's exactly what I intend to keep doing until you say yes. Come on…the place can get along without you for an hour, can't it?"

"This wouldn't be a very well managed inn if it couldn't," Kay conceded with a twinkle. "Let me go up and get my handbag and I'll be right with you."

Alan was standing at a lobby window looking out over Bay Street when Kay came back downstairs. Somehow he was aware of her presence even before she came up to him. He would have sworn that the hairs on the back of his neck bristled slightly, then he turned and she was there.

She was wearing a dress in a soft shade of yellow, with oversize button earrings to match. She'd swept her hair back from her face, anchoring it on either side with a yellow comb. She was beautiful and sweet scented, and he decided she was the most desirable woman he'd ever seen. But, on closer inspection, he saw that she did look tired. The faint shadows under her eyes told their own story, and he suspected she hadn't slept nearly as soundly last night as he had.

They crossed Bay Street and strolled under oak trees just coming into leaf, their branches trimmed with trailing gray wisps of Spanish moss. Iron-and-concrete bridgeways linked the top of the steep riverside bluffs, on which the city had been built, to the upper entrances of the historic buildings on the far side of Bay Street, known as Factors Row.

"The name goes back to the days when cotton really was king around here," Kay said.

They climbed down steep iron staircases to the waterfront, where the streets were paved with large cobblestones.

"A reason why it's a good idea to wear sensible shoes when you're traipsing around Savannah," Kay said, glancing down at the white flats she was wearing. She negotiated a bumpy intersection, then added, "The cobblestones were brought here more than a century ago as ballast in the holds of the sailing ships. I don't think people ever let anything go to waste back in those days. They dumped the stones ashore and then, when they got around to it, used them in street construction."

"Picturesque," Alan conceded. "But I'd hate to try to run a marathon around here."

"Do you ever run marathons, Alan?"

"Not really. I do get in some jogging when I'm home, on a fairly regular basis. And," he added with a grin, "I've finished last in a couple of area road races."

"Come on, now."

"Well...let's say I've been in the middle of the pack. Now and then I think it would be fun to go to Boston some April and see if I could finish in the Boston Marathon, even at a snail's pace. I have no delusions of grandeur in that respect."

"I'm lazy," Kay confessed. "I like to swim, but jogging and such have never appealed to me. I did have visions, once, of being a ballerina. I studied ballet for years, and I still do love to dance."

He'd thought she moved like a dancer, Alan remembered triumphantly. "Do much of it?" he asked.

"No. That's past history. Anyway, I'm too busy these days for much extracurricular activity."

"Haven't you heard that old saw about all work and no play?" he chided.

"Yes, I'm afraid I have."

He chuckled. "You could never be a dull person no matter what you did . . . or didn't do," he told her.

He couldn't have known the effect his statement would have on her, Kay reminded herself. But saying what he said struck a sore point because—for so long—she'd been exactly that. A dull person, because she'd held back from letting herself live life as she intuitively knew she could live it.

Early in their marriage, she'd lost pace with Randy. And she'd never gotten in step with him again because their tempos were too different. She hadn't wanted to get in step with Randy, because her illusions by then had gone down the drain. No one woman, she'd learned, would ever be enough for Randy Dillard.

She supposed one might think learning that would have put the blame on Randy in her mind. Instead, she'd foolishly blamed herself. So she'd shrunk into herself, her isolation only compounded by the fact she'd never had children. It was a long while before she learned that it was Randy who was sterile, not she. Something he'd known when he married her, something that went back to an illness he'd had as a young boy.

She was glad to have Alan interrupt her thoughts by asking, "Hungry?"

"Are you?" she countered.

"I keep smelling all these ambrosial smells," he admitted. "I think I'd gain twenty pounds in a month if I stayed around here, just from sniffing."

They had frosty drinks and crab-cake sandwiches in a small café, then set about exploring the shops that lined River Street. Alan became fascinated by a store that sold nothing but ships' clocks, nautical lamps and

nautical prints. He paused to buy some traditional
Georgia pecan pralines in a sweetshop, which they
munched as they went along. They stopped in a gallery that featured old photos of Savannah scenes, as
well as original artworks. When Kay discovered a
photo of the Randolph House as it had been back in
the days when it was a cotton warehouse he insisted on
buying it for her, and they took advantage of the
shop's special frame-while-you-wait service.

Another former cotton warehouse had been converted into a cooperative art gallery featuring pottery
and enamels, weavings, wood carvings, sculpture and
jewelry. Many of the items offered for sale were really
lovely, and Kay kept expecting Alan to buy some gifts
to take back to Vermont with him, but he didn't.

She decided that either he planned to come back
later to do his shopping . . . or there wasn't anyone in
his life he wanted to shop for.

CHAPTER FIVE

AFTER A TIME Kay and Alan wandered across River Street to Riverfront Park, where a wide brick plaza bordered the Savannah. They sat down by mutual accord on a comfortable bench, and Alan promptly stretched out his legs.

"I warned you walking around here is hard on the feet," Kay teased.

"My feet, especially. We don't have giant-sized cobblestones back where I come from, lady," he drawled.

"How about all those mountains you have to climb?"

"I live in a valley."

"I can't win," she complained, her eyes sparkling. He was good company, fun to be with. She was enjoying this time with him.

Savannah was a busy port, and Alan quickly agreed when Kay pointed out that theirs was a perfect vantage place from which to watch the harbor activity. The river was an active water highway. There were freighters, tugboats, other miscellaneous workboats, a variety of pleasure craft and a triple-decked sternwheeler that went out on sight-seeing cruises, touring the harbor and the nearby intercoastal waterways.

"You might like a little excursion on the *Cap'n Sam*," Kay suggested.

"How about coming with me tomorrow afternoon?" Alan retorted promptly.

"I'd love to," she said, "but honestly, I can't. This is our busy season, remember? Now, if it were July or August...though actually Savannah draws a lot of tourists even in summer, since the restoration."

"You're such a good promoter of your city you'll have me coming back for more," Alan warned.

Would he come back? The unspoken question was tantalizing at first, then became a reminder of why Alan was here in the first place.

The key.

"The 'Damn' she muttered under her breath was quiet, yet Alan heard it.

"What was that about?" he asked.

"I just remembered something."

"Please," he protested, "don't tell me duty's calling you. We just sat down and my feet have never been more appreciative."

"No," she said. "I don't have to go back for a while longer. But...well, I just thought of the key."

Alan had been smiling; now his face became a slate wiped clean. "I wish you hadn't," he admitted. "Not just now."

"It's there, Alan," Kay said uncomfortably. She sighed, wishing she'd held back on her thoughts. She'd been having such a good time with him. Even here on the familiar waterfront everything looked new to her, viewing it with him. The old familiar sights gained a fresh dimension, everything she saw seemed brighter, clearer. The flags flying from windows and storefronts had never been so vivid. She'd been feeling so fully alive, so vibrant. As a result, remembering the key was like a dark cloud cast across the horizon of this perfect day.

Alan said, "I know the key's there, Kay. Have you checked it against the keys in the inn?"

"No, not yet, I haven't had the time."

"If you'd care to turn the inn keys over to me, I could do that for you," he suggested.

"Thanks, but it won't take long once I get to it," she said. "And I will get to it later today, definitely. Though..."

"Yes?"

"I'll be surprised if I strike pay dirt," Kay confessed. "As I said, Randy had very little connection with the Randolph House. So there's little chance this key is a duplicate of one that belongs at the inn."

"Nevertheless, that's a chance you have to eliminate."

"Yes, it is," she agreed.

They both fell silent. Alan watched a sleek white coast guard cutter heading east, evidently ocean-bound. The moods shifted so suddenly and so subtly between Kay and himself that it disturbed him. For a while they'd both been so carefree. He couldn't remember when he'd last felt young like that. But now the shadows were back. The conclusion that, for Kay, the key was somehow connected to those shadows became inevitable.

If anything had been needed to inspire the resolution in him that the object the key unlocked—whatever it might be—must be found, that was it.

Kay, at his side, stirred restlessly. He glanced at her, and saw that she was looking at her slim gold wristwatch. "I guess I'd better get back, after all," she said.

Alan rose reluctantly. "My feet aren't going to like you," he warned, striving for a little levity.

"*My* feet aren't going to like me, either," Kay said, a hint of laughter in her voice again.

They climbed the steep iron steps back up to Bay Street. Outside the inn, Alan said, "I think I'll wander around for a while. Thought I'd take a look in that Ships of the Sea Museum across the way."

"I wouldn't think a Vermonter would be keen on maritime lore," Kay said.

"We Vermonters are full of surprises," Alan allowed laconically.

"True," Kay said, that hint of laughter back in her eyes.

Once, again, he had to resist the impulse to kiss her.

THERE WAS ALWAYS unfinished business to attend to when one ran an inn, Kay had long since discovered. That held true once she'd gone up to her apartment after watching Alan stride back across Bay Street toward the Ships of the Sea Museum. She liked the way he walked. She liked the way he talked—even that slight Yankee accent was intriguing, coming from him. She liked the way he *was*.

She wished so much that they'd met under different circumstances. As she sifted through the day's mail, went over some accounts, checked some orders, Kay found it very difficult to get him out of her mind.

Four o'clock came and passed with no sign of Francey. Kay was about to call the desk downstairs to find out if Francey had left without keeping their tea date when there was a rap at the door.

Maybe it was her imagination, she conceded, but she thought Francey looked even paler than she had earlier in the day, and she seemed jittery. Kay settled her in an armchair with a copy of a new fashion magazine while she went to her small kitchen to make tea.

Earlier, she had ordered some iced cakes sent up from the restaurant, and she put them on a tray with the tea things and went back to the living room. The thick rug muffled her footsteps so Francey didn't hear her coming, and Kay saw that her niece was slumped back in the chair, her eyes closed, the magazine unopened in her lap.

She had never known a time when Francey wouldn't eagerly have clutched a new magazine dealing with fashion, the movies, TV or beauty hints.

Homer was right. Something was decidedly wrong with Francey.

"Well," she said, setting the tea tray down on a low table, "here we are."

She spoke briskly without looking at Francey, deliberately giving Francey the time to recoup a little.

She knew without asking that Francey liked her tea with two spoons of sugar and some cream. Over the winter, Francey had joined her for tea on several occasions. She also knew that Francey liked fancy cakes, which was why she'd ordered up this particular eye-catching assortment. But when she passed the cakes she thought at first Francey wasn't going to take one. Then Francey accepted a pink frosted cake, put it on a small plate and set the plate aside while she sipped her tea.

Kay poured tea for herself, adding a thin slice of lemon. Now the moment was at hand, she had no idea what to say. Certainly she couldn't point out that Homer had commented on Francey's odd recent behavior; that would only be a kiss of death for Homer, as far as Francey was concerned, and Francey was indifferent enough to him as it was. It would be cruel to provoke downright antagonism toward Homer.

Well, she had her own eyes, Kay reasoned. If she'd looked sooner she would have seen for herself that something was amiss with Francey.

She chose to open their conversation with a rather generalized remark. "How are things going for you, Francey?" she asked.

Francey put her teacup down next to the untouched cake. "What do you mean?" she hedged.

"Just that. How are things going?"

"Oh, okay I guess," Francey said. Then she suddenly clapped her hand to her mouth and, before Kay knew what was happening, got to her feet and bolted from the room, heading toward the bathroom.

Kay sat very still, wondering what to do next. She had no doubt that Francey was being sick and the question was whether to go after her or to give her some privacy, at least for a little while. She was a big girl, after all. Chances were she didn't need someone to hold her head, and might even be resentful of a volunteer in that department. On the other hand, if she didn't come back soon...

Francey came back, but a single glance at her was enough to convince Kay she'd been violently ill. She was ashen, she was trembling, and she sank back into her chair shakily, her pale blue eyes looking huge in a face that suddenly seemed not only pinched, but very young.

Kay leaned forward, her concern, her worry, transcending caution. "Francey, dear," she said, "something's obviously wrong. What is it?"

She saw Francey's eyes fill with tears. The tears spilled down her pale cheeks. "If I tell you, you've got to promise you won't say anything to my parents," Francey managed.

"I won't say anything," Kay promised, this only slightly against her better judgment. Knowing Gerard and Tracy as she did, she could empathize with Francey.

"I'm pregnant," Francey began on a sob that ended in a wail.

The tears were now streaming down Francey's face. Kay went to her, knelt down beside her, put her arms around her and drew her close so that Francey could lean against her shoulder. She let Francey cry, and only when the sobs began to lessen did she begin to gently wipe away the tears with a fine linen tea napkin.

Finally Francey said in a weak little voice, "I'm okay now."

Kay nodded, and moved back to her own chair. But she kept a careful, worried eye on Francey.

She let a little time pass, then said, "Want to tell me about it?"

"There isn't much to tell."

"Francey, there must be quite a lot to tell," Kay disagreed. "How far along are you?"

"I've missed two periods."

"Have you been to a doctor?"

"Yes, I...I had to make sure. I went to a clinic down in Brunswick last week."

"You went all the way to Brunswick to go to a clinic?"

"It's only fifty miles or so. I didn't want to go anywhere in Savannah. I was afraid it might get back to my father."

"Francey, sooner or later this is going to have to get back to your father."

"No," Francey protested sharply. "Aunt Kay, you promised...."

"I'm not going to tell him," Kay said swiftly. "That doesn't mean he's not certain to find out. Babies don't evaporate, Francey."

"I haven't made my mind up yet about what to do about *this* baby," Francey admitted. "I guess I should have sooner. I mean, I know it gets harder the longer it goes, but somehow..."

"Are you talking about an abortion?"

"Yes, I guess that's what I'm talking about."

They were getting into deep water. Very deep water. Kay knew she had no basic right to tell Francey what to do or what not to do. She could only think about what she would have done herself, had she ever been in Francey's place. But since she'd never been in Francey's place, that wasn't really valid.

Also...she'd wanted a child more than anything else in the world. So she couldn't envision ever having an abortion, no matter what the circumstances. Which didn't mean that her feelings should be applied to anyone else. Especially a girl not yet nineteen who had parents who were—yes—who were going to go right through the roof when they learned about this.

Kay asked carefully, "Francey, what does the baby's father think about this?"

Francey stared at her. "The baby's father?"

"Yes," Kay said, trying not to let herself become impatient. "The baby must have a father."

"He has nothing to do with it," Francey said quickly.

Could Homer Telfair be the father? The thought crossed Kay's mind, but she instantly dismissed it. For one thing, if that were the case Homer would have known what the matter with Francey was. For another thing, Francey had never given Homer any encouragement; very much the opposite, in fact.

"Francey," Kay said, trying again, "there isn't the stigma today that there used to be about an unmarried woman having and raising a child. In fact, that's the preference of many women, and society accepts their preference. On the other hand, sometimes when something like this happens the two people involved decide they want to get married—something they maybe weren't sure about before—and I personally think that's the best course."

"No," Francey said.

She didn't have to say anything more. Kay read the look on her face and knew without being told that there was no chance of Francey marrying the father of this child. Kay would have given one-hundred-to-one odds that, whoever he was, he was already married and had no intention of divorcing his wife. Which led to the further suspicion that he was possibly someone older, well established. A friend of Gerard's, perhaps?

Francey's eyes filled with tears again and she said, "I am so *scared*."

"Of course you're scared," Kay said quickly. "It's natural for you to be scared. But you're just one of millions to whom this has happened, Francey. You'll work your way through it, it's going to be fine. I'm here to help you. I promise you, I'll help you every step of the way."

"The other night," Francey said, "I went for a walk down by the river. I got to looking at the water and thinking maybe the easiest thing would be to just walk in...."

"Francey!" Kay cried, genuinely shocked. "Dear God, you mustn't even *think* such thoughts. That's your child you're carrying. One day you'll have a little boy or a little girl all your own, and a lot of people in the world will think you're very, very lucky...."

She drew a deep breath. "I made you a promise," she reminded Francey. "I promised you I won't tell your parents and I won't, unless you change your mind and want me to. I admit that's what I hope will happen. But meanwhile, your secret is safe with me. Now I'm going to ask a promise of you."

"Wha ?" Francey asked dully.

"Promise me you won't do anything foolish. Promise me you'll go directly home tonight and you'll *stay* home and you'll take it easy."

"That shouldn't be hard," Francey observed. "My parents are going to be out at a dinner party."

"Do you want to have dinner here with me?"

"No," Francey said. She managed a wry smile. "Right now I don't hold down very much," she confessed.

"That will pass," Kay said. "You'll begin to feel better, then everything will swing into perspective. It's important we get you to a doctor who can see you all the way through this. No, don't look like that. I'm not about to select a family friend who might violate medical confidence—though frankly, I think it's doubtful that would happen."

Kay paused. "Let me think about this," she said. "Come to work tomorrow and we'll figure out what to do next."

Francey nodded and stood up. She trailed across to the door, then turned on the threshold. "I'm glad I told you," she said. "I couldn't have gone it alone much longer."

"You don't have to go it alone *any* longer," Kay promised.

But once Francey had left her, she felt herself sagging and she wondered just what miracle she hoped to pull off for Francey that would make things better for her.

Her eyes fell on the little plate that held the small pink-frosted cake that was still untouched.

The cake was, somehow, the most poignant evidence of all that in a very short time Francey had grown up.

Kay put away the tea things, then made a pilgrimage down to the registration desk to gather up all the assorted keys connected with the inn's operation, these being kept in a back office.

Homer, fortunately, was busy with customers, and she escaped before he got a chance to talk to her. At the moment, she didn't want to get into a question-and-answer period about Francey.

Back in her apartment, she spread out the keys on the low table in the living room. She had already ascertained that the bronze key was not a room key. The room keys at the inn were quite a bit larger.

Now she went through the assortment. She hadn't realized how many keys the inn possessed, cast in a variety of metals, made in an even greater variety of sizes and shapes. A few of them came close to the bronze key. None was an identical match.

Kay put the inn keys back in the brown manila envelope she'd brought them up in, and went out to the kitchen and poured herself a glass of Chardonnay. She settled down on the couch in the living room and tried to arrange her thoughts in order so that she could do some coherent thinking about the possible origin of the key. But she got nowhere. Visions of Francey interrupted her at one moment, visions of Alan Johnston at the next.

Finally she reached for the phone and dialed Alan's room number.

He answered on the second ring.

Kay identified herself, then said, "I hope I'm not disturbing you."

"I was watching the evening news on TV," Alan said, "and nothing very interesting appears to have happened for the past twenty-four hours."

Kay let impulse take over. "I wondered if you could come over and have a drink," she said. "I'm just around the corner from you."

"My tired feet have just sprouted wings," Alan told her.

He knocked at her door so quickly that she said, on admitting him, "You must have flown."

"An old Superman trick," Alan said. "You make a human projectile out of yourself, in this case fired by motivation."

He was sauntering into her living room as he spoke. He looked around at the furnishings—a blend of the old and the new, carefully chosen by Kay to reflect her own personality. The imposing mansion on Oglethorpe Square, filled with family antiques, had never reflected her. He said, "I like your color scheme. Water tones, all the shades of blue and turquoise. They're restful yet vivid enough to make a statement. The colors remind of me of some Egyptian faiences."

He spotted a small statuette on her bookcase. "Well, I'll be damned!" he said. "Nefertiti."

"I bought her on a trip to New York a few years ago," Kay said. There was an edge of bitterness to her voice, because the trip was one of the few business trips she'd ever accompanied Randy on, and so much of the time she'd been left to her own devices. That had been to the good, actually, because she'd visited museums like the Metropolitan and seen and done so many things she never would have otherwise. Even so, his cavalier treatment of her had stung.

Alan picked up the statuette and fingered it carefully. "Nice," he said.

"Thank you. I rather fell in love with it. She was so beautiful."

"Exquisite," he agreed. "Do you know what her name means?"

"No."

"The Beautiful One Is Come," he translated.

"I like that."

"Like most of the Egyptian queens she was famous," Alan said, "but except for her beauty, her fame was principally because she was the wife of a pharaoh—Akhenaton—and the mother-in-law of another famous pharaoh, Tutankhamen. Nefertiti's beauty, though, made her fabulous in her own right. She still endures as a kind of legend of loveliness."

"You make her sound so...alive."

Alan smiled. "A lot that is ancient comes alive when one's an Egyptologist," he said. "The distant past sometimes seems more real than the present...especially when you're in Egypt and you've studied what you are seeing so you know what you are looking at. Putting the pieces of history together becomes so intensely fascinating—

He broke off. "You'll begin to think I belong in a museum," he said lightly. "Or maybe an archive. The dust-covered professor."

"I can't see you as a professor at all," she admitted.

"Why not?"

"You seem like . . ."

"Yes?"

"Well, you seem like a man of action. I can't picture you in musty corners poring over books."

"Perhaps that's because I've been a man of action," he said. "A little too much action, for a while. Also, I still don't spend much time in musty corners, though I've done my share of poring over books. But what I've loved the most—where my work is concerned—are the times when I've been able to be on the site where all the things I've studied about actually took place."

"How often have you been to Egypt?"

"Four times, thus far."

"You hope to go back again?" Kay didn't want to bring the hijacking incident into this and was sure he didn't want to, either. Yet she wondered if he'd be inclined to go in for lengthy air travel after what had happened to him. He'd been on his way back from a trip to Egypt, after all, when the terrible incident had taken place.

He said, perhaps a shade too casually, "I'm planning on going to Egypt again next year. I've even thought of taking a sabbatical and making Cairo my home base, from where I'll set off on a series of excursions. There's so much to learn."

He was still holding the small statuette of Nefertiti. He put it back on the bookshelf, then said, "Now...I've the feeling you called me over here because you have something you want to tell me. Right?"

He was closing the door on the subject of Egypt and his work and his future. Kay followed his lead and said, "Well, yes, I do have something to tell you, but first, would you like a drink? I poured myself some wine but I haven't touched it and—personally I think I could go for something stronger."

"Sounds okay," he said. "Would you have some Scotch on hand?"

She nodded. "Want to fix your own?" she invited him.

Alan followed her into the kitchenette and wound up making drinks for both of them...Scotch on the rocks for himself, bourbon and branch water for Kay.

They went back to the living room with their drinks and settled at opposite ends of the couch. "There," Kay said. "What I have to tell you, unfortunately, isn't much at all. The bronze key doesn't match any of the inn keys."

"Well, that doesn't come as any surprise, does it?" Alan queried. "You said you doubted there'd be a match."

"Yes, I know. I wasn't surprised, but I couldn't help being a bit disappointed. Now..."

"Yes?"

"I don't know where to turn next," she said, then amended that to, "Well, I do know where I probably should turn next, but I don't especially want to."

He chuckled. "You'll have to elaborate on that one, Kay."

"The logical move would be to go show the key to Gerard Dillard, Randy's brother," she said reluctantly. "To see if it has any significance to him. But I don't especially want to do that."

"Why not?"

"It's difficult to put 'why not' into so many words," she confessed.

Alan was watching her closely. "Okay, I don't want to jump to conclusions," he said. "But I can't help but get the idea you're not especially fond of your brother-in-law."

"I have to admit you're right."

"Okay," he said again, "I won't go further into that particular subject unless you want to get into it."

"I don't want to get into it."

"Fine," Alan said, though the rather penetrating glance he directed at Kay made her feel he didn't actually consider it very fine at all. "I do think, though, that you're going to have to approach your brother-in-law. Or perhaps pay a call on your husband's place of business. Unless someone else has taken over. . . ."

"Gerard has taken over," Kay said, "but only with my permission. Gerard and Randy were in business together, with a third man. Originally the firm was Dillard and Sons, and it's an old company, founded only ten or so years after the end of the War between the States. Sons succeeded sons, if you follow me. Only Dillards ran the business. Finally Gerard and Randy inherited equal shares. Then, a few years ago, they began contemplating expansion—it seemed to them the time was right for it—and they decided to take in a partner. They sold a forty percent interest in the business to a man named Bill Abernathy, who combined his own small company with Dillard and

Sons as well as putting in a certain amount of cash. Subsequently the name of the firm was changed to Dillard and Abernathy.''

Kay paused to take a sip of her drink. She disliked talking about any of this, yet she needed to spell it out if she was going to follow any course of action. And if she ever was going to find out what the key unlocked, she was going to have to start following some concrete courses of action.

Before she could speak again, Alan asked, ''Is Abernathy still active in the business?''

''Very much so.''

''How is the ownership divided now?''

''Since Randy's death? Well, I inherited Randy's share, which means that now Gerard and I each own thirty percent of the company, for a total of sixty percent, and Bill Abernathy owns forty percent.

''However,'' she continued, ''I've been pretty much letting Gerard run everything—handle my interest in the company, that's to say. For one thing, I have my hands full at the inn. For another thing, I don't know anything about the textile business. It never has interested me.''

''Wasn't your grandfather involved in it?''

''You're thinking that this building used to be a cotton warehouse, and he owned it. Well, that's true . . . but actually the cotton warehouse was a diversification for my grandfather. Have you noticed that acrid scent you smell around here when the wind's right?''

Alan looked surprised at the change of subject but said only, ''Yes. At moments it overpowers the magnolias.''

"I know. Well, the scent comes from turpentine, which is distilled from the sap of pine trees and is a major business in coastal Georgia. My Grandfather Randolph was primarily in the turpentine business. He bought the cotton warehouse as an investment, and it turned out to be a good one."

"I see."

"So the textile business is not in my blood," Kay said with a slight smile, "and to tell you the truth I have no desire to get involved in it."

"Thus, you're relying on your brother-in-law?"

"Right now, yes. I've been giving some serious thoughts to selling out."

"To whom? Your brother-in-law or his partner, Abernathy?"

"Maybe someone else entirely," Kay said. "I don't know. One of these days, I plan to talk to Gary about it—Gary Madison, he's my attorney. I think I told you it was he and his wife who were so helpful in getting me started here at the Randolph House."

"Yes."

"Alan," Kay said suddenly, "thanks so much for listening to all this. When I asked you to come over I didn't intend to burden you with my problems."

"I consider the key my problem, too, Kay," Alan said. "I brought it to you. If it opens a Pandora's box I want to know about it. I want to be around to help you in any way I can."

"But you can't be around," Kay said more fervently than she'd meant to.

"What do you mean?"

"You're only booked for three days."

"You looked up my reservation?"

"Yes."

"Because you hoped I'd be leaving sooner or you hoped I'd be staying longer?" Alan asked bluntly.

She hesitated for only a second. Then, meeting his eyes, she said, "I think you know the answer to that."

Alan felt his throat go dry even while that treacherous warm tide began washing over him again. He had a lot of willpower, but he didn't know how much longer he could hold on where this woman was concerned. She was sitting less than three feet away from him; he could span the two couch cushions between them in one swift motion. But he didn't. Once again, that gut instinct that he was coming to detest telegraphed that the timing was still all wrong.

He got a grip on himself and asked, "Would there still be room at the inn for me if I could extend my stay a few days?"

"There will always be room at this inn for you," Kay Dillard said.

She wasn't helping him much. He swallowed hard and tried to focus on the issue at hand. "Kay," he said, "it makes sense that maybe the key's to something in your husband's office."

"Yes, I've thought of that."

"Where are the offices of Dillard and Abernathy?"

"Just a few blocks from here, still within the historic district."

"I think you should go there tomorrow."

Kay asked the question he'd hoped she would ask. "I know it's an imposition," she began, "but...would you go with me?"

CHAPTER SIX

"I DON'T KNOW WHY I'm so nervous about this," Kay complained.

They were sitting in Alan's car, parked at the curbside a few doors down the street from the office of Dillard and Abernathy.

Alan said. "It's something you're not looking forward to, something you don't want to do. I think it's understandable you'd be edgy."

"Sure you don't teach psychology instead of Egyptology?"

"Positive." He smiled. "I'd make a lousy psychologist."

"What makes you say that?"

"I'm not that crazy about asking personal questions. Except," he amended, "in certain specific cases."

"Such as?"

"Now you're fishing."

"If you don't cast some bait into the water once in a while you never catch anything," Kay retorted impishly.

Alan laughed. "You do come up with the unexpected," he told her. "I never thought I'd hear anything like that from you."

He became aware that he was talking as if they had known each other for years. Actually they'd known each other for two days, going on two and a half. Regardless, he was intensely aware that he was in danger of falling in love with her.

He couldn't believe himself. He was too old to step out of character like this. He was not the impetuous, romantic type.

He grinned. The hell he was not the impetuous, romantic type. Once they put this business with the key behind them...

Kay said, "You look like that cat—Cheshire cat, wasn't it?—who swallowed the canary."

"No." Alan said, "the Cheshire cat was in *Alice in Wonderland*, wasn't he?"

"I think we're getting our references mixed up," Kay said, speaking with that soft Southern accent he found enchanting, though he'd never especially liked Southern accents before. She sighed. "We can't stall forever," she announced, becoming practical. "Let's get with it."

Alan had turned on the air-conditioning in the car. The contrast to the temperature outside made the day seem hotter than it actually was. The shadowy vestibule in the office building felt cool and damp.

"Look," Kay said, as they waited for the elevator, "I think I want to renege about something."

"Don't tell me you're going to suggest we turn around and walk out of here?" Alan protested.

"No. But I'd rather not show the key to Gerard."

"Then what's the point of this visit?"

"Maybe we can find what the key unlocks by ourselves. Whatever it is may be in Randy's office. For instance, it could be a key to a desk drawer."

"I suppose so."

"I'd prefer to tell Gerard I want to get something out of Randy's desk. If we don't find what we're looking for then, perhaps I'll show him the key."

Alan shrugged. "It's your show."

The receptionist in the outer office at Dillard and Abernathy was a tall, model-slim redhead. Her face had interesting, angular planes. It occurred to Alan that she'd probably be very photogenic. She was attractive. Extremely attractive. Expensive clothes, he assessed, and even more expensive chunky gold jewelry.

She didn't look as if she belonged in a relatively humdrum job. Also, though the hostility in her hazel eyes was veiled as she greeted Kay, he still caught it. Kay returned the greeting stiffly, which puzzled him further. Then, introducing them, she said, "This is Fleur Collingwood, Alan. Fleur was Randy's secretary."

Alan mentally promoted Fleur a notch. She was not merely a receptionist, she was a secretary-receptionist. Perhaps Dillard and Abernathy's only clerical employee? That remained to be seen. Regardless, she still seemed out of sync for the job she was holding.

At Kay's request, Fleur Collingwood summoned Gerard Dillard on the intercom. Gerard came into the outer office immediately. His smile was expansive as he greeted his sister-in-law, and Alan suspected he would have hugged her had Kay not stepped back quickly. Gerard was a handsome man, his well-toned physique set off by a beautifully tailored pale gray suit. There was a strong family resemblance to Randolph Dillard, Alan noted; in fact, he briefly felt as if he were seeing a ghost. But Gerard's face was fleshier and there were crow's-feet in the corners of his dark eyes;

the few years' age difference between his late brother and himself showed.

Gerard led them into his office, a large corner room expensively decorated in an ultracontemporary style. The furniture was ash blond, the color scheme pale earth tones, spiced by splashes of burnt orange.

Sitting down behind his oversize executive desk, Gerard said affably, "This is an unexpected pleasure, Kay. She doesn't come this way often, Mr. Johnston."

Before Alan could comment on that, Kay said, "I wanted you to meet Alan. He's here in Savannah on a short visit from Vermont, where he teaches in a college." She hesitated then, avoiding her brother-in-law's eyes by staring down at his rug, and said, "Alan came down here to see me because he wanted to tell me about Randy."

Gerard's dark eyebrows arched expressively. "Randy?"

"Yes. Alan was also a hostage on the hijacked plane."

There was no doubt in Alan's mind that Gerard Dillard's shock was genuine. "My God!" he exclaimed. "I—I've wondered about the others who were on that plane with Randy. What a terrible experience it must have been for you."

"I survived," Alan said quietly.

Gerard stared at him blankly. Then he said, "Yes, of course. I can see you'd consider yourself one of the lucky ones. Even so..." He shook his head. "It would be enough to haunt a man for the rest of his life."

Alan didn't answer that.

Kay said steadily. "Alan was sitting next to Randy on the plane, Gerard. He says Randy felt sure he was marked for... for execution, by one of the hijackers.

As it turned out, he was right. But I take it from what Alan has told me that Randy was...remarkably calm. That's to say, he didn't panic."

Alan found himself the focus of Gerard's dark eyes and, confirming Kay's halting statement, he said, "That's so. Your brother was a very brave man, Mr. Dillard."

He saw Gerard Dillard close his eyes and shudder slightly. Then Gerard said, "Thank you for telling me that. I've wondered many times how it was with Randy...at the end. I feared maybe he was tortured...."

"No," Alan said. "It was very quick."

"For that I'm thankful."

A thick silence wedged between the three of them. Alan tried to read Gerard's face, but couldn't. He watched as Gerard finally managed a smile, straightened his tie, as if hoping to gain reassurance from a familiar gesture and then, to Alan's surprise, glanced significantly at his desk clock.

"I would like to suggest we lunch together," he said, "but unfortunately I'm already late for a meeting that will extend into the midafternoon. So I'm going to have to ask you to excuse me. How long are you planning to stay in Savannah, Mr. Johnston?"

"I'm not sure," Alan said. "I'm on a leave of absence from my college...."

"Well, then," Gerard said, "I hope you'll bring Mr. Johnston to dinner at our place on Sunday, Kay. Tracy—my wife—would never forgive me if I let you leave town without a taste of her Southern hospitality," he added to Alan.

Before Kay could refuse the invitation, Alan said, "I would like that very much."

Kay gritted her teeth. Coming here, facing Gerard, had been bad enough. She'd plunged into the traumatic subject of Randy's death because she'd suddenly recognized the need to camouflage her real reason for appearing at the office. But the idea of dining at Gerard and Tracy's home didn't appeal to her.

She was hard put not to glare openly at Alan. She felt he'd trapped her.

She remembered her real purpose as Gerard stood, obviously expecting them to follow suit and then to take their leave.

"Gerard," she said, halting him, "while I'm here I want to go through a few things in Randy's desk. Provided, that is, you haven't already emptied it out."

"No," Gerard said slowly. "We haven't touched a thing in Randy's desk, Kay. Everything's just as he left it. I kind of thought going through his things should be up to you, since his office is yours, now... or will be, if you ever care to use it. As I hope you will, one of these days. However..."

"Yes?"

"I really do have to get out of here. Must you go through Randy's things today? The desk has waited this long...."

"I'd prefer to do it now," Kay said. "But there's no reason for you to stay around because of that."

She saw Gerard frown and knew he didn't like this. But, especially with Alan watching both of them, there wasn't much he could do about it.

"Very well," he conceded. "If you need anything, I'm sure Fleur can help you out." To Alan, he said, "Ms Collingwood was Randy's secretary. Now she's acting temporarily as secretary both to my partner, Bill

Abernathy, and to me. She's also filling in as receptionist, as well. Our receptionist is sick."

"Is Bill around?" Kay asked.

Gerard shook his head. "No. He's in Atlanta on business for the company for a couple of days." He paused. "I really do have to be on my way," he said.

"That's all right, Gerard," Kay said quickly. "Don't let us detain you."

She waited until Gerard had left the room and she could hear him speaking to Fleur Collingwood in the outer office. Then she sank down on the nearest chair and said, "Whew! I need a minute to pull myself together."

"You handled it well," Alan commended her. "Very well."

"I don't know," Kay said doubtfully. "Gerard is extremely sharp. I have the feeling he thinks I'm up to something."

"Why should that be?"

"I can't answer that. I just know that for all Gerard's talk I think the last thing in the world he'd want is for me to move in here and play a role as part owner of this company."

She shivered. "Thank God you were here," she told Alan. "There's no way I could have gotten through this by myself."

"Without Gerard making a pass at you?" Alan suggested.

She looked up at him, startled. "Why do you ask that?"

"I saw the way he looked at you," Alan said. "Even when he was being particularly urbane, his eyes were smoldering. Has it always been that way, Kay?"

She nodded. "Yes. The first time—well, Randy and I were just back from our honeymoon and we were having dinner at Tracy and Gerard's. I went upstairs to the bathroom and when I came out Gerard was waiting in the doorway of their bedroom. He had this...this conspiratorial *smirk* on his face and he told me he wanted to show me something. He grabbed my hand and tugged me into the bedroom, and he showed me some earrings he'd bought for Tracy—her birthday was the following week—but that was only a ruse. He took me in his arms and pressed me up against him and he...well, he was fully aroused and it was... terrible."

"Your husband and his wife were right downstairs?"

"Yes," Kay said, "as I quickly pointed out to him. I told him I'd scream for them if he didn't let me go. I think for a minute he didn't believe me, but then he changed his mind. He let me go but he stood back, smiling at me, and he promised that sooner or later I'd see things his way."

"He tried again?"

"He's tried many times over the years, Alan," Kay said wearily. "Whenever he's had the chance, which has been as seldom as I could possibly make it, but there've been moments when, inevitably, we've been left alone together. That, among other reasons, is why I felt it would have been hell to come here by myself...."

"Then I'm very glad I came with you."

"You'll never know how glad *I* am," Kay said fervently. She stood up again. "We'd better go over to Randy's office before Fleur Collingwood starts monitoring us," she said.

Randolph Dillard's office was also a large corner one, at the opposite end of Dillard and Abernathy's suite. Randy had chosen a more traditional decorative scheme. His enormous desk was made of Honduran mahogany, beige floor-to-ceiling drapes framed the windows, and in addition to several chairs there was a couch flanked by a low coffee table, upon which was arranged a small collection of antique paperweights.

There were a couple of oil portraits in heavy gilt frames on the wall. "Two of the earlier Dillards," Kay told Alan then, her expressive face revealing her distaste for this entire caper. She pulled out the swivel chair back of Randy's desk and sat down.

The desk drawers, she quickly discovered, were locked. She fished the key out of her handbag, tried it, then shook her head. "Definitely not right," she said.

Alan, moving around the room, had opened one door that led to a small bathroom and was now opening another, behind which there was a fairly large closet.

Kay joined him as he switched on a light in the closet and surveyed its interior. The shelves were empty, except for a few reams of paper, some file folders and a couple of boxes of pencils. A set of golf clubs was propped in a corner, and a raincoat hung from a hook.

"Nothing," Kay said, her spirits sinking.

"Let's not give up yet," Alan cautioned. "Maybe there's something in one of the desk drawers. Do you suppose Miss what's-her-name would have a key to the desk?"

Kay shrugged. "I can ask her."

She discovered Fleur literally tapping her fingers on the desk blotter. Their eyes met, and Kay felt the odd little chill she always felt when she came face-to-face with Fleur Collingwood.

"Are we keeping you from lunch?" she asked rather coldly.

"I do have an appointment, yes," Fleur said.

"Why don't you go along, then?"

"No. I'll need to put on the security system when I leave here. Gerard won't be back till midafternoon, and I expect to be away a couple of hours myself."

There was an edge of insolence to Fleur's voice that wasn't lost on Kay, who also noted that Fleur didn't bother to conceal the fact that she customarily called Gerard by his first name—except, probably, in front of clients.

A quiet rage that had started simmering a long time ago threatened to resurface, but Kay found herself able to push it back. Fleur, and everything concerning her, no longer mattered. It was a long while since she'd discovered the truth—that Fleur and Randy were lovers and her job as his "secretary" was primarily camouflage.

She kept her dignity in high gear as she asked for the desk key. Fleur gave it to her without a word.

The single key unlocked all the drawers of the desk. As she used it on the top one, with Alan watching, it occurred to Kay that anything of relevance in the desk—especially if it concerned Fleur—had probably long since been removed. Maybe Gerard hadn't gotten into the contents of Randy's office. That didn't mean that Randy's "secretary" hadn't.

As she suspected, there was nothing of any significance in the desk. She found only trivia, and not very interesting trivia. Some snaps of Randy taken at various civic dinners, posing with most of Savannah's leading citizens at one time or another. Some shots of the year before last's St. Patrick's Day parade, in which Randy had played a role—Savannah's St. Patrick's Day celebration had come to be one of the biggest in the United States.

Aside from the miscellany of photographs, there were some address books, mostly filled with business-connected names and phone numbers, a few golf scorecards, some antihistamine tablets, a bottle of aspirin, a couple of minis of Russian vodka, two neckties and two neatly pressed and folded monogrammed handkerchiefs.

Despite the relative innocuousness of the desk contents, though, Kay's hands were trembling as she replaced the final item, closed the drawer and locked it.

Her face was set as she left the office, and she felt as if she were walking like a mannequin taking a series of jerky steps. She paused at Fleur's desk to give back the key, then as she left the office felt as if Fleur's eyes were burning a hole in her back. She no longer gave a damn about Fleur—except for a natural resentment that came with too many memories. On the other hand, she felt pretty sure that Fleur still disliked her intensely, maybe even hated her.

As she and Alan emerged into the bright, hot sunlight, Kay whipped a pair of dark glasses out of her handbag and put them on. Her hands were still trembling as she did so, and she quickly became aware that Alan had noted the trembling.

He clutched her elbow and said urgently, "The two of us need to get away for a while."

Kay was performing by rote. She said dully, "I have to go back to the inn."

"The hell you have to go back to the inn. In case you didn't notice, Homer Telfair was walking in the door as we left."

She frowned. "That early? Homer's not due to come in till four."

"Well, maybe he couldn't bring himself to stay away today. Whatever, he's there. I think you'll agree he can handle things for a while. I'm right in assuming you have a lot of faith in him, am I not?"

"Yes, I have a lot of faith in Homer."

"Okay, then, where can we go?"

They reached the car. Kay stared at him helplessly. "Alan," she said, "there just isn't any place to go."

"Kay, I'm not asking you to take off into space with me. There must be someplace within a reasonable drive from here where we can just relax for a while."

"All right," she decided. "Let's drive over to Tybee Island."

"Is it far?"

"About eighteen miles, but there's a good road all the way. Tybee's the first of the string of Georgia's barrier islands, also the nearest to Savannah. You've probably heard of some of the more famous islands—like St. Simons and Jekyll, which are big resort areas."

Kay settled down in the front seat of the car and gave Alan directions to President Street, where they connected with the Island Expressway. She was quiet, a shade too quiet, Alan thought.

He'd caught those smoldering glances Gerard had given her, especially when he thought she wasn't looking at him, and a certain picture began to emerge.

He wondered if she'd ever said anything to her husband about his brother's annoying overtures. Very possibly she hadn't. He was getting the impression that Kay and Randy hadn't communicated as much as they might have. Also, there had been some definite vibes emanating from Fleur Collingwood. The woman made little secret of the fact she didn't like Kay. He would have said her attitude indicated jealousy. Was she jealous of a dead man? Just where did that put Kay, and where did it put Fleur?

Alan gave up his speculation and chuckled silently. Maybe he should have been a psychologist instead of an Egyptologist, after all.

He concentrated on enjoying the day, the coastal plain they were driving across with its acres of marshland and aquamarine inlets weaving in from the Atlantic, the clear blue sky, the puffy white clouds. Casting away the ghost of Randolph Dillard, which had loomed again with the visit to the Dillard and Abernathy offices, Alan centered upon his prime objective right now, which entirely concerned the woman at his side.

He wanted to bring the light of laughter back into her eyes. He loved that light, and the glint of humor and zest for life Kay had shown him every now and then, which she kept suppressed far too much of the time. He was determined the two of them banish the shadows that had been hovering over them, regardless of the damned key.

They drove across the island to the public beach that fronted the ocean, parked and strolled out onto the boardwalk.

As they walked, Kay mentioned that there was a lighthouse at the north end of the island, as well as

Fort Screven, an old coastal defense. Alan nodded, but admitted frankly that he wasn't much in a mood for exploration.

"Too hot, for one thing," he said.

"You Yankees," Kay protested. "What would you do in July or August?"

"Become an air-conditioning freak," he said, wanting to encourage the hint of a smile that was curving her lips.

The smile soon faded, though. Kay was preoccupied, and the beauty of the day didn't seem to be getting to her at all. Though it was true the sun was hot, there was a caressing offshore breeze that was both gentle and refreshing. The tide was low, and watching the shallow waves break on the sand Alan asked suddenly, "Do you like to wade?"

She hesitated, but then she laughed. "Why not?" she said.

On this early April weekday, the beach was not crowded. They took off their shoes and left them at the corner of some short wooden steps. Alan rolled up his trouser legs. Kay, barelegged, was wearing a dress with a fairly short skirt. Hand in hand they traipsed across the sand, and then, as the water rolled over her toes, Kay squealed.

"It's cold," she complained.

"Ha," Alan said. "You'd never make it in the North Atlantic. To say nothing of a Vermont lake."

In answer she suddenly swooped down and flicked the saltwater dripping from her fingers so that it sprayed across his nose. He sputtered, brushed the drops away and had a sudden impulse to dunk her. Evidently she read his mind, because she warned, "Don't you dare!"

He reached for her, clutching her shoulders. Kay, about to scamper away from him, stood still. Alan's hands slid down from her shoulders, past short cap sleeves, and came to rest on her firm, warm flesh. He tautened, his reaction to her sending a live current of desire through every fiber of his body.

He saw that Kay was staring at him, and her face looked like an ivory mask. Only the eyes were alive, glowing like huge blue sapphires. Then suddenly she reached for him, throwing her arms around his waist. He tugged her toward him, pillowing her head against his chest as he stroked her beautiful, satin-soft dark hair. He bent to nuzzle the hollow back of her ear, then to tentatively touch that tender spot with his tongue.

Kay jerked her head back and he could feel the fire in her, as if she'd suddenly been ignited. To his surprise and delight, she made the next move, pressing even closer against his body. She raised her hands and placed them on either side of his neck, then slowly feathered her fingers across his skin until her touch became a series of small electrical charges.

Alan moaned, the sudden rush of his need for her filling him like wine poured to overflowing. He moved involuntarily, pressing against Kay, so thoroughly aroused that he knew he was on the edge of tumbling past a point of no return.

He felt as if he was drunk on her nearness, her beauty, her incredible sexiness. He saw her mouth, deep rose, full, inviting. He answered the invitation with his lips, his kiss plundering, demanding, passionate—and Kay parted her lips so that suddenly their tongues were touching, probing, putting both of them on an emotional staircase that spiraled upward and upward and upward....

In the distance, Alan heard the sound of laughter. Children's laughter. The sound brought with it the realization that the two of them were standing up to their ankles in ocean water on a public beach in broad daylight ... where, no matter how much they wanted to, they couldn't let themselves topple over the edge.

He wrested his mouth away from Kay's, but he still held her close to him. His laugh was low, husky. "Why can't we blot out the sun and bring on the moon?" he asked her, his voice even huskier. "So that right here, right now..."

She looked up at him, her breath still coming fast, her cheeks tinged with soft color, her blue eyes looking slightly unfocused and very, very sensual. Then she smiled, and there was laughter in her voice as she chided, "Scandalous. Those are downright scandalous thoughts, Mr. Johnston."

Alan could smile back at her easily, because he knew damned well that she shared his scandalous thoughts.

He kept his arm around her as they slowly walked back toward the boardwalk. He wanted the reassurance that she was there, flesh and blood, beautiful and so infinitely desirable.

He also knew he never wanted to let her go.

CHAPTER SEVEN

THEY STOPPED in a small café outside Savannah where they ordered boiled shrimp in the shell and large mugs of draft beer.

Alan, peeling a shrimp, said, "Living in a place like this could get to be a habit. I do go for your seafood."

Kay nearly picked up on that statement to ask him if that was all he went for on her home turf, but she bit back the words and concentrated on peeling a shrimp herself.

Alan had told Gerard he had a leave of absence from his college. Kay had a cousin, on her mother's side of the family, who taught at the University of Georgia, so she knew leaves of absence were hard to come by in the course of an academic year. Alan hadn't said how long his leave was for. He had indicated earlier that he'd stay as long as he could be helpful to her. He'd asked quizzically if there'd be room at the inn for him. . . .

She remembered her statement that there'd always be room at her inn for him and felt herself flushing at the memory.

The flush deepened as she thought about falling into his arms out at Tybee Island. She'd been close to tumbling down into the shallows with him and letting him make love to her. Remembering the "almost" was like lighting a sparkler on the Fourth of July. Little white-hot sparks flew off in all directions.

She had never before cast her inhibitions to the wind as she had out there on Savannah Beach with Alan. Her natural restraint had floated away on the warm spring breeze. She'd been conscious only of Alan, his warmth, his nearness, that telltale masculinity pressed tight against her, and the spiraling desire. . . .

She'd also never before felt as free as she had while they stood clutching each other with the waves lapping around their bare ankles, their mouths merging, their unsuppressed passion soaring. Nothing had mattered except the moment. Today for a little while she'd been true to herself, responding without holding back . . . and it had felt wonderful.

Alan, a glint of humor lighting his eyes, commented, "What I wouldn't give to be a mind reader."

Flustered, Kay asked, "What do you mean?"

"You looked as if you were having a vision of sugarplums," Alan said, the humor creeping into his voice. "What were you having a vision of, Kay?"

She couldn't answer him, but from the way his teasing smile faded and his eyes suddenly darkened she was sure he was getting her silent message.

He confirmed this by saying huskily, "I feel the same way. That was magic out there on the island. It's magic I wish we could hold on to, Kay."

"How can we?" she asked bleakly.

"I'll play devil's advocate with that one. Why can't we?"

Kay twisted her oversize paper napkin. "Magic evaporates when you have to bump head-on into reality, Alan."

"Does it have to?"

"I don't see how it wouldn't have to. It's like Santa Claus. Sooner or later, children find out about Santa Claus."

"That wasn't a myth out on the island," Alan said steadily. "In fact, I'd say that was reality."

"We scarcely know each other," Kay protested.

"I don't buy that."

"Alan...count the hours."

"The hours don't count, Kay. You can't measure everything by...measurements. I feel I know you better than I do many people I've known for years."

She smiled sadly. "Aren't you afraid that's wishful thinking? Wishful thinking can be dangerous."

"I'm willing to risk that kind of danger. Kay, believe me, I'm as aware of everything about our situation as you are...."

He broke off, because, when he permitted awareness to infiltrate, Randolph Dillard seemed to come to stand in the shadows again. Except...Dillard wasn't the threat he'd been, even yesterday. The picture Alan had initially had in his mind of Kay and Randy Dillard as the perfect couple—good-looking, successful, madly in love with each other—had begun at some point to go out of focus, and now there were sections of it that were decidedly blurred.

Kay said intuitively, "The past creeps in, doesn't it?"

Alan met her eyes and smiled a slightly lopsided smile. "Sure, the past creeps in," he agreed. "And you and I have both had our share of a past, haven't we? That doesn't mean we don't have a present...and a future. Speaking personally—ever since I came back from Nam I've been pretty much living a day at a time. Trying to forget about the past and not thinking too much about the future because I didn't see all that much to look forward to."

He shook his head slightly as if chastising himself. "That sounds gloomy and self-pitying," he said, "and I don't mean it that way. I've had good fortune along with the bad. I haven't had to worry about money, for one thing, as so many people do. Not long after I got back from Nam my mother's older brother died, and I was his sole heir. So that freed me to go back to school, eventually to do my doctorate, to take those jaunts to Egypt and other places around the globe. For all of which I'm grateful. But . . ."

"I knew there'd be a 'but,'" Kay said, smiling faintly.

"I like what I'm doing," Alan said. "I like teaching, and most of the kids are great. I like my preoccupation with the ancient past. The 'but' is that at times I get restless as hell, and I think that goes back to Nam. I guess I've never entirely gotten flying helicopters out of my system. That's why I intend, sometime, to convert one fantasy into reality. One of these years I'm going to buy myself a Huey."

"A *what*?"

"A vintage helicopter," Alan said. "The Hueys were the jeeps of the Vietnam War. A lot of us who flew them fell in love with them. Now and then, a Huey comes up for sale at a government auction, and sometimes you can get one for a ridiculously low price."

Kay laughed. "Where in the world would you keep a toy like that?"

"Oh," Alan said, "I could always berth her at the small local airfield we have in Mansfield. Maybe even keep her in my own backyard if someday I own a place with a big enough backyard.''

He was thinking of the extensive grounds around his grandmother's house, as he spoke. He tried to picture Kay in the old family homestead but couldn't. She belonged too much to this exotic, different-tempoed Southern scene. Also, he reminded himself, it was here that she was involved in not one but two business—she was a partner in Dillard and Abernathy, after all, like it or not—and she certainly had a developing career in the inn business.

Kay asked, ''Why did the sun suddenly go out?''

''What do you mean?''

''You looked as if you were having the vision this time. Then...''

''Yeah, I know,'' Alan said. ''You know what?''

''What?''

''I think you and I both tend to be too introspective. What we should have done was to take bathing suits out there to Tybee Island and have a good, rugged swim.''

''Alan, the water still would have been freezing,'' Kay protested.

''I doubt that. Probably the water offshore here right now is considerably warmer than it ever gets up north. Anyway, we both need to do a little cobweb clearing. Cold water's excellent for that.''

Kay said slowly, ''I thought I'd pretty well cleared out my cobwebs...until you showed up with the key.''

''Ouch!'' he murmured.

''I didn't mean it that way,'' she put in quickly. ''It's simply that all of a sudden I had to remember a lot of things I didn't want to remember.''

''Yes,'' he said dryly, ''I can imagine.''

"Please," Kay implored, "don't look like that. Don't you realize that I wouldn't for anything in the world *not* have had you show up?"

"You mean that?"

"Of course I mean it. It's just that . . ."

"You don't have to explain." He stretched and said suddenly, "I think I could do with another beer. How about you?"

"I'm still nursing this one."

The sole waitress in the little café was not in evidence. Alan strode over to the bar himself, beer mug in hand, and Kay watched him, aware that they were skating on thin ice in a lot of their conversation and that the waters under that ice were very, very deep.

She thought long and hard and quickly about what she needed to say to Alan. And once he was settled back in the booth again, she was prepared.

"I think," she said, "before we go any further there is something I should tell you."

"Oh?"

She heard the caution in his tone, but plunged ahead.

"Before Randy left on that trip to Egypt, I consulted Gary Madison about a divorce."

Alan set his beer mug down on the table with a thud and stared at her.

"I was late, very late, in doing so," Kay went on steadily. "Randy and I should have been divorced years ago. I don't think we'd been married six months when I knew it was . . . wrong. Randy didn't have it in him to be . . . faithful. He and Gerard were alike in that respect. Natural womanizers, and with their kind of looks they had no problem attracting women like moths to a flame.

"Maybe if I'd had a child, it would have been different. But, as I was to find out, Randy couldn't father a child, which actually was fine with him. It took me some time to discover that. He let me think it was my 'fault' I couldn't conceive, not his. Not that it mattered so much. The result was the same. So—"

"Kay," Alan said suddenly, "you don't have to tell me this."

"I want to tell you," Kay insisted. "It's all right."

"It's not all right. Do you realize you're tearing that paper napkin to shreds?"

Kay looked down at her hands. Earlier, she'd been twisting the napkin. Now she saw that she was, indeed, tearing it to shreds, and she quickly rolled the shreds into a ball and pushed the ball away from her.

"Look," Alan said, "for a while there you were relaxed. Now this has pushed you back on edge again."

"If I have to be on edge I'll have to be on edge," Kay said. "It's important to me that you know this because I think it's wrong to have you assume that Randy and I were the ideal couple most people thought we were. We kept up a good front. But that's all it was. Actually, for the last three years before he was killed, Fleur Collingwood had been Randy's mistress, and I doubt even she was the only one for him during that period. You must have seen the way she looked at me when we were in the office."

"Yes," Alan said. "I saw."

"In a way, I feel so terrible about telling you this," Kay said. "Because Randy is dead. . . ."

"And you've been brought up not to speak ill of the dead?"

"Yes, I suppose that's partly it."

"But if he'd come back from Egypt, you would have divorced him."

"Yes. Very definitely, yes. My plans for the inn were well under way by then. I could see my way. I'd garnered the strength to do what I had to do...which was something that I had to build up in myself. There is no way I would have stayed married to Randy, there's no doubt about that at all. But that doesn't help the guilt. Do you know what I mean?"

"I know exactly what you mean," Alan told her. "Because I've worked my way through some pretty staggering guilt burdens myself, and sometimes I get hit all over again by feelings of what I could have done but didn't do.

"I can't tell you how many hundreds of times, usually in the middle of a sleepless night, I've told myself that if I had insisted Meiling go to Saigon with me instead of letting her go back to her own village she would probably be alive today. And I'd have a college-age kid.

"Honesty compels me to admit I don't know how we would ever have made it together, Meiling and I. She was a very simple, unsophisticated country girl. I was not in love with her, but there was a war on, we were all of us living from day to day and—to use an old-fashioned phrase—I took advantage of her. When she came to me and told me she was pregnant, I felt I had to marry her because what had happened was my own stupid fault. So I did. I'm sure I would have loved our child. I think Meiling would have tried her damnedest to be a good wife to me, and I'm sure I would have grown very fond of her. But it could never have been the kind of love..."

He nearly said, the kind of love I could feel for you, but realized in time that, for the moment, those words were best left unspoken. He substituted, "The kind of love I could feel for a woman I had a great deal more in common with."

"Did you feel that kind of love for your first wife?" Kay asked him.

Alan didn't answer immediately. He was looking down the years and trying to conjure up a picture of Valerie, who had been pretty and giddy and selfish and had looked on life as a kind of soap-opera existence. He'd been dating Valerie when he was drafted, and he was sure that in her mind he'd quickly become material for a chapter in her own personal soap opera. She'd flung herself into the drama of marrying him, seeing him off to war with a valiant smile, then by the time he was able to ask her to meet him for an R and R period in Hawaii, she'd already gone on to greener pastures and he was, instead, met with her request for a divorce.

At the time he'd thought he was heartbroken. He became intensely bitter and did some serious sorrow-drowning while he was in Honolulu. Later, still stinging, he'd enlisted for another tour of duty. And life had gone on from there.

Now—it was crazy perhaps—but he could scarcely remember what Valerie looked like.

He answered Kay's question. "No," he said, "I didn't feel that kind of love for my first wife. The kind of love I'm talking about requires a certain degree of maturity."

"When I look back," Kay said, "I think Randy mesmerized me. I was young and very impressionable, and it was my grandfather who brought me up after my parents' death, so you might say I was brought up in the style of another generation. My grandfather was an old-fashioned Southern gentleman. He believed in honor and integrity and all those other wonderful values that get lost so often these days. I'm sure he would have challenged anyone to a duel who besmirched the name of a lady in his family. Did you know, incidentally, that the duello code is still not extinct in the South...or so I understand, anyway.

"Grandfather was strict with me. I'm not saying he taught me to believe in hellfire and damnation, but I certainly had some terrible fears about what would happen to me if I ever slept with a man before matrimony.

"That was...unique," Kay continued. "And I think maybe it's what made me so attractive to Randy Dillard. Randy knew how I'd been brought up, and I think maybe the greatest shock of his life would have been if it had turned out I was *not* a virgin when we married, but of course I was."

Kay thought back to her wedding night and grimaced slightly. The expression was not lost on Alan. He could imagine how Dillard had taken her, and that she'd gotten very little pleasure from the act. He wondered if later—

He shut off those thoughts. That, after all, was her own damned business, he told himself savagely.

"I don't think," Kay said slowly, "anyone's ever all wrong in any relationship. In other words, it takes two to...misfire. Randy and I were never meant for each other. We were poles apart. Probably the same can be said of Valerie, and Meiling, and you. Sometimes people can work things out, sometimes they can't. I couldn't. Maybe, if it hadn't been for a war that kept you away from Valerie at a time when you should have been with her, or later if it hadn't been for the wartime tragedy that involved Meiling, you could have—''

"No," Alan said, suddenly certain. "No, I couldn't have."

He looked at Kay, surprised at his declaration. He said reflectively, "I feel like a camel that's just had its hump flattened."

"What in the world do you mean by that?"

"Well, a hump is undeniably an essential part of a camel's physiology, but they always look uncomfortable to me. A camel's saddled with forever carrying around its own burden. I've been carrying around a burden for a hell of a long time, and all of a sudden I feel as if it's . . . been lifted."

He smiled that lopsided smile again. "Maybe you're the one who should be a psychologist," he suggested.

"No way," Kay said. Her matching smile was rather wan. He wondered if maybe she, too, felt a little bit more relieved of her guilt burden since she'd talked about her marriage, but somehow he doubted it. Kay, he suspected, still had a few hurdles to get over.

She confirmed that when she said, "Maybe you can better understand now, why I reacted to the key as I did."

"If you mean have I figured out you're almost afraid to find out what it opens, yes, I do understand that," Alan told her.

"I am afraid," Kay confessed. "Yet . . . I have to find out, don't I?"

KAY ENCOUNTERED an immediate problem at the inn when they returned. The reservations had been over-booked, and two couples had arrived to find that there were no rooms for them.

Homer was being the epitome of Southern charm and graciousness as he tried to mollify the guests, but Kay appreciated that he didn't have the authority to make any concrete decisions.

She stepped in, apologized profusely for what had happened and offered the people drinks in the lounge while she found suitable accommodations for them. She further suggested that they come back to the Buccaneer for a dinner—also courtesy of the man-agement—while in Savannah.

By then the two couples were commiserating with each other, though they'd never met before. They headed for the lounge as a foursome, and Kay ob-served with a wry smile, "Well, maybe something good will come of this. Maybe the four of them will turn out to be lifelong friends."

"I hope so," Homer said. And added fervently, "Was I ever glad to see you walk through that door!"

"You were doing very well," Kay complimented him.

She got busy on the phone in the back office, call-ing both friends of her own and business contacts in-volved in the hotel business.

This was the height of the season in Savannah and rooms were at a premium. The result was that she had to book rooms for them in a considerably more exclu-sive hostelry at Randolph House's expense. Next time around, these people would probably come to Ran-dolph House because of her generosity and would probably suggest her inn to friends, as well.

As she went back to the registration desk, Kay thought whimsically that while she would never make a psychologist, she might very well qualify for the diplomatic service, if she kept on in the hotel business.

Homer was rechecking other reservations on the books, and he looked up to ask, "Were you able to find anything?"

"For a price," Kay said, nodding. "Homer, go into the lounge and tell them I've booked some especially lovely riverfront rooms for them, which will be held till they're ready to claim them. And remind them we'll be expecting them here for dinner in the Buccaneer one night."

With Homer going about his mission, Kay glanced at the wall clock. It was not yet four, which meant Francey should still be on duty.

One more thorn, she thought resignedly.

At that, she glanced up to see that Alan was still in the lobby, seated in an easy chair by a window and scanning the daily paper.

She liked the chance of being able to watch him without his being aware of it. Though she felt somewhat drained by this afternoon's conversation with him, the experience had also been a catharsis. She couldn't say that her hump had been flattened entirely. She still felt the straining kind of burden that only emotional guilt imposes. But talking to Alan—a first for her, for she'd never before talked to anyone about things like that—had helped.

She could see now that her guilt feelings had little to do with the fact she'd become determined to divorce Randy. What did bother her was the role she'd been placed in after Randy's death. Naturally she had grieved. But she had grieved as a person, not a widow, and the sorrowing widow's role into which she'd been cast by almost everyone who'd known the two of them had made her feel such a fraud.

Only Gary and Lucinda Madison, of all their friends, had known the truth. They had stood by her. There were times when Kay felt she'd have lost her sanity without them. And time had passed, helped, healed. Until Alan appeared with the key.

What *did* the damned key open?

What did she think it might open? Kay posed that question to herself and had to admit she had no idea. Was she fearing that maybe whatever the key unlocked would constitute some kind of revenge on Randy's part? That, she knew, was wrong. There had been nothing involved in her life with him that could have caused him to want any kind of retaliation.

As for Alan—he was right when he said that everything couldn't be measured by time. Nor was it possible to explain why just looking at him like this, was enough to make that insidious wanting start to twist inside her all over again.

She disliked the idea that there was some kind of special chemistry flowing between the two of them, because that concept seemed so trite. But she had to admit that there surely was a very special something between Alan and herself, and that something scared her.

It was easy to tell herself that she was a thirty-four-year-old woman who was finally coming into her own in so many ways, and should be able to handle an emotional surcharge, like this soaring feeling that was possessing her where Alan was concerned, without becoming unhinged by it. At this time in her life she should even be able to have an affair, and to take it in stride. To enjoy without letting the world come to an end afterward.

Could she? Could she have an affair with Alan and then bid him goodbye and watch him go back to Vermont while she stayed on here in Savannah and ran her inn?

Kay knew she'd never given to a man even a measure of what was in her to give. She knew that with Alan she'd give it all. There would be no holding back with him, nor would she want there to be. But when he was gone she'd be like an empty well that only he could refill.

She'd never thought of it this way before, but now she realized she was a proverbial one-man woman. And in that kind of dedication there was danger.

Alan looked up and saw Kay watching him. From this distance he couldn't read her expression clearly, but he did know she looked very intense.

He saw Homer Telfair exit the lounge and go back to the registration desk. Homer and Kay became involved in a conversation, broken off only when the desk phone rang and Homer answered it.

With that, Kay circled the edge of the desk and walked across the lobby to Alan. When he started to stand she said, "No, don't. Stay where you are," and sat down in the armchair next his.

Looking at him, she said quietly. "Life really does sometimes seem to be just one damned thing after another, doesn't it?"

He chuckled. "Tell me about it. Well...what's happened now?"

"Homer, as you know, came to work early today, otherwise I wonder if there would have been anyone on the desk this afternoon. At some point, Francey took off. I'm beginning to see I'm going to have to hire more help. I'm not going to be able to count on Francey anymore, and her shift is a very important one.''

"Can't you speak to her?"

"It wouldn't do any good," Kay confessed. She exhaled a short, sharp breath. "Here I go again," she complained.

"Where are you going?"

"That was a rhetorical statement. What I mean is, here I go about to get into problems with you again.''

"You don't have to sound so unhappy about that," Alan advised her. Then he added, "Sharing's important, Kay. I don't think either you or I have ever had so many people around we could really share with. At least, I know that's true of myself. Maybe I'm making a false assumption about you.''

"No," she said. "No, you're not making a false assumption about me."

"Well, I don't think we were, any of us, meant to go it alone. I don't think it's any sign of weakness to admit that it helps to share. There's no need to take everything on our own backs.''

"The camel's hump?" Kay suggested, her mouth curving in that slight smile he'd come to love.

"Yes, exactly. It helped me today to talk about Meiling, especially. Also, I appreciate your having confided in me the things you did. Now don't be so hesitant if there's something else maybe I could help you with.''

"This is a real stickler," Kay said grimly. She looked around, then said suddenly, "You know, I love this place but sometimes it closes in on me. Right now, I wish we were both back out on Tybee Island.''

Alan chuckled. "Don't tempt me."

He saw a flush of color stain Kay's cheeks and loved it. She looked unutterably beautiful to him; there was a charming quality to her confusion. She'd said her grandfather had brought her up the old-fashioned way. Alan wished the old gentleman was still alive so he could personally compliment him on the excellent job he'd done.

He said, "I'm not suggesting an immediate return to Tybee Island—not that I wouldn't like to. Would you like to cut out somewhere for a while, though?"

"I'd love to," Kay said honestly, "but I mustn't. I need to stay around. Homer's very capable, but he's essentially employed as a desk clerk, though I find I've been assigning more and more duties to him. Nevertheless, he's been handling things single-handed most of the day. It's not fair to expect him to do it all."

"I suppose you're right," Alan admitted regretfully.

"Yes, I'm afraid I am. Still...I just can't talk freely down here."

Kay was on the verge of suggesting that he come up to her apartment. She could fix him a drink, have some food sent up from room service if he wanted to have dinner with her.

She knew she was playing with fire. She wasn't sure she could trust herself to be alone with Alan without giving in to some very human feelings and encouraging a repeat of today's scene out at Tybee Island. Only this time there would be no crowd in the distance to distract them....

Alan said, "Kay, Homer's trying to get your attention."

Kay looked up to see a tall, white-haired man standing at the desk, and as she watched, the man pounded the blotter with his fist and said something to Homer she was glad she couldn't hear.

Homer, answering the man, was sending out a visual plea for help.

Kay got to her feet reluctantly. "Looks like more trouble," she said. "Excuse me, will you, Alan?"

Alan watched her walk over to the desk, saw the white-haired man turn toward her, his irate expression slowly fading as Kay began to talk to him.

When Kay stepped behind the desk herself, Alan temporarily gave up. He went to his room, put on the jogging suit he'd brought with him, then headed across Bay Street and climbed down the iron steps. For the next hour or so he tried to let his body take over his mind as he ran at an easy pace along the waterfront.

CHAPTER EIGHT

KAY WOKE UP EARLY Saturday morning after a restless night. She'd been wakened several times by vivid nightmares. She brewed coffee, then settled down with the paperwork that was a regular part of her first-thing-in-the morning routine.

The paperwork out of the way, she checked with the housekeeper, as she always did, and then with the chef. There was always a slight edge of apprehension to invading René LaPlante's kitchen because there was always the chance he'd infuriated or intimidated some of the help, thus causing them to quit when they were needed the most.

Evidently her recent diplomacy had worked, though. The temperamental chef was in an especially benevolent mood and insisted that she try a freshly baked brioche. He walked her to the kitchen door and gallantly kissed her hand in parting.

She was still smiling as she entered the lobby, but the smile faded when she saw Homer Telfair at the front desk with Lissa, the morning clerk, instead of Francey.

Lissa babbled immediately, "We're just so lucky Homer happened to stop by and says he can stay, Mrs. Dillard. Francey phoned in sick, and I didn't know how I was going to handle everything by myself."

Just happened to stop by? Kay noted that Homer avoided meeting her eyes. That was all she needed to convince her that his appearance had been anything but coincidental.

"We need to talk, Homer," she said quietly. "Lissa, we'll be back in the lounge if you need us."

She led Homer to the deserted cocktail lounge, and they sat down at the same booth where she'd sat with Alan just a few mornings ago. She couldn't help but wish it was Alan sitting across from her again. They'd never gotten together again yesterday. She'd seen him set out for his run, but was so busy she hadn't known when he returned. Later, alone in her apartment, she'd nearly succumbed to the temptation to call his room. But she'd resisted, then later wished she hadn't been quite so strong.

Homer said, "I suppose this is about Francey."

Kay wrested her thoughts back to the issue at hand. "Partly," she said. "First, though, I want to find out what happened with those overbooked reservations yesterday. First there were the two couples, then that man from Philadelphia...."

"I know," Homer said. "I've already checked out everything for today and it looks all right. The problem is—"

"I know what the problem is," Kay said tersely. "If the person taking the reservation fails to note it in the book, there's no record. And consequently, no room available when the guest arrives."

"Yes," Homer concurred unhappily.

"Am I right in assuming that it was probably Francey who goofed?" Kay asked.

"Mrs. Dillard, there's just no way of pinpointing that," Homer protested. "Since there's no record, there's no way of telling. In other words, it could have been any one of us on the desk. Maybe right after a call came in to book a room, whoever was on got busy and neglected to write the guest names right down...."

"Stop stalling, Homer," Kay advised. "My educated guess is that it's Francey who forgot, and there's no point in your denying I'm probably right."

"Only probably."

"All right, only probably. Anyway, the damage is done now, and we'll have to live with it. We'll make out as best we can. If people come in who claim they've made reservations and we don't have the reservations, we'll have to try to relocate them as I did the people yesterday."

"You're losing money, in that case," Homer pointed out.

"Yes, but there's no alternative. One thing we have to do at the Randolph House is to stand behind our promises. A reservation is a promise. Maybe some places deliberately overbook because they know they're apt to have some cancellations along the way, but that's not a policy I'm going to fool around with. I'd rather have a few empty rooms."

"I agree," Homer admitted.

"I thought you would," Kay said. "Homer...you have a real flair for this business and it's what you want to follow as a career, isn't it?"

He seemed faintly surprised at her question but said only, "Yes."

"You like working at the Randolph House?"

"I like working at the Randolph House very much."

"Then," Kay said, "I think you're slated for a promotion. As of now, you're my assistant manager."

"Am I hearing what I think I'm hearing?" Homer asked, looking slightly dazed.

Kay smiled. "Yes, you're hearing exactly what you think you're hearing. We'll discuss financial arrangements later on. This will mean you'll have to give up your moonlighting as a sight-seeing guide."

"That's fine with me."

"I'm rather sorry," Kay admitted, "because everyone who's gone on one of your tours comes back with such a feel for this city. But in my own self-interest, I want you here full-time. There's just one thing...."

"Yes?"

"We're going to have to fire Francey."

"No," Homer said. He added, with a stubbornness Kay wouldn't have expected of him, "We can't do that. At least, I certainly can't. Anyway, it would be highly unfair. I told you, Francey just hasn't been herself lately."

"Yes, I know you've told me that. And I agree with you. I've talked to Francey."

"Did she confide in you?"

"Yes."

"Then..."

"Homer," Kay said gently, "Francey definitely has some problems, some very serious problems. But she's going to have to work them out herself, make decisions only she can make. Meanwhile, I don't think she can continue working here."

"I think she needs to continue working here," Homer stated.

"What makes you say that?"

"I don't think Francey gets much support at home, Mrs. Dillard. Oh, I know I'm talking about your in-laws and I suppose I shouldn't. But there just doesn't seem to be any communication between Francey and her parents."

"That's not too unusual in these times," Kay observed. "Do you have any great communication with your own parents, Homer?"

"My parents are dead," Homer said flatly.

"I'm sorry," Kay said. She'd lost her own parents when she was very young, she could empathize with him.

"Do you have family in Savannah?" she asked him.

He shook his head. "No. I have an aunt across the state in Columbus, but we're not close. I've been on my own for a long time, Mrs. Dillard." He smiled wryly. "At this point, it's the only way of life I know."

"Who do you live with, Homer?"

"With myself," he said, with an engaging grin. "I have a room a few blocks from here. It's enough for me for now."

He spoke with a quiet dignity that Kay had to admire. What he was saying also made her aware of how little she really knew about him, except that he had a real talent for the hotel business and was badly smitten with her niece.

"Well," she said, "with the raise in salary you'll be getting, you can probably afford an apartment of your own, if you want one. Now, as to Francey..."

"I don't like to pry," Homer said, "though I don't deny I want to know. Was what she told you really confidential, or is it something you could speak to me about?"

"What Francey told me is highly confidential," Kay said. "If I were to tell anyone about it, I'd tell you, because I think you sincerely have her interests at heart. But I can't tell even you. Regardless of that, though, we're going to have to get other help on the desk, Homer. Especially since you will be taking over other responsibilities. I can't ask you to give up being on the desk entirely. In fact, once Lissa leaves today I'll have to help out myself. According to the books we're going to have quite a turnover. But we do have to assess our personnel needs and then do something about hiring more people."

"I can't see why that means we have to let Francey go," Homer persisted. "Look, I have a suggestion."

"Okay, I'll listen to it."

"Why not reduce her hours? Put her on a part-time shift, maybe from two to six? That would give her mornings free."

Kay looked at him suspiciously. A notorious aspect of pregnancy was morning sickness, though Francey had managed the other day to get thoroughly sick in the late afternoon. Nevertheless, she couldn't help but wonder if Homer knew the real nature of Francey's problem.

"The thing is," he said, before she could comment, "I think it would be hard going for Francey to get another job until she gets whatever's bothering her straightened out. She gets upset very easily... well, I don't have to tell *you*. I'd hate to see her stuck at home, though."

"You think Francey needs an escape hatch?"

"I guess you could say that," Homer allowed, flashing her his wry grin again. "Coming to work four hours a day would get her out of the house, put her into an area where she can be her own person. I think she needs that."

Maybe it was Homer who should be a psychologist! Kay thought. "All right," she agreed, "I'm willing to try out an amended schedule for Francey."

"Thanks," Homer said, and this time gave her a full-fledged smile that was so loaded with charm that it dazzled her.

As she went up to her apartment, she was thinking that Homer had some unexpected qualities. She liked these new sides of him she was seeing. Also, unless she was much mistaken, he was one of those people who was going to get better-looking as they got older. Maturity would bring him into his own. She wondered, too, if he could wear contact lenses, so his gorgeous dark eyes would be clearly visible.

Once she was in her own apartment, Kay called Gerard Dillard at his house. It was ten-thirty. Tracy should have been up and about, which didn't necessarily mean that she was.

Tracy was up, but she sounded sleepy. "Well, hi there, Kay," she said, her suppressed yawn sounding like a small sigh over the phone. "Gerard tells me you're bringing someone real interesting to dinner tomorrow."

Preoccupied with other things, Kay actually had forgotten that she and Alan were to dine with the Dillards on Sunday. Now she wished more than ever she'd been able to decline the invitation before Alan had accepted it so readily.

It was too late to back out, so she said, "Yes. What time do you want us, Tracy?"

"We usually have dinner midday on Sunday, so I can let Josie off later," Tracy said. "How about coming by for mimosas around noon, then we can have dinner around one."

"Fine," Kay agreed, then added, "Actually, Tracy..."

She heard another suppressed yawn and decided Gerard must have been out last night and Tracy must have sat up watching old movies on TV. Tracy had an insatiable appetite for any and all television fare.

"I called," she began again, "because I wanted to find out how Francey is."

"Sleeping," said Tracy.

"What I mean is, how *is* she, Tracy?"

"She came back from your place because she was sick as a dog," Tracy reported. "She must have up-chucked for a whole hour. Now she's asleep, and I hope she stays that way for a while."

"What do you think made her sick?" Kay posed the question knowing that she'd be able to tell from Tracy's answer whether Tracy knew about Francey's pregnancy. Tracy wasn't a good dissembler.

"She ate something," Tracy said flatly, with such conviction that Kay felt sure Francey had yet to confide in her mother. "I keep telling her she's going to ruin her digestion with the junk she eats," Tracy went on, "but needless to say she doesn't listen to much of anything I say. This time, though, I'd say whatever she's got isn't from junk food. I think she's come down with a bad case of food poisoning. Whatever it was, she must have pretty well gotten it out of her system. I think she'll be okay once she wakes up, and tomorrow's her day off at your place, anyway, isn't it?"

"Yes."

"Well, that'll give her some extra time to recuperate."

Kay let it go at that. But as she hung up, she was perturbed. Obviously Francey's deception couldn't go on forever, but the longer it went the worse it would be once Gerard and Tracy found out about her condition.

Long ago, Kay had sensed a latent sense of cruelty in Gerard. She'd witnessed its sting on a few occasions when he had lashed out verbally at either Francey or Tracy, uncaring that he was humiliating them in her presence. She remembered the strength of Gerard's arms on occasions when he'd clutched her. She'd had to use wiles to get away from him, realizing she was no match for his strength. But she'd sensed then that Gerard could be a dangerous adversary if sufficiently aroused, and she had no reason now to alter that instinctive judgment.

She was afraid Francey was going to have a very rough row to hoe with her father. What was important was that she help her. Kay also suspected that Gerard would be highly resentful of anyone who attempted to take the upper hand in a situation that concerned his own family. The Dillard pride ran deep. She'd seen that on more than one occasion with Randy, when what he'd done—or hadn't done—had been motivated considerably more by pride than by logic.

Her phone rang, and she picked up the receiver, ready to confront yet another problem. But the caller was Alan.

"I don't want to bother you," he said. "But I did want to touch base."

Kay said the first thing that came to her mind, which was simply, "I'm glad. Where are you?"

"At the lobby phone. I came down thinking you'd be around. Then Homer said he thought you'd gone back upstairs."

"I had to make a phone call." She hesitated, then made a quick decision. "Alan, I'm going to have to help out on the desk this afternoon. We're shorthanded."

"I wish I knew something about the hotel business," he said. "I'd volunteer to help, too."

"Don't tempt me. I might press you into service."

"I'd love to have you press me into service, Kay," he assured her.

There was no mistaking the double entendre, and her response to the sexy, caressing quality of his voice caused her to sit down fast and grab the phone receiver a little tighter.

"I think you're going to have to censor your answers," she said, trying to make light of the sexual tension strung between them like a fine steel wire. "What I was going to ask," she added quickly, "is if you might care to drive out somewhere for an early lunch. I'm talking about McDonald's, maybe, and snatching a hamburger to be eaten in the car. I can't take much time but . . . I would like to be with you for a little while."

"I second that," Alan said. "My chariot will be awaiting you."

He was parked at the entrance when Kay came out, chatting with Ernest. Ernest opened the car door for her, and his benevolent smile reminded her of a Kewpie doll. She'd found a couple of Kewpie dolls in an old trunk not long ago, and understood they were becoming collector's items.

As Alan drove out into Bay Street, she teased, "I think Ernest approves of you. And you a Yankee yet!"

"I appreciate that," Alan said. "I'll take all the approval I can get. Which way do I go?"

She gave him directions, then settled back, suddenly much more at peace with the world and herself now that she was with Alan.

She realized that getting to enjoy his company so much was a dangerous habit. She tried to tell herself life wasn't much without the occasional spice of danger, but she couldn't be that casual where Alan was concerned. She was too aware that he wasn't going to be in her world very long and, even if she knew him a lot better than she did, she couldn't see any way she could follow him into his.

Pure and simple geography was certain to impose some automatic restrictions on them, for they had two such different life-styles and functioned in two such entirely different places. Theirs, she thought, was like a shipboard romance, good for the length of the cruise. Then, once ashore, the participants kissed goodbye—and that was it. Ideally with no regrets.

Could she hope to have no regrets once Alan left?

She tabled that question and concentrated on the moment. It was a glorious day, and as they drove along, Alan said rather wistfully, "I wish you could play hooky." He added quickly, "Hey, forget I said that."

"No, I'm not going to forget it," she told him. "I wish I could play hooky. But Francey is out sick."

Just the mention of Francey was enough to cause her to frown.

Alan saw her expression and deliberated about whether to comment on it or let it go. He wanted this small interlude for just Kay and himself. On the other hand, he was so attuned to her that her worry communicated itself without her saying a word, and he couldn't negate his own response.

"Want to talk about Francey?" he invited.

Her smile was rueful. "No," she said frankly. "But I think I need to."

"I'm here," he said. "I'm ready to listen. Right now, that's what it's all about, Kay."

She said tentatively, "I know I don't have to swear you to secrecy...."

"That's right, you don't. I would never under any circumstances tell anyone else anything you might confide in me."

"Do you know," Kay said, "I believe that. I have absolute trust in you. Do you know how rare it is to have absolute trust in someone, Alan?"

"Yes," he said, "I do. And if you keep looking at me like that we're apt to wind up in a ditch. You're taking some serious chunks out of the time and attention I should be devoting to driving."

"Then I'll be more circumspect," Kay said a shade too demurely.

This bit of repartee over, though, she frowned again. "About Francey," she said, "it's a very big problem, Alan. She's two months pregnant."

She heard him swear softly.

"Tracy and Gerard don't know," Kay went on, "and Francey seems to have this naive idea she's never going to have to tell them. She's scared to death. Also, she's having a rough time of it. Evidently she's one of those women whose morning sickness lasts all day. She had to take off not long after she got to work. I called Tracy—that's the call I went up to my apartment to make—and Tracy said something Francey ate made her sick."

"You don't think her mother suspects?"

"No, I don't think so. Tracy asked, incidentally, if we could come at noon tomorrow for mimosas before dinner. As she pointed out to me, they customarily dine at midday on Sunday, so she can give her help the rest of the day off."

"Once again, I feel like I've stepped into *Gone with the Wind*," Alan murmured.

"You're going to feel more so once you're at Gerard and Tracy's tomorrow," Kay warned. "They have their own idea of what Southern hospitality is supposed to mean, and I admit they do try hard. It would do no good to point out that we're not living in an antebellum world."

"Hoopskirts and crinolines?" he asked.

She smiled. "Only symbolically. Mixed in with magnolia and honeysuckle. Oh, I don't mean to sound so cynical. But it's a disservice to the South, actually, to behave as if we're still caught up in the fluff of yesteryear, which wasn't fluff at all when people actually had to live through it. The South had some very bad times, and it's only blocking progress to dwell too heavily on the past."

"That's true of anything, Kay."

"Yes," she said, "I know it is."

Once again, the meaning of what they were saying to each other had a far greater significance than the mere words themselves.

They fell silent for a time, then Alan suddenly said, "I know it's none of my business and the name probably wouldn't mean anything to me, anyway. But do you know who the father of Francey's child is?"

Kay shook her head. "No."

"I take it Francey won't talk."

"Definitely Francey won't talk. I'd say the poor kid is being protective in a way you might call ridiculous if it weren't so tragic. Also, my guess is that the father is married, probably someone who moves in the Dillard's own social stratum. So the potential for scandal would be pretty overwhelming if this ever came out. That, I think, is one of the reasons why Francey is running so scared."

"Would there be any chance of getting her to talk to someone—maybe a minister—who might be able to help her?"

"I don't think so. I think she'd be afraid that anyone she might talk to would know Gerard, and feel bound by honor to acquaint Gerard with the facts. Anyway, I get the impression Francey considers this entirely her own burden, and I think she'd do almost anything before she named any names. Matter of fact..."

"Yes?"

"Well, she spoke about walking out in the river. Drowning herself, in short."

Shocked, Alan said, "You don't think she'd seriously attempt such a thing?"

"I don't know, Alan," Kay admitted. "I reacted the way you did. She knew how she horrified me. I implored her not to do anything at all, and I think she heard me. I hope so. But the way I left it, you could say the next move really is mine. I have to come up with some way to help her out."

"Maybe her best bet would be to leave Savannah."

"How could she do that?"

"I could take her back to Vermont with me, Kay. No one would know her there and I could find a place for her to stay where she'd be safe and well cared for. And I'd be there to keep tabs on her, of course."

Kay stared at him. "I don't think you know what you're saying," she said finally.

"Yes, I do. It would be a hell of a responsibility. But for you, I'd do it."

Tears stung Kay's eyes. She couldn't hold them back. "I wouldn't have believed anyone could be that generous," she said brokenly.

"It isn't a question of generosity. Maybe—"

Alan broke off, and she had to ask, "Maybe what?"

"Maybe if I could help someone like Francey I'd feel I was atoning a little bit for some other things."

She knew he was thinking of Meiling. And probably of Randy, as well. The knowledge saddened her. It proved that, honest though they'd been with each other, neither of them had yet to put the past fully behind them.

They stopped at a drive-in for lunch and ate in the car, though Alan protested to Kay that he wanted to do better for her.

"Another time," she promised, and added regretfully, "I really do have to get back to work." The question came impulsively. "What are you going to do with yourself this afternoon?"

"I don't know," Alan admitted. "Just wander around, I guess. There's plenty to see."

"Yes," she said, "and you don't know how much I wish I could show it to you. It doesn't seem right, your having to be so entirely on your own while you're here in Savannah. I know how hard it is to get a leave of absence from a college...."

"I had a pretty good case to present," Alan said, "and the president of our college is a very understanding guy. I explained why I had to be here in April, why I couldn't do this on the regular spring break last month. I made up for what I'm doing, partly, by working on the spring break—course preparations, and so forth, work that had to be done. Also, I was lucky to be able to get a friend who's an authority in the field to trek up to Vermont and take over my classes until I get back. So, it worked out."

He still wasn't saying how long the leave was, and Kay discovered she didn't want to ask him. She didn't want to know when he'd be leaving.

She looked at him, and she wanted to reach over and kiss him. She wanted his arms around her, and she wanted her arms around him. She wanted the kind of closeness they'd had out on Tybee Island yesterday....

"Lissa's going to take a break for a couple of hours and then come back," she told him as he pulled up in front of the inn entrance to let her out. "Then, Homer got hold of Norman—he's the late-night man—and he agreed to come in early. So I should think I'd be able to get away around five or so for a while."

She took the plunge. "Why don't you come up to my place for a drink?" she invited.

It was not until she was on her way across the lobby that it occurred to her they had not once mentioned the key.

CHAPTER NINE

ONCE SHE STARTED thinking about the key again, Kay couldn't stop thinking about it. Every time there was a lull during the afternoon, the bit of bronze metal came back to plague her.

She had failed to match the key with any at the inn. It hadn't fitted the desk drawers in Randy's office, and there'd been nothing else there *for* it to fit. It obviously was not a key to a safe-deposit box or a locker in a bus station or an airport. She doubted it could be a key to a hotel room. The size was all right, but even though hotel room keys seldom had identifying tags attached to them, in this day when thievery was such a risk, they usually did have numbers stamped onto the metal surfaces.

This key was plain.

As if to verify that plainness, once she was back in her apartment, Kay took the key out of the desk drawer where she was keeping it and surveyed it carefully. There was absolutely no identifying mark.

Frustrated, she put the baffling little piece of metal back in the drawer, then set about making a few hors d'oeuvres to offer Alan with a drink.

It was nearly six when she heard his knock. She opened the door and for a moment that stretched on and on they just looked at each other. Then he came in, closed the door behind him and without any further preamble took her in his arms.

Neither of them spoke. He held her, just held her, and after a while her arms stole around his waist. She felt the rough texture of his suit jacket and, beneath it, the taut firmness of his muscles. He smelled of soap and shaving cream blended with the unique scent that makes every person a little bit different. Kay inhaled deeply, and his scent went straight to her psyche. It was frightening to be so easily aroused by anyone. It was also wonderful. A new awareness of life and a heady sexiness mixed in a fast-beating, pulsating rhythm. Even her fingertips felt supercharged. She tested their vibrancy, moving her hands upward along either side of Alan's chest, fanning them out to his shoulders, then anointing his jawline and his ears and finally plunging her fingertips into his thick, sandy hair.

She rubbed his scalp slowly, making small circles. She raised herself almost on tiptoe and kissed him, and as their lips touched she felt the tremor that suddenly surged through him. Their kiss became a savoring thing. A nibbling, a tasting, a coming together, a letting-go then coming together again. But then the kiss plunged into new depths, and Kay traveled with it, letting herself be caught up in the vortex of her whirling emotions.

Alan's hands began to rove, his palms first cupping her face then trailing to the hollow of her throat where his fingers lingered on her pulse beat. Then he began to touch her body, tracing her bones, her contours, her breasts—which were straining against the sheer fabric of her dress, the nipples hard and peaking—and the gentle curves of her hips.

Then slowly, almost lazily, he reached for the zipper at the back of her dress, tugged and stepped back only to ease the fabric over her arms. The dress slithered to the floor, billowing around her ankles. She began to step out of it, but Alan stopped her. He lifted her into his arms and carried her into her bedroom and gently lowered her to her bed.

Kay lay on the heirloom quilt that doubled as a coverlet, afire with an anticipation so intense that it mixed agony with the sheerest kind of joy. Only briefly did the thought cross her mind that she'd never felt like this before, and she dismissed the thought. What had been before no longer mattered. What mattered was now. Not yesterday, not tomorrow. Right now.

She was wearing a wisp of a satin and lace bra, matching panties and a short slip. She closed her eyes, waiting for Alan to finish undressing her. But nothing happened.

Finally she opened her eyes, to see him sitting on the side of the bed. He was looking at her gravely, no trace of a smile on his face.

"What is it?" she whispered, puzzled.

His gray eyes were intent. "I want you to be sure," he said.

The huskiness in his voice told its own story. She smiled. "I'm very sure," she said softly.

An answering smile tugged at the corners of his lips. He leaned across and touched the bare place between the edge of her bra and the top of the half-slip. "So much clothing," he chided.

"You can do something about that."

"Yes, I can," he agreed. "Yes, indeed I can."

He leaned over her, tugging at the elastic band of the half-slip. Kay arched her hips and his hands moved under her, molding every inch of those hips, then her thighs, as the silken fabric of her slip slithered under his touch. His touch in itself was unique. She had not known that fingers could be eloquent.

He tossed the slip on a chair and then again he bent over her. As he slowly, carefully, unclasped her bra and removed it, he followed the gesture by kissing each tautened breast in turn, his mouth lingering on the dark rose nipples, circling their peaks with the tip of his tongue. Kay began to moan and discovered she was clenching her fists and digging her nails into her palms. Dimly it occurred to her she hadn't known very much about the real force of desire, either.

Alan sat back and surveyed her, his gray eyes luminous, his breath coming harder. He didn't need to speak. His expression said it all.

Her wanting, her need, set off a small series of explosions within Kay. Alan had taken off his suit jacket, but he was still wearing a light green sport shirt, open at the neck. Her hands were shaking as she reached for it, fumbling with the buttons.

He leaned closer, making it easier for her, a faint smile on his lips, a hint of tender amusement in his eyes. He waited, once she had tossed aside the shirt, and finally lifted an inquiring eyebrow. Kay's eyes fell to the tan leather belt encircling his waist, centered by a brass buckle. She unfastened the buckle, tugged at the belt and saw that Alan had been exercising the maximum in self-control. Her fingers touched him, felt the hardness, the swelling, and Alan lost all traces of restraint.

In another second they were naked, their bodies merging, then moving to act out the prelude to that ultimate togetherness that is as old as time. They meshed, they clung, kissing and holding and stroking and cajoling as the tension built, as the interplay intensified, as the drama spiraled to the moment when he entered her, filled her. Then they both spun out of reality's realm entirely and into a domain of fire and light and passion's burning colors. Finally those colors muted to glorious pastels that streaked across their personal horizons, lulling them toward peace.

It took a while to come back. They lay, arms entwined, Kay's head pillowed on Alan's chest. After a time he started to speak, and she cautioned, "Don't say anything."

He chuckled. "Never?"

"I mean . . . don't say anything that might spoil it."

"Nothing could spoil it, Kay."

"I hope not," she said. "I hope not."

"As far as I'm concerned," Alan answered slowly, "nothing could ever spoil this time with you. Each hour is a treasure."

The simplicity with which he spoke brought tears to Kay's eyes. Alan saw the tears, began to brush them away, but then his fingers stilled as the pure impact of her hit him all over again.

To his surprise, she reached for him and tugged him closer to her. And slowly, tenderly, they began to enact another wordless drama, touching, clinging, finally fusing. . . .

The early-evening light faded, and darkness crept in to fill the room. For a time Kay slept and Alan held her, her closeness a balm. Eventually his arm began to ache, but he still tried not to move. Finally he couldn't help himself, and his slight movement made her stir. She awakened slowly, staring at him drowsily as she stretched, then sat up in bed.

Kay slipped on a dressing robe and Alan shrugged into his pants, and they left the bedroom. They'd made a couple of drinks, sipping slowly as they munched on the hors d'oeuvres Kay had fixed. They began to talk about a lot of things that related far more to the past than the present. Childhood anecdotes, some funny, some more than a little poignant, little intimate things they exchanged with each other that, with the telling, brought them closer together.

Then finally Kay said very softly, "Alan...there's something...."

"What?"

"Will you stay with me tonight?"

He felt a rush of tenderness toward her and his voice went husky again as he said, "Yes."

He wished he could have added that he wanted to stay with her every night for the rest of their lives, but he knew that was too much to expect and, for so many reasons, was not apt to happen.

He settled for the moment, thankful he had the moment. Long ago he'd learned that happiness, at best, is elusive. The wise man accepted happiness when it was given to him, cherished it, and knew when he had to let it go.

SUNDAY MORNING Kay wanted to order breakfast from room service.

Alan refused to go along with her. "It wouldn't be a good idea," he said flatly.

"Why not?"

"I'm thinking about your reputation, Kay."

She stared at him in astonishment. "My reputation?"

"Yes."

"You're saying they may suspect, down in the kitchen, that someone spent the night with me."

"Yes," he muttered uncomfortably.

"Alan, that is absolutely the most ridiculous..."

"I don't think so."

"I do. Now you're the one who's acting like we're living back in the cherished old antebellum days. Or is this an example of Yankee virtue?"

"No. I just don't want to give anyone the chance to gossip about you, that's all."

"Don't you think you're being a bit too quixotic?"

"No."

"If you were a Georgian, you'd probably still be practicing the duello code," she accused.

He laughed. But there wasn't much levity in his voice as he said, "I'd fight for you, yes."

That struck a chord. What woman wouldn't want to hear the man she loved say he'd fight for her?

The man she loved. The phrase stuck. Troubled, Kay pattered out into the kitchenette, prepared to make coffee.

Over her shoulder, she said, "Well, if you won't let me order up a really scrumptious breakfast for us, I'll see what I can rustle up here." But she was thinking about that word *love*, which gave an entirely new aspect to a relationship.

She'd never had an experience that even touched last night with Alan. She was only too thoroughly aware of the potency of the attraction she felt for him. Also, there were other dimensions to their relationship. She'd confided in him as she'd never confided in anyone before, male or female. She felt as if she could trust him completely, as if he were a real and true friend, despite their short acquaintance.

Did fantastic lovemaking, chemistry, confidence and friendship add up to love?

Once, she'd thought she loved Randy Dillard. It hadn't taken long after they were married to discover that she'd been "in love" with him, but hadn't loved him. There was a vast difference.

She didn't want to make the mistake of confusing desire—yes, and friendship, as well—with love. Especially when, in their case—hers and Alan's—there was an almost automatic time limit to their relationship. Vermont, true, wasn't the end of the earth. But she had her work here, he had his work there. One thing she was sure about, where love was concerned, was that it had to be nourished on a continuing basis if it were to endure.

With hundreds of miles between them, most of the time, anyway, she couldn't see how that kind of nourishing would be possible.

Behind her, Alan said, "How long do you have to run the water before you fill the coffeepot?"

Kay started, then said, "Sorry. I guess I lost track."

She filled the pot, inserted the coffee basket and put the plug in the outlet. "It won't take long," she murmured.

"I'm in no hurry," he said, and there was something in his tone that caused her to swivel around and look at him.

He was wearing his slacks and nothing else. Pale gold hairs sprinkled his broad chest. He had powerful chest muscles, and the muscles in his arms were also strong and well defined. She could picture him on skis in winter, soaring down a snowy slope, each part of his body working in harmony.

Right now he needed a shave. A faint, sandy stubble dusted his jawline. His hair was mussed. She discovered he looked very sexy with his hair mussed, and she forced herself to stop right there. She was damned if she was going to let herself get carried away with him this morning.

As a diversionary tactic, she opened the door of the small refrigerator, peered into the freezer compartment. "Hmm," she observed, "I have a package of frozen croissants. And I can scramble up some eggs."

"Kay," Alan said, "you don't need to fix breakfast for me."

"You'll need to have something to eat before we go over to Gerard's," she said. "Gerard has a tendency to spike the drinks he makes. He'll put a jolt of some kind of lightning even into a mimosa, if I know him."

"Are you sure you do know him?"

She frowned. "What's that supposed to mean?"

There was a table for two in the small kitchen. Alan pulled out a chair and sat down at it. "I don't mean to be critical," he said, "but it seems to me you tend to see things in black and white. Someone's either a hero or a villain. No middle ground. You've cast Gerard into a villain mold. That's a dangerous way to go, Kay. No one's either all good or all bad. When you zero in like that on someone's character you're apt to get burned."

"I've known Gerard Dillard since I was nineteen years old," Kay said stiffly. "I think that gives me a little edge of expertise where he's concerned."

"Did you meet him before or after you met your husband?"

"Right after."

"Where did you meet your husband?"

"At a cotillion." Kay stirred restlessly. Especially after last night, she didn't want to talk about Randy with Alan.

"It was a very social romance, then?"

"I guess you could say so."

"Kay, I'm not trying to pry," Alan said. Then he suddenly admitted, "Matter of fact, I don't know what the hell I'm trying to do. Sort things out, I suppose. Trying to make sense of things. Still trying to figure out why Randolph Dillard handed me that damned key."

The coffee stopped perking. Kay filled mugs for both of them. She sat down at the table and said dully, "The key just won't go away, will it?"

"No."

"I don't know where to turn next, Alan."

"Kay..."

"Yes?"

"Could that be because you don't want to know where to turn next?"

"You're saying I'm afraid to find out what the key opens?"

"Yes," he agreed. "I guess that's what I'm saying."

"All right. I admit it. I want the past to stay *past*. I don't want any old memories revived. I don't want to have to deal with any more traumas."

"I can buy that," he said wryly.

Kay suddenly became aware of him in a different way. It was easy to push back his past—a lot easier than it was, sometimes, to push back her own—because she hadn't known him *then*. Now she thought about the ordeal he'd gone through and said, "This must be very hard for you."

"Being here?"

"Yes."

He shook his head. "No. Yes, the initial encounter with you was hard, very hard. I thought you'd hate me."

She was genuinely astonished. "Why should I have hated you?"

"That's fairly easy, Kay." A trace of Alan's weariness returned. That weariness was one of the first things she'd noticed about him, but it seemed to have dissipated so completely during the course of the week. "I thought you'd hate me because I lived when your husband died." He held up an admonishing hand. "No, don't say anything. My common sense told me I was dealing with what might be called a typical hostage reaction. The psychologists and psychiatrists and scientists who devote their lives to traumatic-stress research have delved very thoroughly into what happens to hostages. There's deep-seated anger. A terrible feeling of powerlessness. You swing on an emotional pendulum that goes back and forth between guilt to rage to helplessness. Believe me, I've been the whole route and I know what it is. But I also..."

"Yes?"

"I've come to terms with the whole miserable experience pretty well," Alan said frankly. "As I understand it, it takes some people a longer time and some a shorter time to readjust. And the length of time one's a hostage doesn't seem to have much bearing on that. Maybe because people are so different, we're all individuals and we react differently to situations, to stress. But I can say one thing. You come out of such an experience stronger... at least most do. You learn to enjoy life in a way you've never enjoyed it before.

You learn it's the simple things that matter the most. You live for the day, and you're a hell of a lot more appreciative of what that day brings you."

He didn't have to add that he was also that much more appreciative of her. She knew it.

GERARD DILLARD'S HOUSE on Oglethorpe Square was a genuine Southern mansion, in Alan's estimation. Although it fitted in beautifully with its neighbors— for this was an area of beautiful homes, many of them historic ones—he could picture it as the focal point of a huge plantation.

As it was, the house was set back from the sidewalk no more than twenty feet or so, the lot bordered by an ornate wrought-iron fence, painted black. The wrought-iron motif was echoed in the stairway rails and the balustrade that ran along a front gallery outside story-high French windows.

The brick facade of the house was painted pale yellow. White azaleas bloomed along its sides, and somewhere there was a magnolia. The heavy, sweet scent hung in the air.

"Randy's house is three doors up the street," Kay said. "It's almost a duplicate of this one, except it's painted white. They both were designed by William Jay. He was one of Savannah's most famous architects—he also did the Gordon House, where Juliette Gordon Low, who founded the Girl Scouts of America, was born."

Kay was rushing her words. Alan had noted this was a habit of hers when she was nervous. But he had to hand it to her, right now, her fast-paced monologue was the only clue to that nervousness.

Her dress was off-white, trimmed with black lace. A black patent belt cinched her slender waist, and the texture was repeated in her slim, shiny pumps. She had coiled her hair into an elaborate chignon, and she wore jet drop earrings. He couldn't imagine how she could ever have looked more beautiful, and he felt that warm, familiar tide beginning to rise again.

It was going to be very difficult to act as if he and Kay were casual acquaintances.

A maid wearing a black uniform with a ruffled white apron answered the door. Kay put on a bright smile and said, "Hello, Chauncey."

"It's really good to see you, Mrs. Dillard," the maid said.

They went into a drawing room where the walls were painted ecru and hung with dark-toned oils in elaborate gold frames. The furniture was a mixture of Victorian and earlier, the couches and chairs upholstered in a striped satin fabric, the occasional pieces polished to a glowing patina. Floor-to-ceiling ivory brocade drapes bordered the tall French windows.

Gerard, wearing a cream-colored suit that blended perfectly with the room's decor, came forward to greet them expansively. He shook Alan's hand with enthusiasm as he expressed his delight at having him as a guest. He slipped an arm around Kay's waist and bestowed a brotherly kiss on her before she could sidestep him.

Tracy was a pretty blond vision in strawberry pink. Her Southern accent totally eclipsed Kay's, and she clung to Alan's hand as she greeted him.

There were four other people in the room. Alan was introduced first to Bill Abernathy, Gerard's partner, and to his wife, Cindy. Abernathy was tall and bronzed. Alan estimated he was probably about his age. He was a handsome man with intense blue eyes and thinning blond hair, which he wore in a rather long but well-contoured style. His wife was tall and very thin, dark haired, dark eyed, and she spoke faster than Kay did when she was nervous. Since she had as much of a Southern accent as Tracy, Alan found her difficult to understand.

Clark Creighton, the writer who was renting the Randolph Dillard house, and his wife, Sally, were the other couple. Creighton was in his fifties, Alan estimated, his hair already turned silver gray. He had a build like an ex-football player and an unexpectedly gentle smile. Sally Creighton was about the same age as her husband. She was short, slim with spiky short brown hair, enormous green eyes and an effervescent sense of humor that came through in almost everything she said. Both of the Creightons were from Maryland, which at this point seemed far more north than south to Alan.

Mimosas were served, and Alan discovered Kay was right. The orange juice-champagne concoction was delicious, but potent. He wondered if Gerard had laced it with vodka. Sinful, to a purist, yet something that could be effective, depending on one's motivation. Maybe Gerard wanted to get everyone loosened up.

After two rounds of mimosas, the party moved on to the dining room, a magnificent room that could have served as a model in any decorating magazine. The mahogany furniture was Hepplewhite in style, and definitely not reproduction Hepplewhite. Silver gleamed on a massive sideboard. The glassware was Waterford, the china Limoges. The buffet was sumptuous and delicious. No doubt about it ... Gerard Dillard and his wife Tracy lived very well.

Alan became aware that, so far, there was no sign of Francey.

With plates in hand, they proceeded to a screened area off the dining room—too elegant to be called a porch—and settled down to eat. Gerard proffered a choice of red or white wines. Alan chose a Beaujolais.

Tracy was sitting next to him, daintily picking at some smoked turkey. "Kay tells me you're an authority on Egypt," she said, her eyes wide.

He couldn't help but think that Tracy probably widened her pretty blue eyes over almost everything. "Egyptology's my field," he confirmed.

"How *fascinating*," Tracy enthused.

He followed her lead and got into a small conversation about his work. But he could see it wasn't taking Tracy long to lose interest, and he was relieved when Clark Creighton, having replenished his plate at the buffet table, sauntered over to join them. Creighton had been to Egypt, "a thousand years ago," he said with a smile, so they had some common ground. They talked about the changes in Cairo, which, Alan said regretfully, were not all to the good, in his opinion.

"We've got the Big Apple here in the States," he said, "so now they call Cairo the Big Mango. Each time I go there the place overwhelms me all over again. It's not just the noise, the dirt, the crowds, the smells, the dust or even the fact that you can take a nickel bus ride—on route 800 to be exact—straight out to the pyramids. I guess it's the vitality of the place that gets to me. It's like nothing else."

"I remember," Clark Creighton said. "And I agree."

"If you felt that way when you were there, you'd feel much more so today," Alan told him.

As he spoke, Alan saw that Gerard had joined them. Gerard had also poured himself another mimosa, and after sipping from his glass he asked Alan, "Would you want to go back to Egypt?"

Alan caught the question within a question. Gerard was thinking about the hijacking, thinking that the hostage experience had probably scared him off. He said, "Yes. Matter of fact, I'll be going back next year."

Kay had been talking to Sally Creighton. But in the pause in their conversation, she heard what Alan said and her heart sank. He'd already told her he was planning to go back to Egypt next year, so that statement came as no surprise. Still...she hated to hear it. She sighed. At the moment, both Vermont and Egypt seemed a million miles away to her.

The buffet table was cleared, and a selection of tempting desserts set out. Coffee was served in wafer-thin china cups. Alan managed to edge close to Kay and to ask, "Where's Francey?" without being overheard.

"Tracy said Francey had a date for lunch and the movies with some friends," Kay answered sotto voce, as she busied herself with cutting a small wedge of pecan pie.

"You think that's so?"

"I don't know," she admitted, "and it worries me."

They lingered by the sideboard. Alan said, "Kay, look, there's something you're going to have to face up to. I know it must have occurred to you."

"What?"

"Whatever that key unlocks may very well be in your house here on Oglethorpe Square."

She had referred to it as "Randy's house." Nevertheless, dammit, it was *her* house now.

"Yes, that has occurred to me," Kay admitted. "But there's nothing I can do about it."

"What are you saying?"

"The Creightons rented the place for a year, Alan. They moved in last September first. Their lease isn't up till August 31, and Sally asked me a while ago if I'd consider renting to them for another year. She isn't sure they can stay, but they both want to."

"So?"

"Well, I said I would."

"What does that have to do with trying to find out if the key unlocks something in it."

Kay said uncomfortably, "It's the Creightons' home for as long as they live in it, Alan. I wouldn't think of invading their privacy."

His lips tightened. "I wouldn't call it invading their privacy," he stated. "Also, I think your peace of mind is worth something. There's no way you're going to regain it till you find out what that key unlocks. You know that."

"I think we're making too much of the key."

"The hell we're making too much of the key!"

Alan was briefly and blazingly angry with her. He wanted to shake her slim shoulders. It seemed to him that each time the subject of the key surfaced it became more of an obstacle between them. The blasted key was getting bigger and bigger and bigger, and there was only one way to reduce it to size. Kay knew that as well as he did.

It was a reprieve to have Gerard Dillard appear in the doorway, saying smoothly, "Hey there, you two. We were thinking about engineering a small croquet tournament on the back lawn. How about it?"

"Great idea," Alan said, and turned to Kay. "Shall we join the others?" he asked politely.

Gerard had already left, so Kay took advantage of the opportunity to make a face at Alan. "Just about the last thing in the world I want to do is get involved in one of Gerard's croquet tournaments," she muttered.

"Join the club," Alan told her with a grin. "But this seems to be the moment for diplomacy."

Before she could protest further, he extended an inviting arm. "Shall we?" he repeated.

CHAPTER TEN

FATE, ALAN KNEW, could be whimsical. And he decided Fate was putting on a good show when he, Kay and the Creightons happened to leave the Dillard house at exactly the same moment.

Clark had won the croquet tournament prize, a bottle of cognac, and as the quartet headed through the wrought-iron gate out onto the sidewalk he was brandishing it triumphantly.

Alan's car was parked to their left. He had no idea whether the Randolph Dillard house was to the left or to the right. He felt that luck was holding when the Creightons negotiated a left turn and the four of them sauntered down the street together, chatting about the weather and Savannah's beautiful azalea display and how much colder it must be in both Maryland and Vermont.

They came abreast of Alan's rented car and halted. Sally Creighton asked, "How long will you be around Savannah, Alan?"

"I'm not sure," he hedged. It was a deliberately open-ended reply. He was hoping Sally Creighton would suggest he and Kay drop by before he left town for a drink or a cup of coffee or whatever.

When Sally merely said, "Well, I hope we'll see each other again before you go," he felt like a deflated balloon.

He wanted to nudge Kay, to make her do something. This was their golden opportunity to get into Kay's former home, which, he was convinced, must hold the key's secret. But Kay was standing at his side, remaining mute, and he was frustrated. He could understand her qualms about the key. But she knew as well as he did that she *had* to find out why whatever it unlocked had been so important to Randolph Dillard.

He heard Kay say, as if the words were being wrenched out of her, "Sally...I've told Alan about the house. I'd love to show it to him one day soon, unless that would be inconvenient for you. Just a quick Cook's tour..."

Alan discovered he wanted to kiss Kay instead of nudging her in the ribs. He wanted to applaud her, because she'd just shown she was made of the strong stuff he'd believed her to be made of.

Sally Creighton said quickly, "Kay, I'd love that. I was afraid Alan must have a full schedule. I know there's so much to see and do around Savannah. Clark and I still haven't managed all of it."

"My time is your time," Alan said with a disarming smile.

"How about supper Tuesday night?" Sally suggested. "We'll pry Clark away from his word processor. I warn you, though, it'll be supper, not dinner. I'm not as lavish in my entertaining as your sister-in-law. Also, this time around I'd rather like to keep it to just the four of us."

"That will be perfect," Kay said. "May I bring something? The chef at the inn conjures up some pretty wicked desserts."

"Surprise me," Sally invited with a grin.

"I will," Kay promised.

The Creightons went on. Kay and Alan got in the car. He inserted the key in the ignition switch, but before turning it he leaned over and kissed her squarely on the mouth.

Kay was startled for a second, but then she instinctively responded to his kiss, and Alan smiled. "That kiss is equivalent to giving you A plus—for effort and performance," he said.

"I'm going to read up on my Svengali," Kay muttered.

"Svengali?"

"He was an arch-hypnotist, among other things, had his way with an innocent young singer named Trilby, if I'm remembering the novel correctly. He possessed some very dark powers, and I'm beginning to think you may be his reincarnation."

"Come on, now."

"You do have a way with you," Kay said. "You didn't have to say a word, but I could *feel* you prodding me. You were right, of course. Randy's house is the next logical step, and I have to take it."

FRANCEY CAME TO THE INN Monday morning, but not to go to work. She presented herself at Kay's apartment at eight-thirty in the morning, as Kay was sipping her first cup of coffee and going over her accounts.

"I think I've come down with a bug," Francey said.

Kay took one look at her, then placed a hand on her forehead. Francey's skin was scorching hot.

She gave Francey aspirin, put her to bed and ordered up a large jug of cool fruit juice, which she insisted she drink.

"It'll make me sick," Francey mumbled.

"If it does, just try again," Kay said unsympathetically. Then added more gently, "You're going to have to push the fluids, Francey."

As she spoke, Kay knew she was going to have to confer with her chef and her housekeeper, as well as some of the other inn personnel. This was the first day of a new week, a time when, after reaching a peak point over the weekend, the inn's activity cycle started all over again. But she hated to leave Francey.

After a short debate with herself, she dialed Alan's room, and was relieved when he answered on the second ring.

"Francey's here, and she's really sick," she reported. "I'm pretty sure she's about to fall asleep. But I have to be out of my apartment for at least an hour, and I hate to leave her...."

"Want me to come and baby-sit?" Alan drawled.

"I have an awful nerve to suggest it but ... yes."

"Give me five minutes," he said.

Kay hung up the phone. Friend, lover, companion, confidant. The words rolled over in her mind. In such a short time, Alan had become all those things to her and more. She couldn't predict their future, but she knew their present was one of the most wonderful times of her life.

Alan had spoken of the philosophy he'd adopted after the hostage experience. People who'd undergone traumas like that, he'd said, learned to live a day at a time and to get the most out of each day.

This is today, she thought. And when tomorrow gets here, it will be today, too. And so will each day, as long as he's here with me. So in a sense that's as good as forever.

When Alan appeared at her door, Kay almost envied Francey. She would not have objected to some of his tender loving care. The thought of Alan's kind of care brought a flush to her cheeks. Alan noted the flush and said, "You haven't caught Francey's fever, have you?"

She shook her head. "No," she admitted, touching a finger to a cheek, "this is something all my own."

"Am I reading your mind?"

"You're playing Svengali again," she accused him.

"Would that I could. Kay..."

The longing in his eyes was as telltale as the color in her cheeks. Her voice quavered a little as she said, "I'd better get out of here."

He caught hold of her hand and pressed her fingers to his mouth. His lips moved against her fingers as he said, "I want you, dammit," and the effect was amazingly erotic.

"I want you, too," she said. "But right now we can't..."

"Does that mean that maybe later on...?"

Her smile gave him his answer.

He said huskily, "You're worth waiting for, you know. You'll always be worth waiting for."

Kay pondered on the significance of that remark as she went about her routine duties.

When she returned to her apartment an hour or so later, Alan met her at the door, and he looked worried.

"Francey's got one hell of a high fever," he said. "She's very restless, a little incoherent. I think she needs to see a doctor, Kay."

"I'm sure you're right," Kay acknowledged. "My common sense told me to call a doctor the minute she walked in here. But..."

"I take it this isn't the moment to bring a family physician into the act."

"Dr. Bardwell is the Dillards' family doctor," Kay said, "but...no...I don't want to call him in. He's a golf partner of Gerard's...."

"There is such a thing as a medical code of ethics, Kay."

"Yes. And I'm sure I'm doing Dr. Bardwell a disservice. But there's a kind of mutual background tie that binds. Dr. Bardwell might consider it the right thing to tell Gerard about Francey."

Alan watched her walk to the living room window and stare out over Bay Street. He asked, "Does Francey's mother know she's here?"

"No," Kay said, her back still turned to him. "I'll have to call Tracy, of course. But if Tracy insists I take Francey home that means Dr. Bardwell will be summoned to the house."

"He wouldn't necessarily find out about the pregnancy, Kay."

"I realize that, but there's still a chance." She turned away from the window. "Dammit," she said flatly. "Dammit, dammit!"

"Who do you call if one of your guests becomes ill?"

"Dr. Boudreau. He's fairly new in town, but I consider him excellent. Also, he's been willing to come to the inn when someone's really sick."

"So?"

"So I'll call him," Kay said reluctantly. "But it will mean coming up with some explanation to Gerard and Tracy about why I didn't contact Dr. Bardwell." She made a sudden decision. "There's no alternative," she decided, and picked up the phone.

The doctor arrived an hour later. By then, Francey was tossing and turning and muttering to herself, and Kay was glad she hadn't waited any longer to summon help. As it was, Alan had pushed her, and she was grateful to him for it.

Alan went back to his own room before the doctor arrived, having extracted the promise from Kay that she'd call him with a report the minute Dr. Boudreau left.

When the examination was concluded, the doctor told Kay that Francey's problem looked like a throat infection, which fortunately would respond to antibiotics.

Kay watched the doctor as he wrote out a prescription, and she liked what she saw. He was a slender, dark-haired man, probably in his early forties, and there was something about both his looks and manner that inspired confidence.

She made a sudden decision. "Can I tell you something in strict confidence?" she asked.

He looked up, surprised. "Of course," he said quickly.

"My niece is pregnant. Into her third month. She's not married. Her family doesn't know and she doesn't want them to know—though, obviously, sooner or later they're going to find out. Right now, I think it's essential she get the right kind of care. She went to a clinic in another town for the diagnosis. She hasn't gone near a doctor since. Would you consider taking her on as your patient?"

George Boudreau didn't give her an immediate answer. He finished writing the prescription and handed it to her. He said almost absently, "You can give her aspirin every four hours, plus lots of liquids. I think by tomorrow morning you'll see a marked improvement. Mrs. Dillard...."

"Yes?"

"I'll accept Francey as a patient because she obviously needs a doctor. Also, because I respect you, so I think there must be good reason for your handling this situation as you are. But I do advise you to try to convince Francey her parents should be told."

"I intend to do exactly that."

"Okay, then." The doctor picked up his medical bag. "I'll stop by to see her in the morning," he promised. "Then we can set up an office appointment so we can get her on the right track re diet and all the rest of it. How has she been?"

"With the pregnancy? Sick," Kay said. "Her so-called morning sickness seems to last a good part of the day."

"Well, that can be helped a bit, and it'll pass anyway in the normal course of events." He held out a firm hand. "Till tomorrow, then," he said.

Kay closed the door behind him and leaned against it wearily. She had just been getting into stride with the inn, as well as putting her personal life together. Alan was the first to upset her relatively tidy applecart, and now Francey was doing the same thing, though in an entirely different way.

Both Alan and Francey would have to be dealt with, though, again, in entirely different ways.

Kay found herself thinking that, of the two, Francey's situation was probably going to be the easier to handle.

KAY DEALT WITH Francey's parents by telling Tracy that Francey had a "bug" that was contagious, so it seemed best if she stayed put at the inn.

Tracy, who was terrified of illness in any form, was more than willing to agree, and evidently the matter was one of indifference to Gerard because Kay heard nothing from him.

She hadn't been speaking a total untruth about Francey's "bug." Dr. Boudreau had warned that it was important to take some ordinary, hygienic precautions—like being careful with the glasses and dishes Francey drank and ate from.

By Tuesday morning, Francey's temperature was down to normal, and though she was weak, she was much improved.

When the doctor arrived, he was pleased with her progress. At that point Kay put a few cards on the table, telling Francey straight out that Dr. Boudreau knew of her pregnancy and was going to take her on as a patient.

"And he will maintain your confidence," Kay added quickly, as she saw the stricken expression that came to Francey's face. "That right, isn't it, doctor?"

Dr. Boudreau nodded. "Yes," he said, "that's right—but I do urge you to tell your parents about this, Francey."

"Maybe, after a while," Francey murmured, her blue eyes, so much like her mother's, looking especially huge in her small, pinched face.

After the doctor left, Francey turned quickly on Kay. "Why?" she demanded, her voice shaking. "Why did you tell him?"

"Because you have to have proper medical care both for your sake and the sake of the baby," Kay stated firmly. "You can trust him, Francey. He's said he'll respect your confidence, and he will. But he's right. You're going to have to get up your courage and tell Tracy and Gerard."

"I can't," Francey said.

"Sooner or later you're going to have to, Francey."

Francey shook her head. "Before I start to show, I've got to get away from here, Aunt Kay. Go somewhere to have the baby...."

"That's ridiculous, Francey. You need to be here where you have family, people who care about you."

"No! Can't you see—if Daddy discovers I'm going to have a baby all he'll think about is finding out who the father is. He'll do *anything* to me to find that out, and I can't let him. He'd kill—"

Francey broke off, looking horrified over what she'd almost said.

Kay didn't press her. She let the subject go, left Francey cuddled up on the bed and went to dial Alan's room. He'd offered to stay with Francey again while Kay tended to hotel business, and though she hadn't planned to take him up on it—actually, Francey was well enough to stay by herself—she changed her mind.

It disturbed her to realize that Francey was thinking about leaving Savannah and striking out on her own, going someplace—God knows where—to have her baby. She knew there was no way she could keep watch over Francey for the next few months if she left town. All she could hope for was to keep her here now, and try to talk some sense into her later.

With her daily rounds over, Kay ordered food sent up to her apartment from room service—enough for both Alan and herself, with some soup and soft custard for Francey.

"It's the middle of the day," she told Alan laughingly after informing him she was having their lunch sent up. "So I do think your reputation is safe enough. Also, Francey's here. We can consider her our chaperon."

"Yeah," Alan growled. "I think you know how much I want a chaperon around right now. And as for my reputation, I couldn't care less, lady."

"Maybe I couldn't care less about mine," she teased.

"Would that were possible. But you have to hang on to your local reputation, Kay, more's the pity."

He didn't pursue the subject. Their lunch came, and Kay toyed with a chicken sandwich, but she wasn't hungry.

After a time, she asked Alan, "Do you think we should postpone our date for tonight with the Creightons?"

"I've been wondering," he admitted. "Francey does seem a lot better. She'd probably be fine staying here by herself, and we can make it an early evening. I think the Creightons would prefer that, anyway, with Clark working on a book. But if you're going to feel uncomfortable about it . . ."

"No, you're right," Kay said. As she spoke, she could picture the bronze key dangling in front of her eyes. It was crazy . . . she'd forget about the key for hours, and then suddenly it would loom up again, larger than life. It was imperative, she knew, to solve its mystery. Alan had made this trek to Savannah, after all, because of the damned key and the strange commitment he'd made involving it. She owed it to him as much as to herself to find out what it unlocked.

She wished she could feel that the key—what it unlocked, rather—might smooth out her path for her. But...a deep-down feeling made her terribly afraid that whatever revelation it might bring about was not going to be a pleasant one.

This, after all, was Randy's final legacy.

They left Francey propped up on an armchair in front of the TV set, watching a sitcom. There was a dish of ice cream on the table beside her and, as Kay told her, plenty more in the freezer.

"Or," she said, "you can call down to room service and order up anything you want."

Francey gave her a wan smile when she heard that, and Kay thought maybe she was going to make a quip about ordering up expensive champagne or something, but she didn't.

As they rode down in the elevator, Kay said worriedly, "She looks so *alone*. And so pale and frail right now...."

"She's just been pretty sick," Alan observed practically.

"I know. Anyway, Homer's promised to look in on her from time to time," Kay said. "He can call me at the Creightons' if there's any problem."

KAY TRIED NOT TO WORRY about Francey once she and Alan were at the Creightons', but it was impossible to entirely shut out a nagging sense of concern.

The Creightons could not have been more pleasant, and she gradually began to relax. Sally, she was sure, realized it wasn't easy for Kay to walk into her former home, so had smoothed the way as much as possible. For that, Kay was grateful.

They had drinks out on the patio. It was a warm and lovely evening, and after a time a mellow moon poked above the treetops. As she watched it, it occurred to Kay that she couldn't remember when she'd last sat out on this patio. She and Randy had seldom used it, except maybe for a summer cocktail party. Yet the setting was so lovely.

Sally announced it was time for her to do something about their supper, then graciously suggested that maybe Kay would like to take Alan on a "grand tour" of the house by herself.

"You know the way," she said with a smile. "Just don't look too closely at the cobwebs in the corners. I'd never get an A in housekeeping."

Kay led Alan to the graceful staircase that curved up to the second floor. He noted that her back was rigid as she climbed the stairs, and he suddenly felt guilty about getting her into this.

"Hey," he said softly, "we don't have to go on, you know."

"What?""

"We don't have to take this grand tour, Kay."

She turned to him, a temporary iciness in her deep blue eyes. "That's what we came for, isn't it?"

"Yes, but..."

"We're here now, Alan," she stated. And he could think of nothing to say to that.

She took him first to a suite of rooms at the far end of the second-floor corridor.

"This was Randy's suite," she said, going into a sitting room furnished in tawny shades of copper, brown and beige. She went on into a large bedroom where the color scheme was much the same, the single, king-size bed covered with a quilted copper spread.

The decor was distinctly masculine, which, Alan told himself, didn't mean that a woman hadn't shared these quarters, at least some of the time.

Kay flung open the door to a large walk-in closet. To Alan's surprise, it was empty except for an assortment of winter clothes, which the Creightons evidently had stored here.

"I guess the Creightons use this suite mainly for guests," Kay said. She glanced around. "There are none of Randy's things still in here," she said. "Nothing, that's to say, that the key might open. There's only this one closet. The bathroom's beyond. You might glance in there."

Her face was stony, her voice completely impersonal. Alan glanced at her anxiously, then went into the bathroom and looked around. But as she'd suggested, there was nothing that might be opened with the key.

Kay's own suite, he discovered, was at the opposite end of the corridor, looking over the patio where they'd just been sitting and the charming back gardens. Her rooms were decorated mostly in blue and white. Again, there were no personal belongings around, nothing the key might have fitted.

"I didn't expect to find anything up here," she admitted, as they went into the two guest rooms along the corridor. "After I left here myself, I told Mellie and Bruce—they're a couple who worked for me for years, and they're retired now—to box up everything of a personal nature and store the boxes in the cellar. They left some of the bric-a-brac so things wouldn't look so bare. I told them to do that. But as you've seen, there's nothing that requires a key."

"Yes," Alan agreed.

He'd caught that phrase, "boxes in the cellar." It occurred to him that if there was anything the key might open, it very possibly was stored in those boxes. But for the moment, he didn't mention that to Kay.

He followed her through the beautiful, spacious rooms on the lower floor. As they peered into the dining room, he could imagine her sitting at the grand piano, making soft music with her lovely, slender fingers. Even that picture, though, suggested loneliness. Funny... but seeing this beautiful house had brought home to him, as nothing else probably could have, how lonely and unhappy Kay must have been for so many years.

Sally appeared in the doorway of the small breakfast room to say, "Well, you two timed that perfectly. I thought we'd eat in here. Four people rattle around in that dining room of yours, Kay."

Kay seemed about to say something, but she didn't. For his part, Alan was glad Sally had chosen the smaller, more intimate room for their meal. She'd put a pretty pale yellow cloth on the table, lighted deeper yellow candles, the wineglasses sparkled and the silver shone. Clark put a cassette on the stereo, and music filtered through the warm spring air. They settled down to an excellent repast, despite Sally's earlier warning that she wasn't much of a cook. Both the Creightons were excellent conversationalists. Time passed pleasantly, and tensions ebbed away.

But over dessert and coffee, Alan realized that their work here, unfortunately, still wasn't done.

He asked casually, "Kay, didn't you mention there was something you wanted to get from those boxes of yours in the cellar while we're here?"

Kay looked at him as if he'd struck her.

Sally Creighton, unaware of the hidden tensions, promptly said, "Kay, by all means get whatever you want out of the cellar."

"Perhaps I'd better," Kay said reluctantly, and rose without so much as a glance at Alan. She knew he didn't deserve the way she was feeling about this— they'd come here for a specific purpose, after all, and she couldn't blame him for pursuing it. But she'd had enough, just going through the house, with miserable memories swirling all around her, and she dreaded going down into the cellar.

She let Alan go ahead down the steep steps, and at the bottom he turned around to take hold of her hand, helping her the rest of the way. But when she reached the floor, he didn't release her hand. Instead, he drew her to him and he kissed her gently and thoroughly, his kiss a blend of such intensity and such sweetness that it brought tears to her eyes.

"Look," he said so huskily that Kay was afraid he was going to lose his voice again as he had that first day at the inn, "I know this is tearing you up and I hate it."

"It's foolish of me to let it get to me so," Kay said. "It's just that I was so…miserable here. I don't think I appreciated how miserable until I came back."

"You never have to come back again, dearest."

"I don't know," Kay said. "I don't know." She added, "Svengali…if you keep looking at me like that we're never going to get to the boxes. In that event, I'd

hate to have Sally and Clark appoint themselves a
search party."

He laughed. "On to the storage space."

Mellie and Bruce had done a good job of handling
the storage. The cartons were labeled; those that held
Randy's things were in one area, those that held Kay's
were in another, and boxes with articles from the various rooms were plainly marked.

Alan dragged out the boxes of Randolph Dillard's
personal belongings and couldn't repress a very odd
feeling once they were opened and Kay started going
through them.

True, Randolph Dillard was not the kind of ghost
he had expected him to be . . . because, by the time he
died so tragically, Kay had long since stopped loving
him. But nevertheless there were moments when Alan
felt Dillard's presence as almost a tangible force.

Kay's hands were trembling and her voice faltered
as she went through boxes of her late husband's
clothes, which, she said, she should have long ago
given to charity. There was a bad moment—for Alan,
anyway—when she unearthed a silver-framed wedding portrait. It was all he could do to look at it, because Kay and Randy Dillard had made such an
extraordinarily handsome couple. And, on their wedding day at least, they'd looked so ecstatically happy.

There were a number of other odds and ends, including a box of assorted cuff links, a college ring and
other miscellany. But nothing a brass key might open.

Kay, at that point, looked profoundly discouraged,
and Alan couldn't blame her. He'd been banking more
than he'd realized on solving the key's mystery here in
Randolph Dillard's house, and the letdown was
intense.

He felt a real sense of defeat. They were no further along in their search, and what was even worse, he couldn't see where they could go next. And he knew, without Kay's even saying so, that she was sharing the same dilemma.

They stayed long enough to have coffee and liqueurs with the Creightons and then excused themselves. The drive back to the inn was through a moonlit night meant for romance, but they both were too dispirited for romance, just then.

Also, they had Francey to think about as well as the key.

Francey was in bed asleep. Kay touched her forehead gently and found it cool. "I guess she can go home tomorrow," she whispered to Alan, who was standing by the bedside with her.

Alan was wishing Francey were at home right then. He wanted to take Kay in his arms and make love to her, he wanted to share her bed through the night and then, with dawn breaking over Savannah, to gently waken her and make love to her all over again. He wanted desperately to be with her so he could try to ease the worry from her lovely face.

Also, there was something he knew he should tell Kay, but he didn't want to because she already had enough on her plate. And, too, because he couldn't risk the danger of Francey possibly overhearing what he had to say.

Yesterday, when he was alone with Francey and she was in a kind of delirium because of her fever, she had begun to mumble, and she'd mumbled a man's name over and over.

"Bill," Francey had murmured again and again.

The world was full of Bills, Alan realized. But he couldn't help but think of the only Bill whom he'd met in Savannah.

Bill Abernathy. Gerard Dillard's partner, who was probably old enough to be Francey's father and had probably known her most, if not all, of her life.

Which, Alan thought, as he left Kay's apartment and stalked down the hall to his room, didn't necessarily mean a damned thing.

CHAPTER ELEVEN

THAT NIGHT KAY DREAMED about keys—a whole chorus line of identical brass keys that performed a dance routine with precise, mincing steps. Then, as they danced, the keys grew larger and larger until, overbalanced, they started falling down. Suddenly she was in their path, and she collapsed with brass keys raining all around her.

She awakened to find Francey, who had been sleeping in the other twin bed in the room, shaking her shoulders.

"You've been thrashing around and moaning like mad," Francey said.

Kay sat up straight, brushed her hair back from her forehead and drew an unsteady breath. "Sorry," she said, then asked curiously, "I was really so loud I woke you up?"

"I'll say," Francey assured her. "You sounded like something was hurting you."

"Well," Kay told her, "nothing did."

She was trying to be very calm and rational, but she was vividly remembering the falling keys, and they had hurt as shards of bronze metal struck her again and again.

She thought suddenly, *For the sake of my sanity, I've got to find out what that key opens.*

Francey said, "How about if I get us some cocoa? That might help you get back to sleep."

"Sounds fine," Kay agreed.

With Francey gone from the room, she leaned back against the pillows and tried to relax. But it was hard to relax when her mind was spinning in circles as she tried to zero in on something that might help solve her problem.

And the key, she thought wryly, wasn't her only problem. There was also Alan. She was coming to care too much for him. Common sense told her they had no place for each other in their life plans. Becoming more involved with him, with each passing day, was only going to create an aching emptiness that would be very hard to live with once he left Savannah. There was also Francey to be concerned about....

Francey loomed up then, carrying two mugs filled with cocoa. She handed one of them to Kay, then sat down on the side of the bed.

She looked better, but still pale and frail. Too young and, yes, dammit, too innocent to have gotten herself into this kind of bind, Kay thought savagely. Francey could be flighty, but Kay would have been willing to swear her niece wasn't promiscuous. The father of her child must really have taken advantage of her, then abandoned her to deal with the pregnancy by herself.

Kay wished she could get her hands on the man who'd done this to Francey. She didn't know what she could do with him—but she'd do *something*!

Francey said, "You look mad as a hornet."

"Just thinking," Kay said quickly, and warned herself she'd have to be more careful about silently venting her emotions around Francey from now on.

"I called Mom tonight," Francey said unexpectedly.

"Oh?" Was it possible that Francey had confided in Tracy about her pregnancy?

"I told her I feel a lot better. I think I can go back to work in the morning," Francey said.

"Francey, there's no need for that."

"Maybe not, but I need something to do."

"I appreciate that. But I want you to take it easy for a few more days before you think about working."

"Aunt Kay," Francey said, "people just can't go around protecting me like this all the time. You. Homer."

"Homer?"

"Yes. He came up while you were out."

"I thought he might."

"He said he'd really been worried about me. He wanted to see for himself how I was."

"Was he satisfied?"

"I guess so. He didn't stay long. He told me you've promoted him to assistant manager. That's great."

"He deserved it," Kay said.

"Yes, I think so, too. You know, it's funny. I've never paid much attention to Homer. I don't think I ever really looked at him till tonight."

"Oh?" Kay couldn't think of anything other than that to say.

"Yes. Actually, he's kind of nice-looking. In fact, he'd be handsome if it weren't for those thick glasses he has to wear. Even with them..."

"Homer's a very fine young man," Kay found herself saying, "and he has a lot of charm. Our guests really take to him. He'll do fine, regardless of the thick glasses."

"Well, I'm glad you're giving him this chance," Francey said. "He really loves the hotel business. He'll go all out for you, Aunt Kay."

"If he just keeps on going the way he's been going that'll be great," Kay said. "Homer doesn't have to prove himself to me."

"I think he knows that, and it makes him feel good." Francey reached over to take Kay's empty cocoa mug. "We'd both better get back to sleep," she said.

It struck Kay that of the two of them, just then, flighty little Francey sounded more mature.

KAY WAS AS BUSY as usual in the morning. She attended to her records, reflecting wryly that her favored combination of math and music wasn't as soothing as it used to be, then held her morning meetings with her chef and housekeeper.

She saw Alan only once. He stopped by the desk, where she was talking to Homer, to tell her he was going off on a tour of old Fort Jackson but hoped they could have dinner together that night.

It was nearly noon when she went upstairs to her apartment. An hour earlier, she'd sent Francey home in a taxi after reminding her that she had an appointment with Dr. Boudreau the following afternoon. Francey promised she'd keep it.

The apartment seemed lonely without Francey. And without Alan. Kay made a small salad for her lunch, but it was no fun eating alone.

This is what comes of getting used to other people's company, she told herself irritably.

She took her coffee into the living room and tried to settle down and watch a TV news program. But she was soon pushing the remote-control Off switch because too many of her thoughts were interfering.

The blasted key had been at the back of her mind all morning. Now it nudged itself forward. And she forced herself to face one of the major things about the key situation that had been bothering her.

If anyone might know what the key unlocked, it was Gerard.

Kay hated to admit that, even to herself…but it was true. Gerard and Randy had been business partners, as well as brothers. As brothers they'd been close in some ways, and had had their differences in others. As business partners, they'd worked as a team—as far as she knew—with Bill Abernathy, the third man on their totem pole. She had never envied Abernathy's position in the firm. Gerard and Randy, united, had always had the power to outvote him and often had.

Since Randy's death, she'd let Gerard handle things at Dillard and Abernathy for her. He had her proxy where anything regarding the firm was concerned. She was sure he must have exercised it more than once during the past year. Having her vote on his side, after all, gave Gerard an automatic majority—he had power over sixty percent of the firm to Abernathy's forty percent.

She had no idea how that sat with Bill Abernathy. At Gerard's house last Sunday, he and Abernathy had appeared to be on good terms. But that could be all front, of course. More than once, she'd seen Randy being outwardly charming and affable to someone he was planning to scalp in business. Gerard was the same type.

Sometimes she wondered why Abernathy had never come to her with an offer to buy her out. Certainly by now he must have realized that she didn't want to become personally involved in the affairs of the firm. It was also rather surprising that Gerard had not, thus far, suggested she sell out to him. Then he would own a controlling interest in his family business and wouldn't have to bow down to anyone.

Maybe Gerard had never needed to bow down to anyone. She didn't know. She didn't know much about her brother-in-law, except that she wanted as little proximity to him as possible.

Regardless, she was going to have to pay him a visit. She needed to show him the key and ask him if it meant anything to him. And this time she wasn't going to involve Alan.

Kay drove over to Dillard and Abernathy's in the middle of the afternoon. She'd thought of calling ahead but decided against it. It seemed a good idea to her to have an element of surprise to this visit, especially when it came to producing the key.

Fleur Collingwood was not at the reception desk when Kay entered the office suite. She heard the sound of voices, coming from Gerard's office, she thought. She discovered Fleur, Gerard and Bill Abernathy all in Gerard's office. Bill Abernathy was perched on the edge of Gerard's massive desk. Fleur sat in a chair pulled up close to the desk. She looked gorgeous in a pearl-gray silk suit, and she was laughing—until she looked up and saw Kay.

Again, Kay witnessed the immediate hostility that came into the other woman's eyes whenever Kay appeared on the scene. There was no mistaking a dislike that, Kay suspected, came close to hatred, and she wondered why Fleur's feelings toward her should still be so intense nine months after Randy's death.

Had Fleur really loved Randy? Was she still mourning him? Was time making her resent, more than ever, the fact that she had never become Mrs. Randolph Dillard? Had Randy promised her all along that one day he'd get a divorce? Kay could well imagine that he had. She could imagine Randy trotting out all the old clichés, the trite promises . . . and being so charming and convincing that Fleur had believed him and cast Kay in the villain role.

Strange, she thought—the idea of all that no longer had the power to upset her.

She knew suddenly that she was free of Randy. Completely free of him. For a long time after his death there had been some invisible shackles, formed mainly from her own sense of guilt. Now she could see she'd had very little ever to feel guilty about. Fleur, in a way, was a witness to that. But the most wonderful part was that it no longer mattered. She was her own person with her own life to lead, convinced that the past was now behind her. She could even smile as she met Fleur's eyes.

"Kay!" Bill Abernathy saw her first, slid off the desk and proffered his hand. His smile was expansive, his blue eyes sparkled. He looked as if he'd just gotten in from playing a round of golf—as maybe he had. His tan was deep, a beautiful bronze. His hair, though thinning, had a nice golden glow about it. Though she'd never cared for him particularly, Kay had to admit he was a very attractive man.

"Well, Kay," Gerard said, slowly rising, "what a pleasant surprise. Two visits from you over the course of just a few days. I'm delighted. By any chance are you planning to occupy that empty office?"

"No," Kay said quickly. She tried to judge the expression that flitted across Gerard's face, but it was gone before she could analyze it. "I just wanted to see you about something, Gerard."

"I am at your disposal," Gerard said, bowing slightly but effectively. When he wanted to, Kay had to admit, he could be the epitome of Southern charm. It was a talent he and his brother had shared.

He glanced from Fleur to Bill Abernathy. "If you'll excuse us . . ."

"Of course," Bill said. Fleur didn't answer, but she followed Gerard's partner out of the office, closing the door behind her.

Gerard sat down again and motioned Kay to the chair Fleur had just vacated. "What can I do for you?" he asked, his caressing dark eyes automatically making the question a suggestive one.

Kay wasted to time. She took the key out of her pocket and placed it on the desk blotter in front of Gerard. "Does this mean anything to you?" she asked.

She was watching him closely as she spoke, and this time he couldn't conceal his expression quickly enough. Without actually moving, he seemed to be recoiling from the key.

Nevertheless, his eyes were direct as he looked at Kay, and when he said, "No," she couldn't help but feel he was telling her the truth.

The conflict between expression and statement puzzled her. Gerard was looking at the key again, and she noted that he had not yet touched it. Before he could do so, she reached over and picked it up and put it back in her handbag.

She saw Gerard frown. Then he asked, a slight thickness to his tone, "Just what is that key supposed to mean to me, Kay?"

"I don't know," Kay said honestly. "I was hoping you might recognize it, that's all."

"Why?"

"It belonged to Randy. It evidently was very important to Randy."

Kay saw an odd expression creep into Gerard's eyes. A blend of alertness, wariness and something that wasn't too far removed from fear. But he said only, "What makes you think it was important to Randy?"

"I know it was important to Randy," she told him. "I'm not going into the details. Just accept my word. The key was extremely important to Randy. So I have to find out what it opens."

"What do you think it opens, Kay?"

"I have no idea, Gerard. If I did, I wouldn't be here," Kay pointed out.

"What could it open?" he persisted.

"I don't know that, either," she said. "I thought you might."

"Why do you think I might?"

"Gerard, please," she said impatiently. "We're not playing a game. As I said, the key was important to Randy. I need to find out what it opens, and I thought you might have some clue."

She stood as she spoke. Gerard stood, too. He was looking at her with no trace of a smile on his handsome face, and his eyes were a deadly black. Gerard had given her some bad moments in the past, making amorous advances she wanted no part of. She'd been somewhat afraid that might happen today, once the two of them were alone in his office with the door closed. But he made no move to approach her. Rather, he looked as if he wanted to back away.

She saw that odd expression creep into his eyes again. But he seemed to be in complete control as he said, "You might leave the key with me, Kay. I can see if it fits anything around the office."

"I already checked Randy's office the other day," she said. "There was nothing in there, so I rather doubt you're going to find anything elsewhere around here the key might open."

"You had it with you the other day?"

"Yes."

There was animosity in those black eyes now. "Why didn't you show it to me then?"

"It slipped my mind," Kay said. "It was the first time I'd been in the office since Randy's death and..."

She was surprised at herself for being able to fib so easily. Strange, she mused, as she left a couple of minutes later after assuring Gerard he didn't need to see her to the door, what one could do when the chips were down.

She didn't even know what the chips were, in this case. But she had a distinct feeling that there in Gerard's office they'd just been tossed down, even though she didn't think Gerard knew any more about what the key unlocked than she did.

ALAN SAID, "Sight-seeing around Savannah is always fascinating but...I was lonely as hell without you today."

They were sipping drinks in Kay's living room. She'd suggested they have something sent up from the kitchen instead of going out to eat. This time, Alan hadn't attempted to dissuade her.

"What did you do with yourself?" he asked idly. Then he added, before she could answer, "That was a stupid question. I've already discovered that running this place could keep at least two managers going full-time, and there's only one of you."

"In just the couple of days since I promoted Homer, the work load's gotten lighter," Kay confessed. "I have confidence in him. He doesn't try to take over arbitrarily, but he's not afraid of a little responsibility. So...I was able to get away for a while this afternoon."

He groaned. "This is a great time to be telling me that."

"Alan...I had an errand I felt I had to perform by myself."

"An errand?"

"Well, something I had to do."

"Okay," he said, "I gather you don't want to talk about it."

He sounded casual enough, but he didn't look casual. Kay had to smile at the miffed expression on his face, and she wanted to kiss it away. But a single kiss right then would have been a spark calculated to ignite a whole conflagration. She wanted the conflagration, but she knew she was going to have to tell Alan about this latest episode involving the key, and she wanted to do that first.

She erased her smile but couldn't erase the urge to kiss him. With an effort, she managed to shelve it temporarily.

She said, "Actually I do want to talk to you about what I did. I went to see Gerard."

Alan had been lounging against the couch cushions. As he heard her statement, he sat up straight. "You went to see *Gerard*?" he echoed.

"Yes."

"By yourself?"

"Yes."

"Weren't you asking for it, Kay?"

"I was afraid I might be," she admitted, "but if I have to I can handle Gerard. As it turned out, I didn't have to. I think I threw Gerard a curve, but it's a curve I can't figure out."

Alan stirred impatiently. "You'll have to do better than that."

"Bill Abernathy and Fleur Collingwood were both in Gerard's office when I got there," Kay reported. "I told Gerard I had something to discuss with him, so they left us alone. I produced the key. I told Gerard it was a key that had been very important to Randy. I asked him if it meant anything to him...in other words, if he knew what it might open."

"Yes?"

"Well, he said he didn't, and I think he was telling the truth. But I also think...well, I'd say I got the impression the key put the fear of God in him, except that doesn't seem to make sense."

Alan considered that. Then he said, "Perhaps yes, perhaps no."

"Please," Kay implored. "Don't start being mysterious now."

"I'm not being mysterious. We all know what keys are for, don't we, Kay?"

"What am I supposed to say to that?"

"It's a simple answer. Keys are for the sole purpose of locking something, wouldn't you say. And, in a reverse process, of opening that something?"

"Obviously."

"Maybe Gerard feels there's something the key unlocks that he doesn't want unlocked."

"What are you saying?"

"Maybe your husband held something over his brother's head."

"That sounds like blackmail," Kay protested.

"Not necessarily. Maybe the hold, whatever it might be, was quite legitimate. Something Gerard was going to have to face up to. Then, Randy was killed, so in that one respect anyway, Gerard was off the hook. Or he thought he was. Now, having seen the key, maybe he isn't quite so sure. Maybe he thinks Randy left something behind—papers, documents of some kind. Something that could be put in a receptacle, a box maybe, and locked up with a key. A key that Randy tried to make sure you would receive."

"I should think anything of the nature you're talking about would have been put in a safe-deposit box," Kay said.

"Did Randy have a safe-deposit box?"

"Yes."

"Do you have the key to it?"

"No. Randy's key must have been on that . . . that key ring you saw him take out of his pocket just before he was . . . killed," Kay said. "Gerard had the duplicate because he was the executor of Randy's estate."

"So Gerard was able to get into Randy's safe-deposit box?"

"Yes."

"Well, that says it all, doesn't it? If Randy had something he wanted to secrete from his brother he would have had to put it in something Gerard didn't have a key to. Right?"

"It would seem so."

"Voilà!" Alan exclaimed triumphantly.

Kay sat back, frowning. "That's all very well," she said after a moment, "but we're back to square one, it seems to me. Suppose there is a box, or some receptacle, that holds information Gerard doesn't want revealed. Obviously the information must have been crucially important to Randy...."

"Yes," Alan agreed. "And it was also something he didn't want you to come across prematurely, I'd say. That's why he told me not to bring the key to you until April."

"This month."

"Yes."

"It sounds like a deadline of some kind," Kay mused. "Something that had to be resolved this month, but not any sooner."

"Not any later, either," Alan said grimly. "Kay, we've got to find the damned thing the key opens."

"The inn, the office, the house. I don't know where else to start searching, Alan," Kay confessed.

She looked so worried as she spoke that Alan's heart constricted. He said gently, "Neither do I, sweetheart. Let's think on it. Maybe something'll spring out of the subconscious. Meanwhile..."

She was staring at a blank wall. He felt as if she'd gone a million miles away from him. He stood and went to her. He put his arms around her and could feel the tautness of her muscles. He said, "How about another drink and maybe a spot of food and then…"

"How about 'then' first?" Kay asked him.

ALAN STAYED WITH KAY again that night and they made love, and it was a mutual experience in which they shared and soared together. His tenderness touched her deeply, because she knew that he wanted her as desperately as she wanted him. But at first she was so tired and distracted that she began to be afraid there was to be no fulfillment for her that evening, and Alan had to teach her she was wrong. He slowly and lovingly coaxed her, stroked her, until finally she escaped her own bondage and was free to let the ecstasy he invoked permeate every atom of her being.

Then, later, it was her turn. She became an explorer, making her own tantalizing discoveries about Alan and his strong, male body. She caressed him as she'd never before caressed a man, and in the process she stirred herself to a fresh awareness, so that when he was ready to climb the heights she was ready with him, and they spiraled side by side.

The tempo slackened as the night passed, as they slept and then, awakening, turned to each other again. But the later, languorous lovemaking was almost better than the first outpourings of pure desire. They moved slowly, hearts and minds and bodies blending, and it was like going from one level of sweet intensity to another, and then still another.

Alan was ardent and patient, giving, demanding, strong and gentle all at once.

By morning, Kay knew without doubt that she loved him.

ALAN WENT BACK to his own room very early. He still had what Kay laughingly called a fetish about guarding her reputation.

"My grandfather would have loved you," she teased him as she let him out her door after first making an exaggerated survey of the empty hall. "You're a gentleman of the old school."

Alan raised a quizzical eyebrow. "So?" he demanded. "Is that all bad?"

"Nothing about you could ever be all bad," she said softly.

She couldn't get him out of her mind that morning. She tried to get back to sleep for a couple of hours, but instead she daydreamed about Alan. Finally she made herself some coffee and then pulled out her account books and started taking care of the inn's business early.

She made her usual checks with the housekeeper and the chef, looked over a couple of rooms that needed redecorating and stopped to chat with Ernest, who was complaining about people who were not guests at the Randolph House and had no right to leave their cars in the inn's parking lot.

"I'd like to put nails in their tires," Ernest grumbled.

Kay laughed. Nothing could sour her mood this morning. The night with Alan had been too idyllic to be swept so quickly from her memory.

It was midmorning, and she was talking with Homer about fixing up an office for him he could call his own, when Alan appeared at the registration desk.

"Could I talk to you for a minute?" he asked.

She quickly came out from behind the desk and walked across the lobby with him to a corner where they could have some privacy.

"What's up?" she asked, puzzled by his serious expression. It was a glorious day. It had been a wonderful night. No one should look so serious. For once, even though the key was still *there*, she didn't give a damn about it.

"I got a call from your brother-in-law a while ago," Alan said.

"Gerard?"

"You don't have more than one brother-in-law, do you?"

"No."

"Okay. Yes. It was Gerard."

"What did he want?"

"He asked me to meet him for coffee at a place up near the Hyatt," Alan said. "I'm on my way."

"I don't understand this," Kay admitted. "It's not as if he hadn't already entertained you at his home and . . ."

"I know. All he said was he wanted to talk to me about something personal."

"Something to do with Randy?"

"It would seem so, wouldn't it?"

"Yes. It's a bit too coincidental, wouldn't you say, that this comes right after I asked him about the key?"

"I'd say so. But there's only one way to find out what he has on his mind." Alan bent and kissed her lightly. "I'll be back with a full report," he promised.

Kay watched him go and wished she could call him back. Though she couldn't imagine what Gerard could possibly do, where Alan was concerned, she basically didn't trust her brother-in-law.

She went back to Homer, who had been insisting he didn't really need an office, and tried to concentrate on convincing him that they should do over a small room back of the registration desk to suit his needs.

GERARD WAS WAITING in the hotel lobby when Alan walked in. They greeted each other and headed for the coffee shop. There, waiting to be served, Gerard talked about the weather, the tourist season, Savannah.

He kept on talking about trivialities while stirring cream and sugar into his coffee. Then without missing a beat he said, "I'm glad you were able to meet with me this morning, Alan. Ever since Kay brought you to the office, I've been wanting to talk to you. It just wasn't possible over at the house last Sunday. This has to be a one-to-one discussion." Gerard smiled disarmingly.

Then he got down to basics with a swiftness that was disconcerting. "You were with my brother when he died," he said. "I don't like to bring up bad memories for you, but I need to know what he said to you."

Gerard was looking straight at him as he spoke, and Alan discovered that those dark eyes could be both keen and calculating.

"Your brother didn't say much," he said slowly. "He didn't have time. We weren't supposed to talk."

"But the two of you did manage to converse a little, didn't you?" Gerard persisted.

"Yes."

The question came fast. "Did Randy give you a key to give to Kay?"

"Yes." There was no point in lying about it.

Alan saw Gerard clutch the handle of his coffee mug, and observed that his knuckles were white. But his soft Southern voice was smooth as ever as he said, "I presume he told you what Kay was to look for? That's to say, what the key unlocked."

"No," Alan said quietly. "He didn't. There wasn't time."

That was true enough, too. And he wasn't about to elaborate, wasn't about to relay Randolph Dillard's "not until April" message to Gerard.

He watched Gerard closely and identified relief.

Gerard said, "Kay came into the office yesterday with a key. She asked me if I knew what it unlocked. I didn't, of course. But when she said the key had been important to Randy, I figured he'd given it to you and you brought it to her."

"Yes."

"I'd appreciate it if you'd fill me in on what happened," Gerard said. Alan suddenly realized that the whole pace and tone of this interview had changed subtly. Gerard, he was pretty sure, really did want to hear, now, about his brother's last few hours on earth.

Alan proceeded to tell him.

CHAPTER TWELVE

"KAY, IT'S THE LOGICAL THING to do," Alan said. It was the middle of the afternoon, and they were sitting on a bench along the waterfront.

"I can't see why you say that," Kay told him.

"Because the damned box or whatever it is *has* to be somewhere, and we know it isn't at Dillard and Abernathy's, there's no reason to think it ever would have been at the inn, which only leaves the house on Oglethorpe Square."

"We went through every one of those cartons I'd stored," Kay reminded him.

"I know you went through the cartons," he agreed. "I think the box must be in plain sight. Or maybe it's something you left behind because it had no significance to you and Sally Creighton moved it."

"I mostly left behind some bric-a-brac so the place wouldn't look bare," Kay said. "Did you see any boxes around, Alan?"

"Not specifically, no. But there were a lot of treasures around that house, Kay. I could easily have missed one of them."

Kay said suddenly, "I don't want to go back."

He let that slide for a minute, but then he had to say, "I thought you told me going back to the house next time wouldn't bother you."

"It wouldn't under ordinary circumstances," she said. "But these are not ordinary circumstances. For one thing, I'd have to make some sort of explanation to the Creightons."

"So?"

Kay stirred restlessly. "I just don't want to go, that's all."

"I think it's very important that you do."

Kay frowned. "Do you know something I don't know?"

"No. Unless it's the idea that Gerard just might try to find whatever the key unlocks before you do."

"Gerard?"

"Come on, Kay. Look, you got some strange vibes from Gerard when you showed him the key. Then he almost immediately followed up with that request for me to meet him for coffee. I also got some strange vibes from him. I've never considered myself even remotely psychic, but I have a strong hunch that Gerard would give a great deal to get his hands on whatever the key unlocks—and he *is* capable of thinking."

"What's that supposed to mean?"

"He may know what it is we're looking for, even though he doesn't know where it is, Kay. That gives him a decided advantage, wouldn't you say? All he has to do is to try to figure out where his brother put the receptacle that you have a key to, and frankly I'd say it wouldn't take a genius to limit the choices."

"Randy could have had a separate safe-deposit box Gerard didn't know anything about," Kay said. "Whatever it is could be in that safe-deposit box."

"Possibly, but I doubt it. In going through Randy's effects either you or Gerard would have come across the safe-deposit key, don't you think? In my experience, safe-deposit boxes always come with duplicate keys, and certainly Randy wouldn't have been carrying both those keys around on his key ring. Speaking of which, was that key ring ever returned to you when—''

"No," Kay interrupted· abruptly. "Not to my knowledge. But Gerard took care of everything when . . . when they sent Randy back."

She suddenly felt so unstrung that she couldn't hold in her feelings any longer. "Oh," she burst out, "I'm so damned sick and tired of keys."

She tossed her dark hair back as she spoke; her eyes were sparking blue flames. Alan already had learned that Kay had a lot of passion in her, but now he was seeing it expressed in a new way. She looked wild and especially beautiful to him. Neither the time nor the place was right for a sudden surge of desire, but just looking at Kay in this mood caused an arousal he was powerless to resist.

He fought back the urge to drag her off to a place where they could be alone and he could make fervent love to her. Cavemen had had something going for them. He wished he had a cave; he wished he could carry Kay away and keep her safe, warding off all predators . . . including Gerard.

The primitive feeling that clutched him, gripping his loins, making his pulse beat faster, came as a distinct surprise. The image he'd evolved of himself as a rather innocuous college professor steeped in the study of the ancient past suddenly seemed to lack validity.

So much for the veneer of so-called civilization, he thought wryly.

Alan made a sudden decision. He was feeling more and more certain that time was running out where the key was concerned, and that if they didn't act soon it would be too late to act at all.

He said to Kay, "Look... if you won't go with me to Oglethorpe Square, I'll go alone."

She stared at him. "Aren't you becoming somewhat carried away?" she asked, her soft Southern accent a little bit more pronounced, as it tended to be when her feelings were running deep.

"I don't think so."

"This is my business, Alan," Kay told him, then saw him wince. Her smile was rueful. "I wish I could take that back," she confessed. "You didn't deserve it."

"It's okay... as long as you didn't mean it. Hell, I know it's your business, Kay, but I can't help but feel I'm the one who got you into this in the first place. So it's my job to see it through."

"Do you always take on responsibility when you don't really have to?"

"I think you know the answer to that," he said levelly. "No, I don't always take on responsibility when I don't really have to. Also, I'm aware that you and I haven't known each other very long—before you get around to reminding me of that—but I'd say we've gotten to know each other pretty well. Time can be pretty much of a variable. In the short time since I walked into your inn, Kay, you've come to mean a great deal to me. Do I really have to tell you that?"

She smiled. "No, but it's nice to hear it," she said.

"Lady," Alan asked, a lopsided grin tugging at his mouth, "are you flirting with me?"

Kay's deep blue eyes darkened. "No," she said. "I care too much about you to flirt with you. And I appreciate the way you're standing by me more than I could ever put into words."

She changed the subject swiftly before either of them could plunge in any deeper. "You're right," she said. "I do need to go back to Oglethorpe Square and take one more look. I'll call Sally Creighton as soon as we get back to the inn and tell her there's something else I still need to look for."

SALLY CREIGHTON EXPLAINED that her husband was nearing a deadline on his book, and so it was important that she keep visitors away from the house in the daytime.

"How about coming for coffee and dessert tomorrow evening?" she suggested, and Kay promptly accepted the invitation for both Alan and herself.

When she hung up the phone, though, she found that Alan was scowling. "For one thing," he said, "I wish we could have made it tonight instead of tomorrow night. For another thing, I wish you could somehow have gotten across to her that she should stall Gerard if he calls her."

"How could I do that without it sounding very, very odd?" Kay protested.

"I don't know. I suppose you couldn't have," Alan admitted.

It was late afternoon, and they were in Kay's apartment.

Alan stirred restlessly. "I need to use some muscles," he confessed. "I guess I'm not the most patient person in the world. When I have to wait for something, my body seems to yowl for exercise. Maybe I'll go for a jog along the riverfront." He chuckled. "I'll be better company later if I let off a little steam now."

"I'm thinking of putting in a swimming pool and a health spa here at the inn one of these years," Kay said.

"Sounds like a good idea."

"Well, if it were a fait accompli you could use it to work out right now," she pointed out.

"There are other ways I could work out right now," Alan said with a grin. "But to be honest, I think we're both too edgy to enjoy each other the way we should."

He was right. Yet Kay felt such a sense of loss when he left her apartment that she thought maybe she should have persuaded him to stay with her after all. Edgy or not, she couldn't envision a time when she and Alan wouldn't enjoy each other. Physically they were so perfectly in tune. She couldn't imagine ever finding with anyone else the kind of fulfillment she found with Alan.

She shivered, contemplating long bleak years without him. Then she asked herself if she really had to settle for those bleak years—wasn't there some way, *some way*, they could share at least a portion of their lives together? This was the jet age they were living in, after all. It wasn't that far from Vermont to Georgia.

Yet...she couldn't imagine achieving any degree of real happiness by indulging in what would become a continuing but sporadic affair.

This afternoon was the first time either of them had come close to making any verbal declaration to the other. Alan had said she'd come to mean a great deal to him. She'd told him she thought too much of him to flirt with him. The word *love* hadn't been spoken yet...but there was no doubt in her mind that she loved Alan as she'd never loved anyone before and never would again.

That, she admitted to herself, was a pretty big declaration when she considered that until a little more than a week ago she hadn't even known Alan existed. And then he'd walked into her life as a stranger, coming under very strange circumstances.

Regardless, dammit, she loved him, she thought. And she knew he cared for her. But whether what he felt for her was *love* was something else again. Alan was forty-two years old. The youthful marriage that had failed was far behind him. The second, tragic marriage, which he admitted had essentially been a mistake, also was lost in the mists of time. Over the intervening years, he'd established himself in his profession, made a good life for himself, a full life. He'd weathered Vietnam better than a lot of people she knew about, and he'd come through last year's traumatic hijacking experience with a residue of little more than tension headaches, which would certainly leave him entirely with the passage of a little more time.

She'd heard that old bachelors were the hardest of all to shake out of their niches, and in many ways Alan could qualify as an "old bachelor." She had to smile at the phrase because Alan, at forty-two, was anything but "old." There was a strong possibility that, regardless of how he felt about her, there just wasn't room for anyone else in his life on a permanent basis.

Kay could feel herself bogging down in her own thoughts—something that had happened to her too frequently in the past, something she was determined not to let happen in the present. She went downstairs and found that Homer needed an extra hand at the registration desk. She told him she'd stay on while he went and got some dinner.

"Have you talked to Francey?" he asked.

"Not since yesterday," Kay said.

"She stopped by earlier, looking for you," Homer said. "She said you didn't want her to come back to work yet. I guess she wanted to talk to you about that, but I told her I agreed with you. I said I thought she should stay off through the weekend."

Kay nodded absently. She was remembering that Francey had had an appointment with Dr. Boudreau today. Was that the real reason she'd come by the inn?

"Do you think Francey wants to come back sooner, Homer?" Kay asked, hoping that Francey had kept the medical appointment, while at the same time remembering her saying she "needed" to work.

"I couldn't tell what she wanted," Homer said frankly. "She's got something on her mind, that's for sure. I wish I could help her." He shrugged, the movement eloquently expressing his frustration. "Hell," he said bitterly, "I wish so many things where Francey's concerned, Mrs. Dillard."

Kay didn't know what to say to him. Francey, in her most recent observations about Homer, certainly had seemed to be more appreciative of him than she ever had been before. On the other hand...even if Francey could be made to see Homer in an entirely new light, Homer, in all honesty, didn't deserve to be placed in a position of having to assume a major problem that by rights wasn't his.

Bill. Alan had told her that when Francey was muttering feverishly while he was with her, she'd repeated the name *Bill* over and over.

Was Bill Abernathy the father of Francey's child?

Kay gritted her teeth, wishing there were some way she could find out, while at the same time wondering what she could do about it if she did find out. Bill Abernathy was a "respectable" married man, highly thought of in local society.

Homer suddenly said, "Excuse me. I didn't intend to gripe like that."

"You weren't griping, Homer," Kay said impulsively. "I understand how you must be feeling, maybe better than you think. Francey does have some serious problems, I admit. But she's going to have to work them out herself, Homer."

Which, unfortunately, was probably very much the truth.

"It's hard to stand by and not to be able to help when the person you love is involved," Homer said almost under his breath.

Kay was spared a reply by the arrival of a party of four, and both she and Homer got busy registering the new guests.

She was at the desk when Alan came back from his run. He was wearing a loose-fitting gray sweat suit. His hair, clinging damply to his forehead, showed a slight tendency to curl. The run had heightened the color of his complexion so that he looked as if he was glowing. Kay, watching him come toward her, wanted him with a deep, sweet ache that went all the way through her.

He said, frowning slightly, "I didn't know you planned to work tonight."

"Homer needs a helping hand," Kay said. "With Francey off, we've been juggling hours, so there's no one else on with him tonight."

"I see," Alan said. But Kay knew he didn't like what he saw, nor could she blame him. He read her too well. He probably suspected that she'd deliberately sought out an escape route via the registration desk and would have been there whether Homer really needed her or not.

"Maybe we can touch base later," Alan suggested, and let it go at that.

They didn't touch base later. Around eight o'clock, business slackened off, and Kay insisted that Homer go down to the Buccaneer Room and have what she called "a decent dinner." For once, he took her up on the suggestion. It was after nine when he returned, and at that point she went upstairs to her own apartment.

She thought about phoning Alan's room and then decided against it. She felt very out of sorts. Her thoughts were veering in all sorts of different directions. As Alan had put it earlier, she was "edgy" and was probably better off by herself tonight.

She more than half expected, though, that he'd try her room phone before it got very late. When he didn't, she experienced a letdown and a disappointment that she tried to tell herself was disproportionate to what was actually happening.

She thought briefly about taking one of the sleeping pills the doctor had prescribed at the time of Randy's death, then decided against it, telling herself she preferred to toss and turn to getting to sleep in an artificial way.

Tossing and turning through the night was, as a result, exactly what she did.

KAY MANAGED TO REMAIN outwardly calm as she and Alan shared coffee and a rich chocolate cake with the

Creighton's the following evening. But inwardly she was impatient, anxious to get at the task at hand.

Alan was right. There was a strong possibility that whatever the key fitted was here in the Oglethorpe Square house, after all. It almost had to be, because there simply wasn't any other logical place.

The only way to find out whether Sally Creighton had moved any of the bric-a-brac Kay had left behind was to ask. Kay waited until they were on a second cup of coffee before she came to the point. Then she said, "Clark, Sally, I really appreciate your letting us come back tonight."

"It's our pleasure, Kay," Clark Creighton replied quickly, and Sally put in an added affirmative.

"Thanks, regardless," Kay said. She drew a deep breath. "You know I was looking for something I thought I might have packed with the cartons in the cellar, last time I was here," she began. "I didn't find it. I thought, after that, I'd probably been mistaken about it being here at all. But as Alan has pointed out to me, this whatever-it-is almost has to be here somewhere. . . ."

Clark didn't attempt to camouflage his curiosity. "That's a provocative statement if I ever heard one," he said. "If I were a mystery writer, you'd have me right on the edge of the chair. Even so. . . you're making me think there's a plot here that's starting to thicken."

"Clark never can hold back on that imagination of his," Sally said. "It's funny, you know. Gerard Dillard called this morning and said he needed to go through a couple of things in the cellar. . . ."

It was Alan who spoke. He leaned forward and asked Sally, "What did you tell him?"

"Well, frankly, I told Gerard I'd have to check with you first, Kay, before letting him go through anything in the cellar, because this is, after all, your house. I put it a bit more diplomatically than that," Sally added with a smile, "but I don't think he was too pleased."

"Did you mention we were coming tonight?"

Sally looked surprised at the urgency of Alan's tone, but she said only, "As a matter of fact, I didn't. Kay, what *is* this all about? Is Gerard looking for the same thing you are?"

Clark chuckled. "What was it you said about imagination?" he chided.

Kay smiled, but she spoke seriously. "Gerard may be looking for the same thing, Sally," she said honestly. "I really don't know. You see...Alan was on the same plane Randy was on last year."

Both Creightons stared in disbelief.

"I thought that might come out Sunday, when we were all at Gerard's," Kay admitted, "but maybe Gerard didn't want to cast a cloud on the day. I don't know. Anyway...Alan was with Randy at...the end," she went on. "Randy gave him a key and asked him to bring it to me...but not before April. And...well, this is April. So Alan brought the key to me, but we can't find what it unlocks."

"Wow!" Clark managed.

"I've looked through everything in Randy's office, and as far as I could tell there was nothing missing. There was no reason for the key to fit anything at the inn—Randy was never at the inn—but I've looked through everything there, anyway. It seemed, at that point, that the logical place to find whatever-it-was would be here. But when Alan and I went over the house the other night—and, after dinner, checked through the cartons in the cellar—we couldn't find anything the key fitted. This," Kay admitted, a desperate edge to her voice, "is just about the last chance, I guess. Did you move anything a key might fit, Sally? Store anything away you didn't want around?"

"Yes," Sally said.

She stood, her small figure tense with excitement. "Clark, as you may have already realized, uses the library to write in," she said. "There was quite a bit of bric-a-brac in the library—some lovely things—but I packed a lot of it away because Clark needed more space for his own gadgets. You probably didn't notice any gaps the other night because Clark's pretty well filled them up. But I stored the things in a back pantry that's pretty empty."

Kay nodded. "I took a lot of the things from that pantry over to my apartment at the inn," she said.

"Most of the things I moved were relatively small—nothing you'd use a key on. But there's one fairly large, lacquer box.... Come and look," she invited.

The box was Korean in origin, an exquisite work of art, lacquered in shining black and red, elaborately ornamented in gold.

The bronze key fitted perfectly.

Kay started to turn the key in the lock, and all of a sudden her fingers fumbled, then refused to move at all. Her hands were deadweights. Her bones felt like jelly, in contrast, and her legs were strung together with rubber bands that threatened to snap at any instant.

Alan came to her quickly, took the key out of her hand before she dropped it and literally pushed her into a nearby chair.

"You're white as a sheet," he said. "Clark, would you have some brandy around?"

"Give me a minute," Clark said, and was as good as his word.

Alan took the brandy snifter from Clark and said to Kay, "Here, swallow some of this."

She laughed shakily. "I feel as if I've stumbled into an amateur theatrical production," she protested.

"Yeah, I know, and you're the heroine with the vapors. Dammit, Kay, drink some of this, will you?"

"Alan, I don't need it, I'm all right," Kay said, and swayed as if the script had called for a fainting spell.

Alan held the glass to her lips, and she was all but forced to let some of the brandy's fire trickle down her throat. She sputtered, gulped...then rallied. "All right," she said weakly, "you've made your point."

She glanced at the Creightons. "Clark, Sally," she said, "I feel like an absolute idiot."

"No need," Clark assured her. "Look...why don't Sally and I clear out so you and Alan can open the chest in private?"

"I'd suggest maybe we don't open the chest at all right now but take it along with us," Alan said. "It might be a good idea for Kay to be back in her own place where she can tumble onto her own bed if she pulls a faint on me."

"Please," Kay protested.

"Alan's right," Sally Creighton said. "You are still white as a sheet, Kay, and I think he should take you home. But I'll warn the two of you right now...Clark and I are going to have to find out the ending to this drama, agreed?"

"Agreed," Kay said.

It was a relief to get out of the house, to let Alan help her into the car and then stash the chest on the back seat. But once they pulled away from the curb, Kay said, "I feel like such a fool."

"No reason you should," Alan told her.

"I reacted out of all proportion to what was happening," Kay said.

"Did you? I thought maybe you remembered the chest once you saw it."

"Are you saying you think I know what's in it?"

"I thought you might."

Kay tried to tell herself there was no reason why Alan's supposition should anger her...but it did. "If I'd recognized the chest I would have said so, dammit," she sputtered.

"Haven't you ever seen it before?"

"I'm not sure. That library—well, it was all Randy's. His sanctum sanctorum. I just about never went into it. I couldn't have told you what was there and what wasn't there. I supervised the things to be packed away in the bedrooms, but I asked Mellie and her husband to put away any of the personal things in the library. I guess the chest was locked and it's pretty. They must have decided to leave it where it was for decoration. Believe me, Alan..."

"There's no question of believing you, Kay," Alan said. "Of course I believe you. The main thing is...the key fits, and so the mystery, as Clark Creighton put it, is about to be solved. What worries me is perhaps you're not ready for that."

"I'm going to have to be ready for it, am I not?" she asked him.

"I suppose so," Alan admitted grudgingly. He felt unbelievably frustrated because now they'd found what the key unlocked, there was so little he could do for her. He wished he could handle the contents of the chest for her, whatever they might be, because he had a gut feeling that Gerard was mixed up with whatever was in the chest, and its effects weren't going to be pleasant.

He wanted to shield Kay, protect her. He supposed that was the way men had felt about the women they loved from the beginning of time and always would.

Love. Alan turned the word around and thought about it and knew it was the only word that fitted his feelings for Kay.

This was indeed a for-keeps love he was feeling for her. He admitted to himself somewhat incoherently that he would be loving Kay tomorrow, and for all the tomorrows for the rest of his life.

He was thinking about that and wondering what he was going to do about it as they walked into the lobby together, Alan carrying the chest.

Homer was standing at the desk, about to dial the telephone. Alan saw Homer's glance move toward Kay, and then Homer was rushing across the lobby, his voice hoarse as he said, "Thank God you're here! It's Francey, Mrs. Dillard. She came in here a while ago and she was crying. I didn't want her to be by herself, so I got her to lie down on that cot in the back room. I just went back to look at her and she's passed out, and I found an empty vial of pills on the table next to her. It's a prescription made out to you, Mrs. Dillard, I think for sleeping pills. Francey has taken all of them. I was just about to call the rescue squad...."

CHAPTER THIRTEEN

KAY RODE TO THE HOSPITAL with Francey in the rescue squad ambulance. Alan and Homer followed in Alan's car. Once at the hospital, Francey was taken beyond the reach of all of them, into an emergency room where a team of doctors and nurses began to work over her with swift precision.

The horror of Francey's having attempted to take her own life was terrible enough. But it was multiplied, for Kay, by the fact that the girl had taken *her* prescription medicine. Medicine she'd kept in a bathroom closet and never given much of a thought to except on those occasions when, most frequently, she'd decided against taking any of it herself.

She mumbled some of this to Alan as they sat side by side in the waiting room. Homer, unable to sit still any longer, had gone outside. Kay could see him through the floor-to-ceiling window, pacing up and down at the edge of the parking lot.

She said despondently, "Oh, God, Alan, Homer looked at me as if I'd *poisoned* Francey...."

"That's ridiculous, Kay," Alan snapped. "Homer knows damned well you didn't have anything to do with this. He's pretty distraught, that's all. Don't make any assumptions about what he's thinking. Right now, he doesn't know himself."

"But she took my pills," Kay moaned. "Those damned sleeping pills. I should have gotten rid of them a long time ago."

"I looked at the label," Alan said. "Fortunately they weren't megadoses. There's every reason to think Francey will pull through with no bad effects from this, though it's been a hell of a scare for all of us. Which makes me suddenly wonder—did you call Francey's parents before Homer and I got here?"

Kay shook her head. "It just didn't occur to me," she confessed. "It just hasn't occurred to me," she amended. "I'll have to call them, of course."

She started to get up, but Alan gently pushed her down again. "I'll do it," he said decisively, and started across the room.

Kay was willing to let him make the decision. She was willing to lean on his strength right now because she felt so totally unraveled by what had happened to Francey. Somehow, it all tied together—Randy, Gerard, Bill Abernathy and what had happened to Francey tonight. There'd been a pattern to the kind of life Randy had lived that seemed duplicated in the kind of life Gerard lived, and probably in the kind of life Bill Abernathy was living, as well. Right now it seemed to Kay that Francey had been the unwitting victim of all of them. She'd never had a father she could turn to. She'd never had an uncle who paid much attention to her. And, as for Bill Abernathy...

He was a conceited man. He would have fed on Francey's adoration.

Maybe I'm blaming him unjustly, Kay reminded herself. Yet though she'd racked her brains, she could think of no other "Bill" who could have been as close to Francey as Abernathy might have been.

In a few minutes Alan came back from the phone and said, "Gerard and Tracy will be over shortly."

He added, "I also spoke to the emergency room doctor. I felt he needed to know that Francey's pregnant, and he's assured me her secret's safe with him."

"Thank you," Kay said, and wondered what she'd do without Alan right now.

She'd manage... but having him by her side made managing so much easier. She'd never really had anyone by her side before, in this sense. When crises had arisen in the past, she'd handled them herself, primarily because Randy had automatically avoided anything unpleasant. Family illnesses, family deaths... Somehow Randy had always arranged to be absent at times like that.

Yes, she'd manage again, if she had to. But it was good, so very good, to have someone else around who cared.

Homer came in and took the seat Alan had vacated. "Any word?" he asked, taking off his glasses and rubbing his eyes, which were red rimmed. Kay suspected that Homer had been shedding a few tears in private, and her heart went out to him.

"Nothing so far," she said. "But, Homer..."

"Yes?"

"Dreadful though it is that Francey took my pills, maybe it was better *my* pills than anything else she might have gotten hold of. Alan pointed out they're not what he called megadoses."

"Mrs. Dillard," Homer said wearily, "I didn't mean to imply that any of this was your fault. It was just such a shock seeing that empty vial by Francey and realizing what she'd done. If I'd had any idea I would never have left her alone."

"I know that. But how could you possibly have had an idea, Homer...?"

Kay saw that Homer was waiting for her to finish her sentence, but she stopped in midstream. She'd come close to confiding Francey's real problem to him. Somehow it seemed to her he had a right to know, feeling about Francey as he did. That might be so, but it might also not be so, she acknowledged now. This was not the moment for such a confidence. For one thing, she had no way of anticipating how Homer might react. For another thing, it was Francey's business.

By the time Gerard and Tracy arrived at the hospital, Francey had already been pronounced out of danger. It was Dr. Boudreau who came out into the waiting room to reassure Alan, Kay and Homer, and it was Homer who quickly asked if he could see Francey, even for just a minute.

The doctor nodded, and arranged for Homer to be admitted to the room where Francey was being treated. Then, returning to Kay and Alan, he gave Kay a long look that she read correctly.

"No," she said, "Homer is not the father of Francey's child, doctor. Rather, he's someone who cares a great deal about her."

"Then more's the pity he isn't the father," George Boudreau commented. He added, "You know, Mrs. Dillard, Francey's parents should be informed about her condition. No," he continued, as he saw the alarm on Kay's face, "I'm not about to tell them. I said I wouldn't, and I won't. But I think you should talk to Francey once she's calmed down a bit."

"She did keep her appointment with you today, didn't she?" Kay asked.

"Yes. Aside from her so-called morning sickness, which is not at all unusual, she's coming along well. She's into her third month, and that means in a few more weeks she's going to start to show." The doctor paused. "I pointed that out to her," he said, "in the effort to make her realize she needs to confide in her parents. Perhaps I shouldn't have. I can't help but feel maybe it was that knowledge, suddenly thrust on her, that added to her desperation, put her into a panicky frame of mind..."

The doctor's words trailed off, and momentarily he looked stricken. Kay felt a stirring of sympathy for him. "You did what you thought best," she said impulsively.

"Yes, and none of us always know what's best, do we?" he countered with a wry smile. "Anyway...the important thing is for those of you who *are* close to Francey to support her as much as you can from here on in. I would like to think her parents might be included in that number, but you know them better than I do."

Kay wondered what Dr. Boudreau's impression of Gerard and Tracy was, once they arrived on the scene. Tracy was sobbing, almost in hysterics. Gerard looked grim and tight-lipped. Kay was thankful when the doctor told them he was admitting Francey so they could run a few checks on her the following day.

"Just to be on the safe side," he said. He added, "You can see her, but for just a minute, please. She's been through quite an ordeal."

Homer emerged, passed Gerard and Tracy, neither of whom recognized him. Kay took the opportunity to tell her in-laws that she and Alan were going, and a moment later she, Alan and Homer left the hospital.

It had started to rain, a faint, misty drizzle. The air was warm, but still Kay shivered. Alan put his arm around her as they walked across the parking lot and said, "I think the worst is over, sweetheart. I doubt Francey ever tries anything like that again."

"I hope to God not," Homer muttered vehemently. "She looked whiter than a lily, and so frail."

"She's going to be okay, Homer," Alan said, "but I think you ought to know she's going to need a lot of help from both you and Kay."

Homer, who'd walked on slightly ahead of them, turned. "What do you mean?"

"Francey's pregnant, Homer. In her third month. Her folks don't know about it. She went to the doctor today. Her first visit, and I guess the whole thing sort of...swamped her, which is why she did what she did. Now...something tells me she's going to face up to it and do very well. But she's going to need people who care about her."

Kay saw that while Alan was speaking Homer stood stock-still, then slowly clenched his hands into fists. There was a surprising menace to his tone as he said, "I don't suppose you know who did this to her?"

Kay thought suddenly of the South's famous duello code. At that moment she could picture Homer fighting a duel over the woman he loved.

She thought about Bill Abernathy and hoped that if he was the father of Francey's child, Homer never found out about it. And it was unlikely he would. Kay had a strong, strong feeling that Francey was never going to tell.

She looked from Homer to Alan and experienced mixed feelings. It would be easy to take offense at Alan for having assumed the initiative as he had. She

could say that he'd had no right to divulge Francey's
secret, something she'd thought about doing herself
only to conclude that she had no right. On the other
hand...she felt a decided sense of relief now that
Homer knew. And she had to thank Alan for that.
Alan, when the chips were down, actually had used
good judgment. Francey was certainly going to need
people on her side. This, in a way, would be a test of
Homer's caring. Right now, he must feel pretty
shaken. Yet his initial impulse had been anger at the
man with whom Francey had been involved rather
than at Francey.

On the way back to the inn, they dropped Homer
off at the rooming house where he lived. When he
protested and said he should be getting back to the
registration desk, Kay very definitely overrode him.
"Norman will be coming on in an hour or so for the
late shift," she reminded him. "In the meantime, I can
handle things."

"I'll help her," Alan told Homer, and Homer
smiled.

"Next thing you know, Mr. Johnston, she'll have
you getting into the hotel business," he said.

Kay listened, and thought very briefly of how things
might go for Alan and herself if Alan did take a sudden liking for the hotel business. But common sense
told her that was something as far removed from reality as her suddenly becoming an Egyptologist.

As they pulled into the inn's parking lot, Alan said,
"Homer's quite a person, Kay. You have a treasure
there. I don't wonder you promoted him. Something
tells me he's going to be your real right-hand man."

"He has a talent for the business," Kay conceded.

"More than a talent," Alan said. "He's intensely loyal. To you, to his job and also, I think, to Francey. You know, though, frantic as he was, he wouldn't leave here to go to the hospital until he latched on to Ernest and got him to take over the desk."

Ernest was still at the desk, and one had only to look at him to know it was not his favorite milieu.

"I took the liberty of calling Norman and asking him if he could come in early, Mrs. Dillard," Ernest said, once he'd asked about Francey and had been assured she was going to be all right.

"Good," Kay replied. She was only beginning to appreciate the toll this evening had taken on her. She felt as if all her strength had been siphoned out of her. First, the discovery of the box at the house on Oglethorpe Square, then Francey...

She stared at Alan. "My God!" she exclaimed. "I forgot all about the box."

"I didn't," Alan informed her. "Homer put it in the inn safe for me before we left here. If you know the combination, we can get it out and take it up to your apartment—"

He broke off and looked at her more closely. "Kay," he said quickly, "maybe it would be better to let this ride till morning."

"No," she said. "No... I wouldn't sleep, knowing the box was still to be faced up to." She tried to smile for him. "Not that I'm going to be guaranteed a good night's sleep once we've opened it," she admitted.

Alan let his worry show. "Sweetheart," he said softly, so he couldn't be overheard, "you look totally done in. If you'll let me have my way, we'll go up to your apartment and I'll put you to bed. I mean just that—put you to bed, nothing more. I'll fix you something hot to drink, and I think you're so damned tired that nature will take over, after that."

Kay shook her head. "It wouldn't work," she told him.

"Sweetheart..."

"Alan, we've come this far," she said, also speaking softly, even though Ernest had left the registration desk now, and there was no one else around. "Whatever's in the box *should* mean the end of the search."

As she spoke, Kay suddenly realized what she was saying to Alan actually meant. Once they'd examined the contents of the box, the search would be over. And though she had no idea what those contents would reveal, she more than ever dreaded finding out. She felt, clear to her bones, that whatever it was was going to be unpleasant, especially if it involved Gerard.

Also, there was another reason why she dreaded turning the key in the lock. With the key's mystery solved, the major reason why Alan had decided to stay on in Savannah would no longer exist.

NORMAN CAME ON DUTY nearly an hour early. Kay worked the combination on the inn's safe, but once the door was open she let Alan withdraw the lacquered box. She warned herself she was getting paranoid about it, but she didn't even want to touch it.

In the apartment, Alan set it down on the kitchen table. "It's quite a work of art," he said, admiring the exquisite decoration and the highly polished lacquer finish.

"Yes," Kay conceded.

"Kay, would you still happen to have some bourbon on hand?"

"Yes."

"Would you mind if I fix us each a drink?"

"No."

"Will you sit down before you fall down, for God's sake," Alan said, exasperation and concern for her blending. "You're behaving like a zombie, Kay," he added gently, the gentleness taking the sting out of what might otherwise have been an accusation.

Kay looked at him and said, "I'm sorry."

Watching her, Alan felt something melt inside him. It occurred to him that he'd been living for years with a lot of inner ice floes and now the last of the ice was gone.

He said huskily, "Come here, sweetheart," and reached out to her. She came into his arms and he held her very close, her soft, fragrant hair brushing his chin, giving him the crazy feeling that he'd stumbled into a field of velvet wildflowers.

He heard her mumble something and he drew back to ask, "What was that?"

"I was just thinking out loud," Kay said.

"What were you thinking out loud?"

"I guess I was wondering out loud," she amended. "I was wondering why life has to be so...mixed up."

"Maybe it doesn't," Alan said. "Maybe we make it more mixed up than it needs to be."

"Do we?"

"I don't know," he admitted honestly. "You see..."

"Yes?"

"Well...I'm not much of an authority because I'm just beginning to realize how out of the mainstream I've been," he admitted. "I've touched more on the lives and emotions of other people since I've been here in Savannah than I had for...well, for longer than I like to think about.''

"Since the hijacking, you mean?''

"No, not since the hijacking. Since Nam, actually,'' he said slowly. "I guess a lot of us who were in Nam tried to put all that behind us once we came home again, and maybe we put a lot of ourselves behind us, as well. It's hard to explain. I know I became pretty much immersed in myself, my life, my career....''

"You're sounding as if you're a selfish person. You're not a selfish person, Alan.''

"Not selfish, no. Just not going beyond myself. It's hard to explain.'' He tried to find the right words to say to her. "Since I've been here, it's like having a new lens put in a camera,'' he said. "I'm seeing things in a different way. The pictures have a different perspective. I—''

He broke off, and after a moment Kay asked, "You what?''

"I was thinking it's going to be pretty strange to go back to myself and Egyptology,'' he said.

Kay felt as if her heart had suddenly become a deadweight in her chest. For a second, she nearly asked, Then must you go back to yourself and Egyptology? but she suppressed the question before she could verbalize so much as the first word. *Of course*, he must go back to himself and Egyptology. What had she expected?

She said suddenly, "We'd better open the box and get it over with. I'll get the key.''

Going back into the living room and over to her desk gave her a moment to regroup...and she badly needed to pull herself together. She stared down at the

slender piece of bronze metal and resented the power
it had over her. This key and her destiny had become
entwined. She wished they'd never found the damned
lacquer box. She wished she'd had the forethought to
take this key down to the riverfront and toss it out into
the depths of the Savannah and let the search end
there.

Instead she carried it back into the kitchen with her
and handed it to Alan. "You do it, will you?" she
suggested.

Kay knew her fingers would be shaking if she tried
to insert the key into the lock. In contrast, Alan's hand
was rock steady.

He opened the box, lifted the lid, then turned and
said, "I think maybe you'd better take over."

Kay pulled out a chair and sat down. Her hands
were icy as she pulled the open box across the table.
She stared down at some neatly typed papers and two
signatures leaped out at her: Randy's name and Gerard's name, both inscribed in flowing black ink. The
signatures had been notarized. There was an official
seal stamped next to them.

She still made no move to touch the papers. She sat
staring at them until Alan urged, "Kay..." Only then
did she pick up the first sheet, and as she read she became more and more dumbfounded.

Finally she raised her eyes to Alan's and said, "I
don't understand this. I guess maybe I don't want to
understand it. Read it, will you."

Alan pulled up a chair, sat down and took the papers from her. He read slowly, carefully, then finally
shoved the papers aside.

"Well," he said heavily, "now I can see what your
husband meant by waiting until April."

"What did he mean?"

"Gerard was heavily in debt to Randy, Kay. It looks as though Gerard has been doing a lot of gambling over a period of time and suffered some pretty heavy losses in the course of it."

"Gerard's always liked the horses," Kay admitted.

"Well, I'd say this was horses and more," Alan said. "What we have here is an affidavit from Gerard that states that for a period of years he was taking money out of the textile business to cover his losses. Evidently, to a certain point, he later replaced that money. But a few years back, Gerard got so heavily into debt and took so much out of the company till that they would have gone under, except for some very definitive action. That's when Gerard and Randy took Bill Abernathy in as their partner and sold him a forty percent interest in their firm."

"They said they took Abernathy in because they wanted to expand."

"Did they expand?"

"As I understood it, the expansion was still in the planning stage. . . ."

"As maybe it was, maybe it is," Alan said. "The crux of the situation, though, was that Gerard's neck—and the firm itself—were saved simultaneously by taking in Abernathy. But Gerard failed to learn a lesson, from what I'm reading here. More recently he went into the hole again. Randy went to his rescue once, but this time around Randy paid off Gerard's debts out of his own funds and he insisted on full security. What we have here is a legally binding promise from Gerard, stating that if he fails to pay off the funds Randy advanced to him by the end of one calendar year, the thirty percent he owns in Dillard and

Abernathy goes to Randy—or, as it now happens, to Randy's heirs.

"That year's up on the last day of this month, Kay." Alan put down the papers and concluded bitterly, "No wonder Gerard was pumping me. No wonder you thought he was antsy about something. No wonder he called Sally Creighton and wants to go over to your Oglethorpe Square house to look through the things in the cellar."

For a long moment Kay sat stunned, trying to digest what Alan had just told her.

Alan said, "I think it's about time I mixed us that bourbon I talked about a while ago."

Kay didn't answer him.

He made drinks for both of them and brought the glasses over to the table. "Come on, sweetheart," he urged Kay. "Right now, this is medicinal."

She said, "I don't know. I'm afraid right now a sip of anything might make me sick to my stomach. Do you think Gerard wanted to get hold of these papers before we found them so he could destroy them?"

"What do you think?"

"I think Gerard wanted to get hold of the papers and destroy them," Kay said bitterly.

Alan shrugged. "Look at it from his viewpoint. He must have felt he was home free by the time I arrived on the scene. The papers hadn't shown up among any of Randy's effects. He must have had a good idea you didn't know anything about them, just from your attitude. Then you showed up with the key. It's a wonder he didn't panic right on the spot."

"I think in a way he did," Kay said, remembering that scene in Gerard's office with him. "But Gerard is smooth, Alan, he's very smooth. He's a past master at subterfuge."

"Well, I doubt he's going to be able to deny what's certain to come up next," Alan said. "There's probably not a chance in hell that he can pay up by the end of this month. There are only a couple of weeks to go. That means that as of April thirtieth he'll be out on his ear, and you'll hold the controlling interest in Dillard and Abernathy. Sixty percent, to be precise."

"I don't want the controlling interest in Dillard and Abernathy. I don't want *any* interest in Dillard and Abernathy," Kay protested.

"Then maybe you can sell out to Abernathy or get someone else to buy your shares," Alan pointed out. "Which doesn't alter Gerard's situation. He must be a pretty desperate man, Kay."

"Afraid," Kay said. "Yes, Gerard was afraid when he saw the key. I can see that now."

"Afraid, desperate—they can merge into the same thing," Alan said. "I don't like the idea of your having to deal with him, yet you're going to have to. But through your lawyer, I'd advise. What's the name of the lawyer you've spoken to me about?"

"Gary Madison."

"I'd suggest you contact him first thing in the morning, Kay. Above all, don't get yourself in a position of meeting with Gerard alone anywhere."

Kay frowned. "I can't believe what you're saying. You think I'm actually in *danger* from him?"

"I don't know. I'm not trying to push the melodrama button, but men have done some pretty bizarre things for lesser stakes than this one. Dammit," Alan said suddenly, "I'm staying here with you tonight, and I don't care who knows it. I'm going to hang around with you until you turn these papers over to Madison, and then he can tell Gerard he has them and take it from there."

"Alan," Kay reminded him, "I'm here in my own inn, for heaven's sake. Where could I be safer?"

"Your inn has doors and windows like other places. There are a lot of ways someone could get to you if he wanted to," Alan said. "I'm not trying to frighten you, but I do want you to be realistic, Kay. I'm staying with you, all right?"

Kay smiled wearily. She wanted Alan to stay with her... not just for tonight, but forever. There was no denying that. Yet the circumstances of his staying tonight cast a shadow. She didn't want him to feel responsible for her. She didn't want to have to think that her own brother-in-law might actually be considering doing her harm. She didn't like to remember that tonight Francey had been so desperate she'd tried to take her own life.

The shadow lengthened, casting out the joy that would have come, normally, with sharing her bed with Alan. They lay side by side, listening to the rain pattering down on the roof, and he reached over and took her hand. But he didn't try to make love to her and after a time he fell asleep. Kay stared wide-eyed at the ceiling as she listened to his steady, even breathing.

CHAPTER FOURTEEN

GERARD TELEPHONED at nine o'clock the next morning.

"I need to talk to you, Kay," he said. "Tracy and I are worried sick about Francey."

Kay and Alan were sitting at the kitchen table, drinking coffee. She'd been unable to follow her usual routine this morning. Waking up after a very poor night's sleep, she'd been more tired than she was when she went to bed. She'd had to defer dealing with the account books and business correspondence and handling the variety of other details connected with running the inn until she could get her second wind.

Now she prefaced her answer with Gerard's name, so Alan would know with whom she was speaking. "Gerard, I have my hands full this morning," she said. "We're going to be shorthanded at the registration desk with Francey out and—"

"I need to talk to you, Kay," Gerard repeated. "I'll be at your place in fifteen minutes."

Gerard hung up before she could answer him. Kay turned to Alan, her distress causing her words to come out in a feverish rush. "I don't know what I'm going to do about this," she said. "He's on his way over here. I don't want to talk to him, I don't want to deal with him."

"Call Gary Madison," Alan instructed promptly.

Kay called Gary's home, only to find out he'd just left for the country club to play some golf, this being a Saturday.

"Is it urgent, Kay?" Lucinda Madison asked. "You sound kind of frantic."

"I am," Kay confessed. "And yes, I'd call it urgent."

"Then I'll try to intercept Gary before he gets started, or else have someone go out on the links after him," Lucinda decided promptly.

Kay hung up the phone and impatiently pushed some stray locks of hair back from her forehead. "I'm acting as if I'm expecting Gerard to come in here and do something terrible to me," she said. "Tell me my imagination's going overboard."

Alan said levelly, "I don't think Gerard is going to do anything terrible to you, but I'd rather have you wary, and yes, even scared, than to open the door for him as if this were an ordinary encounter. Because it isn't."

"I know that."

"Kay, give me the box."

"Why?" she asked, puzzled.

"Because I'm getting it out of here and into my own room, okay?"

"Why not put it in the downstairs safe?" she suggested.

"The safe could become too accessible," Alan said grimly. "The closet in my room has a lock. I'll put the box on the top shelf and lock the closet door. Look, while I'm stashing the box away, go get some clothes on, will you? And hurry up. It may not take him fifteen minutes to get here."

Kay nodded. Though Alan had showered, shaved and dressed, she was still wearing a lounging robe. She headed for her bedroom but asked on the way, "Are you coming back?"

"No," Alan said.

She turned, dismayed. "Alan . . ."

"Get going," he instructed tersely. "I've got to get out of here, or Gerard'll walk right in on me with this damned box in my arms. Kay, I'll be sitting by the phone. I'm sure Homer's already on the desk. Tell him to call you here in ten minutes. If Gerard hasn't gotten here yet, tell Homer to keep calling you at five-minute intervals. Once Gerard is here, when you answer the phone say, 'I'll have to see about that,' if you need me. In that case, have Homer call my room and I'll be here in about three seconds. If Homer doesn't get any answer, tell him to call both me and the cops. If you feel you really don't need me, say, 'That's all right, Homer.' Got it?"

"Oh, God, I think so."

"Go on, Kay," Alan urged. "Call Homer first, then get something on." He was trying to be as brisk and matter-of-fact with her as possible, but the need for doing so was tearing at him. He wanted to take her in his arms and assure her everything was going to be fine. He wanted to protect her. He wanted to beat the hell out of Gerard Dillard if Gerard gave her any grief.

He forced himself to say again, "Hurry up, Kay." And let himself add only, "Everything's going to be all right, sweetheart." Then, before she could answer him, he beat a hasty retreat, clutching the lacquered box.

Alan put the box on the closet shelf, locked the closet, but then instead of taking up a position by the telephone he went to the window and looked out over Bay Street.

April was going by much too fast. In a few more days he had to get back to Vermont, back to the college, and in that respect the only good thought he could latch on to was that by the time he left, Kay's problems with her brother-in-law, or the major part of them, should be over with.

He didn't doubt that she'd probably have to deal with Gerard in court, and that wasn't going to be pleasant. But by then, at least, there should be no further threat of danger for her.

Alan didn't doubt that Gerard Dillard could be a powerful adversary. He didn't know whether Gerard would go so far as to threaten Kay physically—in fact, he doubted he would—but he didn't want to wait to find out.

If Gerard tried to harm so much as a hair on her beautiful head...

Alan gritted his teeth, went over to the bed and sat down next to the phone.

He stared at the mute instrument willing it to ring, while at the same time wishing it wouldn't. Because if the phone didn't ring that meant—should mean—that Kay was safe.

KAY GAVE INSTRUCTIONS to Homer, adding that Gary Madison was not only to be sent up to her apartment when he arrived, but also should be given a key to it. "I'll explain later, Homer," she said quickly. "I don't have time now."

She dressed quickly, wondering at herself for thinking about seeing to it that Gary had a key. She didn't like the implication of her own thought. If Gary needed a key to get in when he arrived, it would mean she couldn't answer the door herself either because she wasn't physically able to or because Gerard was preventing her from doing so.

Neither idea was a pleasant one.

She combed her hair hastily and dabbed on a little lipstick, then heard the knock she'd been waiting for.

Gerard brushed past her as she opened the door. Nevertheless, her first impression was distinct—he looked terrible. Dreadful. Pale, his eyes deep-set and dark-circled. And there was a tautness to his body that was echoed in the jerky way he moved across the room.

Kay, closing the door, tried to take the initiative. She said, "I'm very sorry about Francey, Gerard. But..."

He swung on her. His dark eyes, so like Randy's blazed across the distance that separated them. He said, "You know damned well I'm not here about Francey, Kay."

Kay neither denied nor affirmed what he was saying.

Her silence provoked an exasperated sigh from him. He muttered something under his breath, then growled abruptly, "I could use a drink."

"All right," Kay said, forcing herself to speak evenly, to keep her voice low. But her pulse was hammering. "Come on out to the kitchen," she invited.

She was so conscious of him following close behind her that she could feel the gooseflesh rising on her arms and legs. It took real discipline to keep control over her voice as she asked, "Would bourbon be okay?" She wanted to scream.

"Yes," Gerard said. "Bourbon's fine."

She gave him the bottle and a glass and let him make his own drink. He gulped down a liberal straight shot, shuddered, then followed the whiskey with a water chaser.

Kay pulled out a chair and sat down at the kitchen table. She managed this bit of action smoothly, but her legs were shaking so badly that she doubted she'd have been able to stand up another minute without Gerard's becoming aware of her fear.

"Why did you want to see me?" she asked him.

He poured himself another shot of whiskey before he answered her, but he didn't drink it. He gripped the glass and glared at her. "You found those documents, didn't you?" he accused.

There was no point in denying it. Better to admit she'd found the papers, to put this all out in the open and get it over with, Kay thought wearily. "Yes," she said.

"Where are they?"

The fib came easily under these circumstances. "In the safe downstairs," she said.

She tried to analyze Gerard's expression. She thought he looked skeptical as he heard that, but warned herself this could be her own imagination. There was no reason that he shouldn't believe her...and, she added to herself wryly, if she'd had any sense she *would* have taken the box back downstairs last night and returned it to the safe.

"I want those papers, Kay," Gerard said flatly, still gripping the glass of whiskey. "They are the only evidence that exists to the goddamned travesty that went on between Randy and myself. No one else knew about that neat little agreement Randy coerced me into making with him. The whole damned thing's illegal, anyway, but I want those papers out of the way. I want them destroyed."

Courage came from unexpected places. The fact that Gerard had just told her a patent lie gave Kay a sudden jolt of courage. She felt as if her spine actually had been stiffened, as if she could face this man who looked right now like the villain in a melodrama.

"Someone else knew about those papers, Gerard," Kay told him, "and I would say they are perfectly legal. They are witnessed and notarized."

"Fleur Collingwood notarized them, for God's sake," Gerard spat contemptuously. "She'd have done anything for Randy." His laugh made him seem more villainous than ever. "She *did* do everything for Randy," he said significantly.

White-hot anger flared in Kay. "I'm not interested in that," she stated.

Gerard's laugh became even nastier. "No, I don't suppose you are interested," he agreed. "You must have been looking the other way for a long time."

"There's no point in getting into that now," Kay said stiffly.

"Isn't there? I think there's a hell of a lot of point getting into it now, little sister-in-law, because it's the reason those damned papers ever came into existence. Why do you think Randy'd been paying off my gambling debts year after year? Because there was always someone, my dear Kay, some lady he didn't want you to know about, and I didn't mind keeping his secrets for him if he helped me out. Fleur, though, lasted the longest. She's still living in the nice little place he bought for her outside of town. She thought, poor fool, that Randy was going to divorce you and marry her. Haven't you ever noticed the way she looks at you when you come into the office? Haven't you felt that hatred? It comes across from her like a tidal wave."

"Fleur's feelings make no difference to me," Kay said.

"Oh, believe me, we're in agreement there, dear sister-in-law," Gerard said, with exaggerated politeness. "I don't give a damn about Fleur's feelings, either. Except it might have been nice if she'd gotten mad enough at you somewhere along the line to take that nice little pearl-handled revolver Randy gave her one time—so she could defend herself if she had to—and use it at what, let's say, would have been an auspicious moment."

Kay felt her jaw tighten, her teeth clench. "You *are* a bastard," she hissed.

Gerard raised a dark eyebrow in that same provocative way that had been one of Randy's trademarks. "Does that come as any great surprise to you?" he asked. "Your husband and I were cut from the same cloth, after all. Oh, don't look so shocked, Kay. You know what Randy was. So do I. Maybe you're superstitious about speaking ill of the dead. Is that the problem?"

Before Kay could answer him, the phone rang.

Gerard swore, and for a moment she thought he was going to cross the kitchen into the living room and answer the phone himself. Then he commanded, "Let it ring."

"No," she said quickly, already on her feet. "It's probably either the chef or the housekeeper. They both check in about this time of day. They'll know I'm here."

She was at the phone, picking up the receiver, trying to keep her voice from trembling as she asked, "Yes?"

Homer said, "Mrs. Dillard, are you okay?"

"Yes," Kay said, and tried to remember Alan's instructions. But her voice quavered as she said, "That's all right."

She was aware that Gerard had come to the kitchen door and was watching her intently. And she had the deep conviction that one false move on her part might tumble Gerard over the edge. An edge, she was beginning to realize, that he wasn't all that far from.

He was a big man, strong—far, far stronger than she was. The only viable weapon she had to use against him was her wits.

At the other end of the line, Homer said, "Are you sure you're okay? Mr. Madison hasn't shown up yet."

"Really," Kay said, "I don't have time for it right now, Homer. I'll get to you later and we can go into it then."

She hung up before Homer could protest further.

Gerard asked suspiciously, "What was that all about?"

"It was Homer, on the registration desk," Kay said. "Just a couple of routine problems I'll need to go over with him."

"Homer." Gerard frowned. "Homer Telfair, isn't it?"

"Yes."

"Wasn't he at the hospital with you last night?"

"Yes, that's right. He was."

"Is he the one who's been shacking up with Francey?"

Kay yearned to reach out and slap her brother-in-law's handsome face. "No," she said coldly.

"Don't look so outraged," Gerard advised. "We stayed with Francey till they got her in a room over at the hospital last night. She'd pretty much come to by then, and she blabbed. She told us she's with child, shall we say.'' Gerard jeered. ''She said that's why she tried to take an easy out.''

Kay was so appalled that she couldn't hold back her scorn. ''Is that what you call it?''

''Don't you?''

''No, of course I don't. Your daughter was terrified. She felt she had no one to turn to. I should think if you had a shred of decency in you that might bother you terribly, Gerard. Francey has been a bitterly unhappy girl, and someone—someone I think you know very well—took advantage of that fact. As a result, Francey has been abandoned. Yes, abandoned, as much as if she were some little stray waif,'' Kay went on, waxing eloquent as her spirit and temper mounted. ''She's been left to face this pregnancy alone, and she *knew* how you and Tracy would react to it. She knew she couldn't expect an iota of support from either of you. You've never, either of you, given Francey anything of *yourselves*—''

She saw, as she spoke, that Gerard's face was losing every trace of expression. She broke off, and the stillness was so intense that it rang in her ears. Then Gerard said, ''Randy always said you were a meddler. I guess that's one of the few things I have to agree with my late brother about. Get it straight, Kay. How Tracy and I bring up our daughter is none of your damned business. What you're saying about Francey getting involved with someone I know, however, is *my* business. Who, Kay?''

It was Kay's turn to smile a not very nice smile. ''Even if I knew for sure, I wouldn't tell you,'' she announced.

Gerard said levelly, with no change of expression, "I'd like to choke the words right out of your beautiful throat, little sister-in-law. You never have wanted to give me the time of day, have you? Never would give me a chance, would you, to show you all the Dillard men don't put on the same kind of performance?"

"Gerard!"

"Oh, stop looking so shocked," he said disgustedly. "I do have to hand it to you," he added. "You don't scare easily. I would have expected you to start whimpering about now."

How was she managing this? Kay couldn't believe her ears when she heard herself saying, "Sorry to disappoint you."

"Oh," Gerard said, "you're not disappointing me. I've always been kind of interested in you, Kay. Right now, you're kind of whipping up that interest. But we have to deal with those papers, before anything else. I'll go downstairs with you, Kay, and we'll go back to your safe and you just take those papers out of the safe and hand them over to me. That'll be all there is to it. We can go on just as we've been going on. You with thirty percent of the firm, me with thirty percent, Bill with his forty percent. That keeps the controlling interest with you and me, and believe me, I'm going to do everything I can to roll up a big profit for the two of us."

"Where have you found the money to back your gambling since Randy died, Gerard?" Kay asked. "Oh, the papers do spell out your problem where gambling's concerned. Also, that Randy got tired of covering up for you, which is why he demanded you make good by this April or your shares of the company were to go to him... or, now, to me, as it happens."

Gerard's sneer was ugly. "Where the hell do you think I've been getting my financing, Kay?" he asked her.

"From the company funds, I would imagine."

"Go to the head of the class," he applauded. "Problem is, we're due for an audit before long, so I've got a little bit of juggling to do. I can manage. I've managed before. Abernathy'll be none the wiser, which is what matters now. But I've got to have you on my side, Kay."

"I'll never be on your side, Gerard."

"I thought you'd say that," Gerard said slowly. "All I can do is tell you you're making it very damned hard for me, Kay. This brave front of yours is great. I could even admire it if I weren't the one who's going to pay the piper unless you come to your senses. But I am the one who's going to pay unless you get smart, Kay, so you ought to start thinking about that. These days, it's so damned easy to snuff someone out. People go out without a whisper, know what I mean?"

"I'm not even listening, Gerard," Kay said evenly, "because I can't believe you're that big a fool."

"I wouldn't count on that, little sister-in-law," Gerard said, his eyebrows lifting slightly. "Now... shall we go downstairs?"

"No," Kay said.

He sighed, and said, "You make me feel I'm dealing with a stubborn little kid. You don't have any choice about this, Kay. You see, Fleur doesn't have that little pearl-handled pistol Randy gave her any longer, because I have it right here in my coat pocket. But if I use it on you, the gun'll be traced to Fleur, and since Tracy knows and I know and even Abernathy knows how much Fleur hates you, there'll be a nice ready-made suspect for the police to deal with. I sent Fleur off on an errand this morning, just in case something like this should come up. I sent her to get some stuff at a house where there's no one home, which means she'll have no alibi." Gerard chuckled. "It's kind of like one of those mysteries you see on TV, isn't it?"

Kay would never have said that Gerard was brushed by madness. Now she wasn't sure. Right now he looked calm, self-assured. Maybe the whiskey had settled him, because he looked a lot better than he had when he'd walked in earlier. But she suspected a caldron must be boiling inside that handsome exterior.

She'd heard that everyone in the world is capable of murder under certain conditions and circumstances. Also... Gerard *was* proud and vain; his image meant everything to him. He stood to lose his social prestige, his business reputation, his beautiful home on Oglethorpe Square, probably his wife—Kay doubted Tracy would be one to stay around if the going got rough—and everything that meant anything to him, if the papers in the lacquered box got to Gary Madison and Gary instituted legal proceedings.

Realizing that made Kay aware of just how deep Gerard's desperation could be.

She said slowly, reasonably, "Gerard, if you so much as touched me you'd never get away with it. Homer knows you're up here..."

Gerard chuckled. "Ah, no, he doesn't," he contradicted her. "Neither does your man Ernest, who is usually such a guardian of the gates. I parked up the street and I came in via the Buccaneer Lounge. Way back it occurred to me I might want to come in that way sometime, and it wasn't too hard to get a key to the lounge one day when I stopped by to check with Francey when she was on the desk.

"Just now, your man Ernest was busy out in the parking lot helping some people with their suitcases. I waited until Homer and that girl you've got on went out back for a minute, and that's all it took to slip by the registration desk. I used the stairs, not the elevator." He chuckled again. "Guess one does get a little knowledge out of watching those TV mysteries," he said.

The phone rang.

"Again?" Gerard queried, his tone now definitely suspicious.

"This is a business I'm running, Gerard," Kay pointed out testily. "Mornings, I deal with the housekeeper and the chef and some of my other employees and—"

"Spare me the details," Gerard said. "I've never been interested in the hotel business. All right... answer the damned thing, will you? But be brief about it and be careful what you say."

It was that admonition that frightened Kay more than anything else had. Nevertheless, she had control of herself as she heard Homer's anxious voice.

"Mrs. Dillard? You okay?" Homer asked.

"Yes."

"Mr. Johnston's been ringing me up every two minutes to see if Mr. Madison's gotten here yet. Is there any way I could contact Mr. Madison for you?"

"No, that's okay," Kay said. She was trying, desperately, to remember Alan's quickly formulated "code," but she couldn't. Primarily she didn't want to make Homer suspicious enough to summon Alan. Seeing Alan just now, she feared, might be the straw that broke the camel's back for Gerard.

She glanced toward him and saw his frown. He made an impatient gesture with his hand that obviously signaled that he wanted her to end the call.

"I'll get back to you later, Homer," she said, wondering if Homer would possibly catch the frustration—and the fear—in her voice. And hung up.

"Well," Gerard said, both eyebrows raised now. "And just what was that all about?"

"Hotel business," Kay said. "I keep telling you, Gerard..."

"I should have had the sense to listen in on your bedroom extension," Gerard said. And Kay knew, sickly, that was exactly what he'd do next time the phone rang, and there was no way she could prevent him.

She saw a telltale muscle twitching in Gerard's jaw, a visible sign of the nervousness that, until now, he'd managed to conceal. He said suddenly, "You've got to get that Homer off the desk before we go down. He could be trouble. The way he looked last night...he's stuck on Francey, isn't he?"

"I don't know," Kay muttered.

"The hell you don't know. You've always been a lousy liar, Kay. Look, what I want you to do is call down to him and tell him Francey's taken a turn for the worse and she's been asking for him. Tell him he's to go right to the hospital."

"Homer will know that the hospital hasn't called here, Gerard. The only calls that have been put through since you've been here are the two he made himself."

"If you can sound convincing enough he'll be so rattled he won't think about that. No..." Gerard paused then continued. "I have a better idea. You tell Homer that Tracy just came here. You just let her in and she's crying and she said she just came from the hospital and Francey's very sick and she wants to see him. I think you could also be a pretty good actress, Kay, if you put your mind to it. Now's the time for the test."

Kay shook her head. "I can't do that, Gerard. Homer would never believe me, anyway."

"He'll believe you if you put it across," Gerard said hotly, "and I advise you for your own sake to put it across. Tell Homer to go ahead. You'll come down to the desk in a few minutes and take over yourself."

"All right. Suppose I do that? What then?"

"You can send the girl on the desk on an errand."

"What about Ernest?"

"You can get rid of him the same way. Send him somewhere. This isn't going to take that long, Kay. All you've got to do is open up the safe for me, give me the papers and I'll be out of here. Then I'll get in touch with you tomorrow, and we'll get together for lunch and make some plans for Dillard and Abernathy. You've been making money on this place. It just occurs to me maybe we could buy Abernathy out. I don't think he's as crazy about the textile business as he was when he got into it. He hasn't been getting back that big a profit."

The knock on the door was loud and decisive. Kay heard it, and a shot of relief mixed with fear spread through her veins, with all the push of a jolt of adrenaline.

It must be Gary at the door, she thought. He knew she was here, and she had to let him in. On the other hand, she suddenly was overwhelmingly conscious of the pistol Gerard was concealing in his pocket.

She heard Gerard mutter something and knew that in another minute he was going to prevent her from opening the door. If she didn't act fast she was probably never going to get a chance to act at all.

But Gary deserved a warning. Until she could give it to him, she'd keep her own body between Gerard and Gary... and she'd have to just trust that Gerard would have enough common sense not to pull the trigger....

She moved swiftly to the door, so swiftly that she had her hand on the knob and was turning it before Gerard could catch up with her.

She faced the man standing on the threshold and was appalled. Because it was Alan Johnston standing there, not Gary Madison, and it was Alan's life she was placing in jeopardy.

CHAPTER FIFTEEN

ALAN'S HEART LURCHED as he looked down at Kay. Her lovely face was a white mask of fear, yet her eyes were shining with courage. He saw Gerard Dillard only a few feet behind her, saw Gerard's hand thrust into his coat pocket and suddenly and accurately assessed the situation.

Gerard had been threatening Kay. Gerard had a weapon. Whether he was actually prepared to use it was a moot question. That he *wouldn't* use it—that all his upbringing, his moral values, his sense of ethics were against a use of blatant force—was a risk that couldn't be taken.

Alan remembered Vietnam, where many times he had witnessed desperation and what it could do. He looked at Gerard, and knew he was seeing a desperate man right now.

He forced calm, forced himself to smile at Kay and ask, with exactly the right note of politeness, "Am I interrupting something?"

Kay's eyes flickered. He sensed she was imploring him to—what? Do something? Say something? No, he realized suddenly, she was imploring him to go away. And with that kind of mental overdrive and energy that seemed to possess him, he knew why.

She feared for him. She wanted to protect him. If he had needed any verification of his love for her—which, Alan thought wryly, he surely didn't—this valiant gesture on her part would have tipped the scales.

He managed to look amused, just faintly amused. "*Am* I interrupting something?" he asked again.

He knew that Kay realized she'd lost her small battle to try to guarantee his safety. "No," she said, and drew back so that he could come into her apartment. "Gerard and I were just discussing a few things. Gerard was about to leave, anyway."

Getting closer to Gerard, Alan smelled the strong odor of whiskey on his breath. Though it took even more of an effort than he would have expected it to, he greeted Gerard Dillard pleasantly and then turned back to Kay.

"You were going to fill me in on some of the local sight-seeing tours and such that I shouldn't miss," he said, as if reminding her of a promise. "I wondered if maybe we could do that over an early lunch?"

He added, in an aside to Gerard, "I only have a few more days in Savannah."

"Oh?" Gerard asked. "You're heading back to Vermont?"

"Yes." Alan was walking on into the living room as he spoke, and at least Gerard made no move to stop him. "It's going to look pretty bleak in Vermont after Savannah," he said, making himself keep on with a conversation that sounded totally inane to him under the circumstances yet was the safest—the only—route to take right now. "Nothing much'll be out yet.

Spring's a latecomer up there, not the beautiful season you have down here.''

"I take it you've enjoyed your time in Savannah," Gerard suggested.

"Very much so."

"I find that rather surprising," Gerard observed. "It was a sad errand that brought you down here. Not the best of beginnings for a vacation."

Alan waited, wondering what was coming next.

"That key," Gerard nudged. "The key Randy gave you just before he died..."

"Yes?"

"I suspect he told you more about it than you've admitted."

Alan froze internally, but somehow managed to keep on his bland, smiling mask. "No," he said. "Naturally I realized the key must be important. At least it was important to your brother, which doesn't necessarily mean much."

He saw Gerard frown. Gerard said, "I don't understand you."

"People in desperate situations attach importance to things that may not be very important at all," Alan said, which was true enough. He'd observed that particular phenomenon in Vietnam, too.

He said quietly, "I was in Vietnam. Were you?"

They were of an age, after all, Gerard only a couple of years older, if that.

"No," Gerard said.

"Well, a lot of the time you lived...close to the core," Alan said. "A lot happened quickly that tore up many of us who were there.... I'm not talking about physically, I'm talking about emotionally, psychologically."

"So I've understood," Gerard said dryly.

"So things became important that weren't important. Similar circumstances could explain why the key suddenly had such significance for your brother."

"No," Gerard said. "There was another reason why the key was important to my brother. As I knew, and as Kay has found out—"

The telephone rang again.

"I'll get it," Kay said quickly.

Alan thought for a moment that Gerard was going to stop her, but he didn't.

She picked up the receiver and heard Homer say, "Mrs. Dillard, are you alone up there?"

"No," she said. "That's all right, though, Homer. We can straighten it all out in a little while."

"I tried Mr. Johnston's room. He doesn't answer his phone. Is he with you?"

"Yes."

"Someone else?"

"Yes."

"Mr. Johnston talked to me a little bit about this," Homer said. "I know there's trouble. I also know that if things get bad, I should call the cops. Shall I call the cops?"

"No."

"Mrs. Dillard—" Homer broke off. "Mr. Madison's coming in the door," he said. "Shall I give him a key?"

"I don't think it will be necessary," Kay replied, "but . . . you might as well. And, Homer . . ."

"Yes?"

"I think you better go ahead and do what you just suggested, after all."

Kay, turning away from the phone, was thankful that Gerard—because he had Alan to keep track of as well as herself—hadn't gone into the bedroom and listened in on the other phone there. She also hoped that Homer had heard her message correctly and was at this moment phoning the police.

She heard a knock at the door and felt a new wave of fear wash over her, because now there was the concern that she was letting Gary Madison in for real trouble. A lot could happen in a matter of minutes, seconds even. She could see that Gerard was tight as a drum; if anything, there was an added edge to his desperation. Seeing Gary might be all that was needed to push him over that edge.

He growled, "Go ahead. Get the door," and she complied just as Gary was about to open the door himself with the key Homer had given him.

She saw Gary's light hazel eyes move from Alan, whom he'd not yet met, to Gerard and then Gary smiled. Kay knew him well enough to know it was purely a superficial smile, and she became certain that Homer had cued the lawyer to the fact that something odd, at the least, was going on in Kay's apartment.

Gary said, "I'd hoped to get here sooner, Kay. Lots of weekend traffic out."

Kay nodded, afraid to look at Gerard. But then, out of the corner of her eye, she saw his hand come out of his pocket and he was holding the pearl-handled revolver in it.

The tableau they were making, Kay thought, belonged in a wax museum. She was standing to one side of the door, rigid. Gerard was facing her, still as a statue. Nothing about him moved. Gary Madison was just inside the door, holding his briefcase, a tall, mild-mannered man whose intelligent face showed that he was getting some astonishing messages and was thoroughly on the alert.

Gerard snarled at Kay, "You bitch! Goddamn you, you sent for Madison. I'll—"

Gary said quietly, "Don't be a fool, Gerard. In a couple of minutes this place is going to be surrounded by the police."

"Please," Gerard said wearily, "don't underestimate my intelligence, Madison."

"He isn't underestimating your intelligence, Gerard," Kay said, her voice distinct even though it was quavering slightly. "That was Homer on the phone again. He'd asked me if he should call the police. The first time I said no. Then, just now, I told him to go ahead. . . ."

Alan's voice rang out. "Hold it, Dillard," he commanded. "Don't crucify yourself."

"He's right," Gary Madison concurred. "Whatever your problem, Gerard, it can't be as bad as what you'll face if you pull that trigger."

Gerard looked at the lawyer, and from his expression Kay had the feeling that he was faltering. But only for a moment.

Holding the pistol in a tight grip, he said, "Not much could be worse than what I'm going to be facing if this bitch of a sister-in-law of mine has her way. I'd advise you to step aside, Gary. You, too, Johnston. Don't either of you try any heroics. Kay, go in front of me. We'll take the elevator down, providing it's empty. If it isn't, we'll wait for it to come back up again. Once we're in the elevator, I'll put this gun back in my pocket...but believe me, I'm quick on the draw and I won't hesitate to pull the trigger."

Gerard drew a deep breath. "Once we're downstairs, you're to tell your boy Homer that you found what was lost—make up anything. I don't care what, as long as it sounds logical enough so both Homer and the cops will be convinced. After that, all you have to do is say something in the safe is mine, and we'll go get it. I'll walk right out the front door with the papers...and then we'll have that little lunch tomorrow as I suggested and talk things over." Gerard paused. "Do you hear what I'm saying, Kay?" he demanded.

Kay said, "Yes, I hear you. But what you're suggesting won't do any good, Gerard. You've made a serious mistake."

Gerard's laugh was harsh. "You never do give up, do you? No, Johnston, I've got eyes in the side of my head. So forget about trying to make a move on me. Come on, Kay, before my patience gives out. Let's get this little caper over with."

"Gerard," Kay said, "the papers are not in the safe."

His laugh was a shade harsher. "You're expecting me to believe that?" he queried. "Kay—come on, little sister-in-law. Give me credit for a little more than that in the way of smarts."

"Gerard," Kay insisted, her strength somehow returning so that her voice was steady, "the papers are *not* in the safe. I repeat, *not*. We can go down to the lobby and I'll do what you say if you insist on playing it that way, but it will do you no good. I'll open the safe for you, but the papers are not in it." She started for the door. "Since you don't believe me," she said over her shoulder, "come on. You can see for yourself."

She saw Gerard hesitate and pressed her advantage. She said, "Several of the hotel employees know the combination to that safe, Gerard. That's necessary, because our guests store valuables in the safe, and whenever they check out they want their things back. That means that anyone who's on the desk needs to know how to get into the safe."

"So?"

"Once I read those papers and understood what I was reading, I didn't want them in the safe where anyone else could come across them and read them," Kay said.

This time, she had no doubt that it was uncertainty she was seeing on Gerard's face. Nevertheless, he blustered, "You're putting me on, Kay. Don't think I don't know that."

Kay's sense of calm settled in a degree deeper. Her common sense told her that Gerard—unless he was completely deranged, which she doubted—was not going to make a move against her now unless he found out whether she was telling him the truth about the papers. If he were to use that gun, maybe he could—by exercising a small reign of terror—force Homer to open the safe for him. But if that were done, if he then discovered that she'd been honest with him, where would he be?

Thank God for Alan, Kay thought. *Thank God he had the foresight to take the papers with him.*

She became aware that Gerard's eyes were sweeping around her living room, taking everything in, and there was a wild look in them. "All right," he snapped, "suppose I buy your story for the moment. If the papers are not in the safe, that means they're here."

Gerard brandished the pistol at Kay as she spoke, and for a terrible moment she was afraid he was going to lose control and press the trigger involuntarily. It took a mustering of that renewed strength to say, "They're not here, Gerard."

"Somewhere," he muttered. "Your kitchen, your bedroom. Somewhere. I'm going to turn this damned place inside out."

Gary Madison had a quiet, mellow voice, an excellent courtroom voice. Now he used it to full advantage as he said, "That would be futile, Gerard. I have the papers."

Gerard swung on him. "You're lying through your teeth."

Gary shook his head. "No," he said. "Kay turned the papers over to me."

Kay plunged in quickly before Gary could make what would amount to a tactical error by describing a wrong, invented scenario to Gerard.

"After I failed to find anything the key opened at Randy's office, I knew the only logical place where there could be anything must be at the Oglethorpe Square house," she said rapidly, which was true, thanks to Alan. "So I made arrangements with Sally

Creighton to go through the things there and I found a box...."

She didn't have to try to sound convincing, Kay suddenly realized. She sounded convincing because she was telling the truth. She had no intention of filling Gerard in on all the details. Nor was she going to describe the lacquer box for him. Enough for him to know that there'd been a box, the key had unlocked it and she'd found and read the papers.

She told the first fib. "I took the papers to Gary immediately," she said.

Gerard focused on the lawyer. "Okay," he said. "So where did you put them?"

"In an extremely secure place," Gary Madison said. "An *extremely* secure place. Not my office safe, though under ordinary circumstances I would consider that safe enough, so there is no need for you to force me into my office at gunpoint. I can assure you they are not hidden in my home, either. If you want to verify either of those statements for yourself, you can. I will lead the way. But you will find nothing. And I am not about to tell you where the papers have been placed for safekeeping. My advice, Gerard, would be to hand that gun over to me and then get the hell out of here, and if you don't have faith in your current attorney you'd better go find yourself a good one, as soon as you can."

"Damn you," Gerard said evenly. "Don't think you're going to get away with this, any of you..."

For a moment, Kay was afraid he'd become unbalanced enough to use the gun on all three of them, after all. Then the phone rang again.

Gerard swore violently. The phone kept ringing. When Kay made no move to go near it, he turned on her. "You've been quick enough to pick up that receiver before," he snarled. "So what are you trying this time? Want to make sure the cops come pounding on the door? *Answer it*, dammit!"

Kay spoke into the receiver and heard Homer's voice. "The police are on the scene," Homer said, as if calling the police to the Randolph House was an everyday occurrence. "Do you want them up there?"

"Not yet," Kay said.

"Mrs. Dillard?" For a moment Homer's self-control sounded as if it were fraying. "Are you all right?"

Was she all right? Kay looked from her brother-in-law to Alan to Gary Madison. "Five minutes," she said. "Five minutes by the clock, Homer."

Alan looked at Kay, realized what the instruction she'd just given Homer meant and wished he had been the one to grab the phone receiver. In that event, the Savannah cops would have been pounding their way upstairs right now.

Kay was being as brave as hell, in fact maybe a shade too brave, in his opinion. What happened in the next five minutes depended on the state of Gerard Dillard's mind, and that was something only someone with considerable psychological training could hope to determine with any degree of accuracy.

The sight of the gun in Gerard Dillard's hand forcibly reminded Alan of Vietnam. And there had been guns, again, on the plane last summer. All in all, he'd had enough of guns to last him a lifetime, and his loathing rang through clearly as he rapped out the order, "Put that pistol on the table, Dillard. Now!"

Kay looked at Alan and saw that his eyes were as cold as gray steel. He looked as if he were ready to spring across the space between Gerard and himself and knock the gun out of Gerard's hand, if he had to. She saw the latent strength in him, the sureness and an element of ruthlessness that surprised her. And she knew Gerard was no match for him.

Her eyes swerved to Gerard, and she saw that Gerard knew it, too. "Three against one," she heard him mutter, and knew also that what he was saying wasn't the point. Right now, actually, it was one against one. Alan against Gerard. And at that point, Gerard was beaten.

He lowered the pistol to the coffee table, then edged back, staring at the gun as if it had burned his fingers.

Alan said to the lawyer, "Mr. Madison, the police will be coming up here in about three minutes. Is that what you advise?"

Gary Madison said quietly, "No. I suggest you inform Homer to tell the police to hang around a little longer. We'll have to concoct a plausible story for asking them to come here at all. Meanwhile, I suggest that Gerard leave and get to his attorney as quickly as possible. We will, subsequently, be meeting in court."

Alan went to the phone, placed his hand on the receiver, but before he picked it up he turned toward Gerard to ask, "Dillard?"

"I'm on my way," Gerard Dillard said thickly. And he turned away from them and walked out the door.

Gary Madison waited until Alan had made his call. Then he turned toward Kay and Alan, his face a mask of bewilderment.

"Now," he said, "will someone kindly tell me what this has all been about? Just what *papers* are we talking about, and where the hell are they?"

CHAPTER SIXTEEN

"THE HOSPITAL PHONED," Kay said. "Francey can come home. The thing is, she asked them to call me. She wants to come here and stay with me."

Alan groaned inwardly. He tried to tell himself he was being selfish, and he supposed that was true enough—okay, he was being selfish. But, dammit, his time in Savannah was running out, and he didn't want to share Kay with Francey or anyone else.

"How do you feel about that?" he asked.

"How do I feel about having Francey here?" Kay echoed. "Well, I think it would be a terrible moment *not* to take Francey in, don't you agree?"

"Yes," he said. "I agree." He did agree...which didn't erase any of the *buts* surging through his mind.

To his surprise, Kay laughed. "Too bad you're staying at my inn," she said mischievously. "Maybe you could move to another hotel and I could visit you there."

She saw the expression on his face and realized he didn't think that was very funny. She said apologetically, "I was only trying to make the best of an awkward situation."

Alan didn't comment on that. Instead he went directly to an entirely different point.

"Kay," he asked her, "what are we going to do about *us*?"

Kay was tired almost to the point of exhaustion. Much as she loved Alan, the issue of the two of them wasn't one she was prepared to deal with.

"Please," she protested wearily. "Not now."

She would have given a lot to retract the words the instant she'd uttered them. She saw she'd hurt him, and impulsively she got to her feet and went over to him. She put her arms around him and felt his shoulders stiffen beneath her touch. "Dearest," she said, "I didn't mean that the way it sounded."

"You don't have to explain," he said. "I understand."

He spoke gently, but he sounded like a stranger.

"Look," she said, "I want to explain. That's to say...I want to talk about us as much as you do. I just can't right now, that's all. And I couldn't have the people at the hospital relay the message to Francey that she couldn't come here. Do you realize that in addition to her other problems she doesn't know anything about Gerard—about this mess her father's gotten into?"

"What are you going to tell her, Kay?"

"I don't know," Kay admitted. "Dammit, I don't want to tell her anything about Gerard. It's not up to me. It's up to *him*, or if not him, it's up to Tracy. But God knows what Tracy will do when this comes out."

"What are you going to do about Gerard?"

"I am going to listen to whatever advice Gary gives me," Kay said. "I am not going to bail Gerard out, if that's what you may be thinking. My God...he pulled a gun on us." She paused, then added, "That sounds so melodramatic I can't believe it."

Alan said slowly, "A lot of people do things out of desperation."

She stared at him, her brow furrowing. "Are you excusing Gerard?"

"Of course not. I'm only saying he must have been close to the end of his rope to pull out that pistol."

"The gun Randy gave Fleur to protect herself with," Kay observed wryly.

"What?"

"That's what Gerard told me before Gary got here. He filled me in on the Randy-Fleur story, but it wasn't news to me. I knew she'd been Randy's mistress, but by the time that happened I didn't care anymore."

Alan heard her and felt his heart sink a little. He'd never heard Kay sound cynical before. Now he wondered just how much injury her unhappy marriage to Randy Dillard had inflicted on her. Was she soured on marriage—maybe so deeply that she'd be turned off to the idea of ever really committing herself to anyone again?

In those moments when they'd been together, she certainly hadn't seemed so. Which, he realized, was to say she certainly hadn't been turned off lovemaking. In fact, she'd seemed to him like a beautiful flower, long denied both sunlight and water. He'd bathed her in the glow of his love, slaked her thirst with a passion she'd come to share in a glorious way he'd never forget.

But there was a big difference between making love—even loving someone—and making the kind of commitment a marriage entailed if it were to have any chance of success.

Kay said suddenly, "Alan, I'm so sorry you had to get into all this. It's such a sordid scenario, and it's far from over yet. Somehow, things have to be worked out for Francey. Somehow Gerard has to assume respon-

sibility for what he's done. I feel very sure he can't
come up with the money he owed Randy. As I said, I
am not going to bail him out. I do know one thing for
certain . . . there is no way I would ever be involved in
any business with him.

"Anyway. . ." She pressed her forehead, as if pushing back a headache, and gave him a tired smile that
only heightened his frustration where she was concerned. "Anyway," she repeated, "I need to go down
and talk to Homer. He deserves a decent explanation
for what's been going on here . . . and he also deserves
to know that Francey'll be back here as soon as I go
over to the hospital and pick her up."

"Could I do that for you?"

"No," Kay said. "I appreciate the offer, but no. I
think this is something I'd better do myself."

BY MIDAFTERNOON Francey was taking a nap in Kay's
apartment, and Homer was under strict orders not to
put any phone calls through until Kay told him Francey was awake again.

Kay, realizing she'd had practically nothing to eat all
day, went down to the kitchen then and let René
LaPlante exercise his Gallic temperament while she
munched on a delicious croissant sandwich he made
her.

Alan had gone off somewhere, and she had no idea
where. It seemed to her he must have done all the
sight-seeing he wanted to do around Savannah and
more by now.

Kay usually preferred working in her own apartment, but that afternoon she used the downstairs office she intended to have refurbished for Homer. She

had just finished attending to a couple of business letters when Gary Madison called her.

"At least Gerard took my advice," Gary said dryly. "Evidently he went directly from your place and rooted out his attorney, Saturday off or no Saturday off. Everett Solomon. Do you know him?"

"I've met him," Kay allowed.

"He's well thought of," Gary said, "and I can't imagine he's exactly ecstatic about having Gerard as a client in this matter. Nevertheless, they've had a preliminary conference."

"Fast work."

"I'd say Gerard had the fear of God in him, Kay, when he left the Randolph House. Anyway... Gerard has made us an offer."

"Does Gerard have the right to make us an offer?" she demanded.

"No. But the name of the game in law, Kay, is compromise, more often than not. It would be better for everyone in this case if we agree to a compromise rather than insist on going to court and dragging all the Dillards' dirty linen out in public. At least, that's the way I feel about it."

"I can see that."

"Well, then, Gerard agrees to turn over his thirty percent of Dillard and Abernathy to you without protest, provided I arrange what will appear to everyone else to be a sale. To make it legal, you can pay him a dollar for those shares."

Before she could respond to this, the lawyer continued. "I know and you know that those shares would technically become yours anyway as of April thirtieth, unless Gerard paid up by then. And there's no way he can pay the sum involved. Solomon's certain of that, and I believe him. This way, obviously Gerard is saving face. He is going to leave town, Kay, if you'll agree to his offer."

"Gerard—leave Savannah? It's hard to believe he'd do that."

"The only thing Gerard has to back him up, in Savannah, is his affiliation with Dillard and Abernathy," Gary said. "I doubt there's a businessman in town, to say nothing of a bank, who would loan him a cent, which is why it's such a certainty he could never come up with the amount of money Randy loaned him.

"In leaving, though, what primarily interests him is saving face. His story will be that he's going into another line of business in Atlanta and can't resist an offer that has been made to him. Matter of fact, he'll *have* to go into another line of business in Atlanta, and he may have a certain leverage after a time if his Oglethorpe Square house sells."

"Gerard is putting his house up for sale?"

"Yes. And you—Dillard and Abernathy, that's to say—will be the prior creditor. He got into the till again, these past few months, to cover up on gambling losses. He *will* have to make that money good."

"How does Tracy feel about that?"

"Solomon got the impression that Tracy is in the throes of a nervous breakdown, but I'm sure she'll snap out of it once she thinks things over. She has the sense to realize—if you agree to Gerard's terms, that is—that the story could be very different. She could be married to a man facing a prison term. You'd have adequate grounds to file charges against Gerard, Kay, based on his behavior this morning. Also, Tracy will come to realize that Atlanta's a lot bigger place than Savannah, and I think she'll thrive on the life there.''

"Gary, I'm getting the impression you really think I should go along with this. Do you?''

Gary Madison hesitated. Then he said thoughtfully, "I realize it may seem to you at first that we'll be letting Gerard get away with a great deal if you agree to accept his terms, Kay. Actually, what I'm thinking about is you. Both Lucinda and I have been so delighted with the way your career at the Randolph House has blossomed. We both care a great deal about you, Kay, and these past few months . . . well, you've become an entirely new woman, in our estimation. I can't help but think that getting involved in a court case with Gerard Dillard would be a highly traumatic experience . . . and we don't know what aces Gerard may have up his sleeve.''

"What do you mean?''

"He may be able to come up with something, maybe able to claim that Randy got him to sign that paper under duress, under circumstances he might be able to invent that he just also might be able to get the court to believe. Kay . . .''

"I'm listening, Gary.''

"I'm not saying any of that would happen. I'm saying stranger things have happened. Yes, the more I think of it, my advice is to let Gerard sign over his shares of Dillard and Abernathy now, instead of lowering the boom on him on April thirtieth. Pay him the damned dollar and let him get out of town. Maybe there'll even be a chance for him to do something with his life, if he goes somewhere else and starts over. Unless he lets his love for the horses and other forms of gambling get the best of him again.''

"There's another factor, Gary," Kay said.

"What might that be?"

"I don't want to own sixty percent of Dillard and Abernathy. I don't want to own *any* of Dillard and Abernathy. I especially don't want to be in business with Bill Abernathy."

"You're not surprising me, Kay. I expected you to say something along those lines."

"Then what do you suggest, knowing how I feel?"

"Assume Gerard's shares and then let me find a buyer for your sixty percent. I have contacts, both here in Savannah and farther afield. In due course, I'll come up with someone who'll buy you out. One thing I'll say for Randy, Dillard and Abernathy was a good company as long as he ran it. Abernathy, though I don't like him personally any more than you evidently do, is not a bad businessman, but that's neither here nor there. I doubt he could afford to buy you out even if you were willing to sell to him."

"I don't want to sell to him, Gary. I don't want anything to do with him." As she spoke, Kay was thinking about Francey. She was more sure than ever that Francey was never going to reveal the name of her child's father, and she had to admire her for having the courage to shoulder her burden alone. Nevertheless…she was also more certain than ever that Bill was the father. Gary was right. She never had liked Bill. Now she also resented him.

"I'll handle the sale of your Dillard and Abernathy interest," her lawyer promised her now. "Just let's take first things first . . . though that's sometimes the most difficult thing in the world to do."

THE MOST DIFFICULT THING in the world to do, as far
as Kay was concerned, was to stand with Alan at Savannah's airport a few days later, waiting for his flight
to New York to be called. He was going to be in New
York for a couple of days for a meeting with an Egyptologist connected with the Metropolitan Museum of
Art, then he'd be flying on to Vermont to resume his
post at the college.

These past few days had been totally frustrating for
Kay. Francey had inevitably taken up a large share of
her time and attention. Tracy had appeared on the
scene to blurt out the whole story of what she termed
Gerard's ''gambling addiction'' to his already harried
daughter. Tracy, frequently dissolving into tears, had
played the martyr role, claiming that she'd been
keeping Gerard's terrible secret for years.

Kay conceded that might be so. But she didn't admire Tracy for adding to Francey's burden, which was
heavy enough.

Francey, though, was doing admirably. She insisted on putting in her stint at the registration desk
each day, and she seemed to have suddenly become
aware of the fact she was carrying another life inside
her and was responsible for that life. She started paying careful attention to her diet and more attention to
herself. Though she'd lost some of the old Francey
bubble, there was a new loveliness about her. And as
she watched Homer when he was watching Francey,
Kay could see that he was more smitten than ever.

It was also good to see that Francey was treating
Homer very differently than she had in her more
carefree days. Often Kay found the two of them in
deep conversation when there was no one else around,

and Francey told her that Homer was teaching her a lot about the hotel business.

The necessary preoccupation with Francey, though, had taken a toll on the time Kay could spend with Alan after the morning of that terrible confrontation with Gerard. They'd had almost no chance to be alone, what with Francey, consultations with Gary Madison about the Dillard and Abernathy situation, and Kay's needing to attend to the demands of running an inn.

Alan hadn't attempted to get back to that all-important subject of "us," and what they were going to do about each other, and Kay wondered if at this point he even wanted to get back to it. He'd seemed preoccupied lately, somewhat remote. She knew he was genuinely enthusiastic about his upcoming meeting in New York. She also had the uneasy impression that he'd be glad to get back to Vermont and into teaching again.

One night, when Kay had asked him to join Francey and herself for supper in her apartment, Francey had led Alan into a discussion of his work. She had been fascinated not only by the subject matter but also by his stories about happenings on some of his trips to Egypt.

Some of his love of his native state came through, too, when he told Francey—who like Kay had never been in New England—about Vermont and the college town where he taught.

"To think," Francey exclaimed rapturously, "you were lucky enough to find a college town right in your home state where a wealthy man who was an Egypt freak just like you are had made a large endowment!"

Alan had laughed, and Francey had said, abashed, "Alan, I didn't mean by *Egypt freak*..."

"That's okay, Francey," Alan had assured her. "I know what you meant, but I *am* an Egypt freak. Sometimes I feel I know those ancient pharaohs better than I do my own friends."

He'd been teasing, of course...yet there'd been a ring of truth to some of the teasing. Alan did love Vermont and he did love his work, and he'd made a good life for himself. As Kay waited with him at the airport, all of that was hitting home to her, and she felt strangely tongue-tied.

She wanted to tell him how much she regretted the swing things had taken during the latter part of his stay, but she couldn't seem to find the right words. She wanted to thank him—not that she hadn't a number of times—for staying on in Savannah in the first place, and for his tremendous help and moral support first with the key, then with Gerard.

She wanted to tell him how much she loved him, how much she wanted him, but now that the hour of parting had come she didn't seem to be able to find the right words for any of those things, either. There was something so anticlimactic about watching while he checked his luggage through and verified that he had the right tickets and got his seating assignment and boarding pass and accomplished all the rest of the trivia connected with travel. Then, as the minutes ticked by, he and she seemed to have less and less to say to each other.

Kay walked with him to that point beyond which only airline passengers could go. People milled around them, heading for the metal detectors and final checkpoints. Kay could feel the tears brimming, and she didn't want to cry. She wanted to send him off with a smile. She wanted him to remember her waving to him with a big, happy smile on her face....

It came to her that she was acting as if they were never going to see each other again.

She blurted the words at the very last instant. "I want to go with you."

Alan was separating his boarding pass from a clutter of other papers. He stared down at her. "Am I hearing you right?"

"Oh, yes, no, I don't know." The tears came, despite her best efforts.

Alan looked stricken. "Dearest," he said. "Kay, dearest...if I see two more tears I'll never be able to leave you."

Kay was tempted to tell him she'd shed a whole bucket of tears for him...if that might mean he'd stay.

Instead she said, "I'm never any good at farewells."

The words came out like a generalized statement, but this was certainly not a generalized situation. Did he understand that?

His eyes darkened. "I guess none of us are," he said unsteadily.

Was that a generalized statement? Or did he mean what she thought he meant?

He swept her in his arms and his lips claimed hers, his kiss intense, demanding. She answered the demand and they rocked together while people brushed past them.

They heard the final boarding notice announcement being made, and Alan muttered something vehement under his breath, released her and then kissed her again.

Then without a word he was gone, and Kay watched his tall figure going in a direction she couldn't follow.

FRANCEY SAID, "I had my hopes up."

It was the Sunday after Alan had left, and they were in Kay's apartment, skimming through the Sunday paper.

"What do you mean?" Kay asked.

"I would have sworn it was the real thing between you and Alan Johnston," Francey said. "I thought for sure he was going to scoop you off to Vermont with him. So did Homer. We both thought he was going to ask you to marry him, and I said you were going to say yes, but Homer wasn't so sure."

It came as a slight shock to Kay to learn that Homer and Francey had been discussing the relationship between her and Alan. She sat up a shade straighter and said, "He's a wonderful man, a delightful person, but his world is there, Francey, and mine is here."

Francey chuckled. "The War between the States ended a long time ago, Aunt Kay," she observed. "I know you're a dyed-in-the-wool Southerner and Alan's a dyed-in-the-wool Yankee, but does it make that much difference? This is also the jet age, after all. People can arrive at the place they're going almost faster than they leave the place they're coming from. Then there are such things as telephones, which both you and Alan seem to be disinclined to use."

Kay looked at her pretty young niece and blinked. For one thing, Francey was coming on almost like the old bubbly Francey, except that there was a nice added depth to this new Francey, and what she was saying was suddenly making a lot of sense.

Sunday morning. Alan had been due back in Vermont two days ago. What might he be doing right now?

There was one way of finding out, Kay told herself.

She rummaged through her desk for the phone number he'd given her, reached for the phone and dialed.

CHAPTER SEVENTEEN

VERMONT WAS BLEAK. Alan had expected Vermont weather to seem bleak after Savannah, but he was experiencing a different kind of bleakness.

Everything seemed so *empty*. There was no enjoyment to eating alone, he discovered, and since eating was something most people did three times a day, that became important. There was no enjoyment in going places or seeing things because there was no one to share his impressions with.

No one?

He amended his complaint. Everything was bleak, empty, unenjoyable because *Kay* was not around to share with him.

Certainly much of the time he was not alone. His days were filled with people. The college had welcomed him back, as had his students. In the short time since his return, the invitations from faculty wives were proliferating. Though he liked people, he'd never felt less like socializing, but he was beginning to run out of polite excuses. Anyway, whether he was by himself or with someone else, a constant sense of loneliness plagued him.

New York had been great. But not great enough. Everywhere he'd gone, everything he'd seen, even the conferences with his colleague at the Met Museum, had only served to make him wish Kay were with him.

Now that he was "home," that held true more than ever. There was so much he wanted to show her. Like his Egyptian faience collection of vases and tiles in glowing blues, greens and violets. His scarab collection. Another collection of papyrus art, including some ancient Egyptian versions of comic strips. An assortment of exquisite figurines. He looked at the shelves on which the figurines shared space with books and could imagine Kay's little statue of Nefertiti coming to take its place among them. Kay's Nefertiti would look just great keeping company with his things.

That conclusion brought with it a question. How would Kay, herself, fit into his milieu? Could he ever possibly make her happy? What, after all, did he have to offer her? A silent argument about that began to rage in him. He was forty-two years old, he'd been married twice, but he'd lived by himself for so many years now that he was admittedly set in his ways. He'd carved out a niche in this small Vermont community where it could be blazingly hot in summer but was as cold as hell's opposite in winter, and until now he thought he'd found contentment with his job and his books and his stereo and his studies. But he was learning that having the freedom to do pretty much what you wanted to do when you wanted to do it wasn't necessarily all that great.

His apartment was on the second floor of a big frame house in the center of town. He'd never paid too much attention to furnishing it, now and then buying something he needed or wanted without being overly conscious of the decor. Now he compared his rooms with the quiet elegance of Kay's Randolph House and her apartment, and the lack was obvious.

Also, over the years he'd lived here, he'd acquired a lot of stuff. The place, he observed with a candid eye the Sunday after he got back to Vermont, was extremely cluttered, and it was no wonder his housekeeper complained that there was just nowhere to put anything without it bumping into something else.

He'd liked this comfortable confusion he'd surrounded himself with. He still liked it, for that matter, but the lack of expressed care in what he was seeing—decorwise, planwise, *every*wise, he thought wryly—was evoking some odd thoughts.

He surveyed his domain and saw that it looked like exactly what he was. What he'd become, anyway. His apartment was a place where a crusty old bachelor with no one to think about but himself hung his hat. A place where no one cared if maybe the dishes were stacked up in the sink over a weekend, or the bed left unmade, or if a couple of streaks of shaving foam were left drying on the bathroom mirror.

No one cared if he went around the house wearing an old woolen shirt with a couple of burn holes. The burns had been acquired last year when, after the hostage experience, he had for a short time taken up pipe smoking again, before making the decision to renounce tobacco for once and for all.

He never entertained. As a faculty bachelor he wasn't expected to entertain. The shoe was very much on the other foot. As he'd told Kay once, the faculty wives always liked to have an extra man around. This Vermont town was no exception to the national norm. Single women, at least middle-aged single women, outnumbered middle-aged single men.

Most of the time, his housekeeper fixed a casserole of something or other for him to heat up for his dinner. Sometimes he settled for a can of soup. Sometimes he drove past the pickup window of the local golden arches establishment, indulging in things like sausage biscuits or cheeseburgers and french fries, usually accompanied by a chocolate shake.

He didn't think much about diet, though, basically, his diet wasn't all that unhealthful, and he'd never had a weight problem. He jogged only when the spirit struck him, but he did get in a fair bit of regular swimming. The college gymnasium facility had both indoor and outdoor pools, so swimming could be an all-weather exercise.

His comfortable old armchair, positioned for a good view of the TV, was contoured to the shape of his body, he saw. The imprint of his butt was clearly visible.

Well, all that was fine. His life was fine. Not exciting, except when something new came up in his chosen field of Egyptology, or when he was in Egypt himself, but fine. But as he was analyzing himself and his total performance record, in fact, he felt as if he were watching a video, which only served to prove one Alan David Johnston, Ph.D., was a man who lived in a rut. A rut that was getting deeper and threatened to become a chasm he'd never be able to climb out of if he didn't do something about it.

Did he really want to do something about it? That was an extremely big question. It would be strange, after all these years, to have to defer to another person about everything from what television program to watch to what to have for dinner. Or to have another person insist that he really should get rid of the old wool shirt or have the comfortable chair reupholstered.

On the other hand, it would be unutterably wonderful to wake up every morning and find a woman with beautiful, tousled dark hair sleeping at his side. To smell that faint but pervasive smell that was female and perfume mixed. To suddenly have deep blue eyes assessing him, and then to reach over and kiss a mouth that would be warm and soft and inviting. . . .

Alan forcibly broke off his analysis.

Earlier that morning, he had made a foray to the bakery uptown and then to the pharmacy and brought back both a couple of almond croissants and the Sunday *New York Times*. He was abandoning his self-inventory and thinking about starting in on the *Times* crossword puzzle, and had just poured himself a cup of coffee and was putting the cup down on the table, when the telephone rang.

He picked up the phone, heard Kay's voice and knocked over his coffee cup. Hot, creamy brown liquid cascaded over the *Times* puzzle and he vented a heated "Damn."

"Well," Kay said.

For an awful moment, Alan was afraid she was going to hang up on him. "Wait!" he commanded.

"I'm not going anywhere," she said, and her soft, Southern voice tore at his heartstrings. She added with a chuckle, "What just happened?"

"I spilled my damned coffee," Alan confessed. "I mean, when I heard you say my name . . ."

"You knew right away it was me?"

"Yes."

"Do I have *that* kind of influence on you?"

"You'd be surprised at the influence you have on me," he said thickly, and added, "Dear God, but I've missed you."

He heard Kay's voice pitch a tone higher, the way it sometimes did when she was trying to rein in her emotions, as she said, "Francey and I were sitting here mulling over the Sunday papers and we were wondering how you were...."

"And Francey suggested you give me a call and find out?" he finished for her.

"Well...yes."

"It would have been nice to think you were motivated all by yourself," he said. "But I'm grateful, regardless. Give Francey a hug and a kiss for me."

He paused. "Kay..." he said then.

"Yes?"

"I know I haven't called you. I know I should have called you. But I've been thinking of you every second, dammit!"

"Is it that bad?"

"That's not what I meant."

"Alan..."

"Yes?"

"About not calling. Look, there are no obligations. No strings, you know?"

Wasn't *that* the truth! he thought ruefully.

"I wanted to call you," he said. "I got caught up in things. Also..."

He groped for the right words. "I didn't know what to say to you," he confessed finally. "No, that doesn't sound right, either. What I'm trying to say is...that was a lousy parting in Savannah."

"Yes," Kay agreed softly. "Yes, it was."

"So much happened in such a short time down there," he said. "Then, at the end, there was just no chance for the two of us to really talk things over. Talk about us, that is, as I mentioned to you at least once. You had other priorities to concentrate on.''

''No,'' Kay said. She waited a minute, then went on, ''Francey, bless her, is being the soul of discretion. She just told me she had to go downstairs and check with Homer about something, and she left so I could talk to you by myself.''

''How is Francey doing, Kay?''

''Remarkably well . . . and I think Homer's helping her a great deal. She's working several hours on the desk each day, she looks great and she seems to be feeling fine. She and Homer talk to each other a lot when there are no guests around. I notice that when I'm passing by the desk, at various times, Homer gets her to laughing. He's so much in love with her, Alan. But I don't think that's really hit her yet. I'm wondering what will happen when it does. It seems to me it's bound to.''

''Maybe Francey's story will have a happy ending, Kay. Do you think Homer would accept her child?''

''I'm sure he would. And I think Francey really appreciates Homer these days. Love, of course, is something else. But I hope so much that Francey will realize what Homer could really mean in her life.''

''What about her father?''

''Gerard has already left town. He's gone to Atlanta. I agreed to 'buy' his interest in Dillard and Abernathy for the munificent sum of one dollar.''

''That was pretty decent of you, Kay. You could have given Gerard a very bad time.''

''I might have,'' Kay admitted, ''but for Francey. It would have been very hard on her to have her father dragged through a court case . . . and I guess my desire for revenge wasn't as strong as I would have thought it might be. Gerard's out of the firm, out of Savannah...that's more than enough. Tracy is still at their house, but the house is up for sale and I understand Tracy is in the process of packing the things she wants to take to Atlanta with her.''

"So Francey will continue to live with you?''

"Only for the present. She's talking about getting herself a little apartment. We'll see.''

"Are you going into the textile business, Kay?''

"You mean am I going to take an active interest in Dillard and Abernathy? Good heavens, no,'' Kay said, sounding appalled at the idea. "Gary is in the process of finding a buyer who'll either buy out my interest or maybe buy the whole firm. There are indications Bill Abernathy would not be against selling.''

"You could buy the whole firm yourself, then,'' Alan pointed out.

"I think,'' Kay said, "that's about the last thing in the world I'd ever want.''

She waited, hoping that he might ask her what was the *first* thing in the world she'd want, and wondering what she'd say to him if he did. *You*, would sound pretty blatant.

But Alan said only, "Yes, I saw firsthand that running an inn is a full-time occupation.''

Kay listened to what Alan was saying, but it wasn't what she wanted to hear. She knew she'd made a full-time occupation out of running the Randolph House, at first because she'd needed the kind of therapy devoting herself wholeheartedly to a project furnished.

Kay sighed. They didn't seem to be doing any better at long-distance than they had at the end of his stay in Savannah.

Had she really expected it to be otherwise?

Alan said suddenly, "Kay, school lets out in just a few more weeks. For the summer, that is."

"You mean you're taking off for the summer?" As she asked that, Kay wondered if maybe he might be about to go trekking off to some far corner of the world again. Maybe Egypt. No...she remembered he'd mentioned Egypt was on his schedule for next year.

"No, not the whole summer. I have some writing to catch up with, and this'll be the best place to do it. Everything I need for what I'll be doing is right at the college. But..."

"Yes?" she asked, wondering why he was sounding so hesitant.

"I thought I might come down, once the college term ends," he said. "Maybe in early June, maybe a bit later than that."

"It'll be pretty hot here by then," she said automatically. Hearing her own words, she was aghast. *Why*, in heaven's name, had she said that? She sounded as if she didn't want him to come.

Fortunately he didn't seem to be taking it that way. He said, "I don't care about the weather. I want to see you. I need to see you."

Alan's voice was rough with emotion. Kay felt a surge of answering emotion, and tears suddenly moistened her cheeks as she clutched the phone receiver a little tighter.

"We'll work it out," Alan said. "I'll be in touch." And then he added, so softly that she could barely hear him, "I love you so much."

Kay heard a click at the other end of the line and stared dumbly at the pale blue phone receiver she was still clutching as if it were her last grip on life.

Alan had finally said the magic words she had wanted to hear more than she'd ever wanted to hear anything. Then he'd hung up before she could answer him.

Hadn't he been sure of what her response would be?

Probably not, Kay had to admit. She'd been so harried, so upset about so many things those last few days he'd spent in Savannah that their wires definitely had become crossed, and for a while there the vibes between them had been all wrong.

When, minutes later, Francey came back, Kay had hung up the receiver but she was still staring at the phone.

Francey, seeing her, said, "You look like you're in a state of shock."

Kay's laugh was wobbly. "I don't know what kind of a state I'm in," she admitted.

"I think Alan just kissed you long-distance," Francey teased.

Kay felt as if Alan had more than just kissed her. He had said he loved her. The words rang around and around in her head forming a beautiful carillon that pealed out his message over and over.

It was a while before she thought about the other part of Alan's statement.

"We'll work it out," he had said.

Had he meant they'd work out a time for him to visit Savannah? Had he meant a lot more than that? Could they ever work out things between the two of them?

Kay tried to tell herself that only time would answer her questions. Time, and Alan. But she'd always been impatient by nature, and now she wondered just how long she could wait.

ALAN WENT AROUND in a daze for an hour or so after that telephone conversation with Kay.

When he realized he had, in effect, hung up on her, he nearly dialed her back. But anything he could say would be so...anticlimactic. And the truth was he was almost afraid to hear her answer to his unplanned declaration.

Kay had shown herself to be capable of all the caring, passion, emotion, a man could ever want from a woman. But she'd never mentioned the word *love* to him.

Restless, Alan felt that the apartment had become too small to hold him. He wadded up the ruined *New York Times* crossword puzzle, tossed it in the garbage can, then picked up his car keys and headed out.

When he started driving, he had no real destination in mind. Within a few minutes he had put the town behind him, and he was heading through hilly country studded with magnificent pines, where turns in the road opened up vistas of the beautiful Green Mountains in the distance.

He was almost at the turnoff to his grandmother's old house when it came over him that this was where he'd subconsciously been intending to come all along. Then, as he made the turn and continued along a narrow dirt road, he was wondering what he'd do if the For Sale sign had been taken down.

It hadn't been. It stood at the edge of the property, and Alan pulled up his car and parked alongside it and let his eyes wander over the huge old house and the acres of adjacent land.

Much of this property had been worked as a farm for many years. There was a fairly large tenant's house perhaps five hundred feet from the main house. There were barns, outbuildings and the main house itself, which was, in a way, a Victorian monstrosity, three storied, with a wide veranda running around three sides of it.

The latest owners had let the house go a bit. A fresh paint job was needed, maybe some new shutters, possibly a new roof. But Alan knew from memory that the house was solid, having been built by Vermonters in an age when pride in craft was a way of life.

He knew the house was vacant. He got out of his car and slowly walked around it. Finally he climbed the steps to the front veranda and peered in the windows. He saw furniture covered with white sheets. Evidently the previous owners were selling the place at least partially furnished, which would help anyone buying it get started.

From the veranda, he stared out across the land. Some of the acreage was remarkably level. He remembered telling Kay that one day he wanted to own a Huey helicopter, and there'd be plenty of room for one in a far field that could be converted into a small helipad. The rest of the land was rolling enough to be intriguing and very picturesque. There was an old apple orchard, where the trees were just beginning to show green, and a small stream that tumbled over flat rocks just beyond the orchard.

Alan wandered through the orchard to the stream and remembered the day when, while visiting his grandmother as a youngster, he'd stood on the banks of this stream and caught a trout. He had a sudden vision of a son of his doing the same thing, and in his vision the son had dark hair like Kay's and gray eyes like his, and looked like a mixture of the two of them, except that he slightly favored Kay.

Alan warned himself that he was taking quantum leaps, rushing ahead like the proverbial fool heading in where angels fear to tread. But, with the late April sun filtering down on this place that was, after all, a family homestead, he discovered that it could be pretty great to daydream.

KENNETH CROCKER HAD BEEN a real estate agent in Mansfield for years, and his office was in an ell at one side of his home, a large yellow-painted house on Main Street.

Alan had no idea whether Mr. Crocker worked on Sundays, but he didn't pause to find out. He drove directly to the realtor's house, noted that the office ell looked closed—the window shades were drawn three-quarters of the way down—and so went directly to the front door of the house and rang the bell.

Ken Crocker answered the bell himself. He was a big, jovial man with silvery hair, bright blue eyes and such an expansive girth that he could have played Santa Claus without having to stuff a red suit.

"Well, Dr. Johnston," he addressed Alan. "Heard you've been away."

Alan nodded. "I got back just a couple of days ago."

"South?"

"Yes. Georgia."

"Pretty down there this time of year," the realtor allowed. "Noticed this morning, though, the hyacinths and tulips are coming out by the back porch. Won't be much longer till we see some real spring."

He paused. "Something I can do for you?" he asked Alan.

"Yes," Alan said. "I just drove by my grandmother's old house. I see it's still for sale."

"So it is," Crocker agreed. "Thought I had a sale on it a couple of weeks ago, but it fell through. I'm confident, though, it won't be on the market much longer. That's a once-in-a-lifetime kind of place, and at the price the owners are asking, it's a steal. I expect it'll sell by summer."

Alan shook his head. "No," he said, "not by summer. It's already been sold." He met the realtor's questioning expression with a rather lopsided smile, because he'd never before in his life done anything like this on the spur of the moment. "To me," he finished.

CHAPTER EIGHTEEN

ALAN BECAME THE OWNER of his grandmother's house in the middle of May. The sale had been expedited, papers passed, and what people around Mansfield called the original Johnston family homestead once again belonged to a Johnston. Alan called his elderly aunt in Rutland, and she was ecstatic.

He kept his rented apartment in town but gave notice that he'd be giving it up by the end of June. By then, he expected to have his new-old home in reasonably good shape. His long-range plan was to convince Kay to come up to Vermont for the Fourth of July holiday. By then, he wanted to have the house looking the way he remembered it looking in his grandmother's day. He wanted Kay to fall in love with his house. He wanted Kay to tell him she already was in love with him.

No, he corrected, he wanted Kay to tell him she *loved* him and would forever and ever.

He realized he was behaving like a kid trying to plot an ending to a book he'd read only halfway through. But he still couldn't think beyond just getting Kay to Vermont and having the house ready for her coming.

Then the picture changed radically. The afternoon Ken Crocker handed him the keys and he went out to claim the house as his own was a tremendous letdown, and he decided he'd made a terrible mistake.

It was a rainy day, more cold than merely cool. Alan pulled into the driveway at the side of the house and wished Kay were there with him so they could walk through the front door together. A few minutes later he was glad she wasn't with him. The house was damp and musty smelling, and spiders had been building their castles all over the place, so there were filmy webs everywhere. When he turned the tap on the kitchen sink the water that ran out was rust red, explaining the stains that marred the porcelain finish, and he quickly discovered the furnace was out of oil.

The electricity had been turned on and, since the kitchen stove was electric, it worked. Alan brewed himself a cup of instant coffee, mainly to ward off some of the chill that was seeping through his bones, and told himself he'd been all sorts of a damned fool.

For one thing, the house was huge. He hadn't really remembered how big it was.

He found himself muttering, "The place should be a hotel!"

The words stuck, and he ran them over and over in his mind.

Could he offer Kay a hotel, rather than a house? It was a tantalizing idea, but after a few minutes of entertaining it, Alan was disgusted with himself. What the hell would Kay do with a Victorian monstrosity of a hotel in the backwoods of Vermont?

He warmed his hands on his coffee mug as he trailed from room to room, lifting the sheets to view the furnishings that had come with his purchase. He turned on lights as he went and made a mental note to replace the dim bulbs with some brighter ones. Soon he realized he'd acquired a very mixed potpourri, as far as the furniture was concerned. The town dump would be the best place for a lot of it. But there were a number of pieces that could be reupholstered and wouldn't be all that bad, and here and there he discovered a table or chair that might have some real value as an antique.

The same could be said of glassware, china and the miscellaneous assortment of kitchen utensils and stainless steel cutlery that had been left behind. Nothing much matched, yet there was an occasional piece of glass or china that looked as if it might have some genuine beauty, once it had been given a thorough soap-and-water treatment.

The place would be a challenge, and maybe even a delight, to someone interested in renovation, in restoring a house to its former glory. Kay, though, had already been through the restoration experience. Viewing his house and thinking about the Randolph House, he appreciated as he hadn't fully before the extent of the work and study and talent it had taken for her to have achieved the beautiful inn she owned today.

It also occurred to him that he'd mostly viewed this place through the relatively uncritical eyes of a child. The window seat upstairs had been a great place in which to curl up and read a book on rainy days, like this one. There was a big attic, filled then with old trunks and boxes, that had been a paradise to play in on cold winter days when he'd come to visit his grandmother during a school vacation. He remembered the warm old handmade quilt on his bed that had been so cozy to snuggle under. And the acres around here had been as exciting to explore, then, as delving on the scene into the mysteries of ancient Egypt was now.

He lingered in the living room after his survey, sitting down in an armchair that immediately emitted a puff of dust when it felt his weight. And he knew, though reluctantly, that now he'd gotten himself into this mess he was going to have to make some clear-cut decisions about where to begin to put things in order.

The Fourth of July holiday, which just a couple of hours ago, he'd thought of as far in the future, now seemed right at hand. Discouraged, he knew he could never even begin to have this place the way he wanted it to be by then.

Better to go to Savannah for the Fourth of July, if not sooner. One way or another, he had to see Kay before much longer.

He called her frequently, and if she didn't hear from him for a day or so she called him. They talked about a lot of things in the course of those telephone conversations. She kept him up-to-date on the Dillard-Abernathy situation and on Francey and on Homer and on the inn and even on Tracy, as well as telling him about various rumors that were floating back from Atlanta about Gerard. He told her about his classes, about the writing he planned to do once college was out, about the current state of the flora and fauna in Vermont, about his students. But they both tended to shy away from the personal, as if mutually sensing that when finally they got onto the subject of "us," this time they were going to have to do something definitive about it.

Alan didn't tell Kay about buying the house. That wasn't because he was trying to keep things from her; in fact, that Sunday afternoon when he'd impulsively told Ken Crocker what he was going to do, he'd intended to call Kay and tell her about it. Then he decided he'd better wait until the sale was a fait accompli—the owners could always back out at the last minute and change their minds about selling. Since then he'd decided to wait to talk to her about the place until he'd first really looked it over.

Well, now he'd done that. And had learned the bitter lesson of acting on impulse with only nostalgia to back him up.

He returned to his apartment and was tempted to call Crocker to tell him to put the place back on the market. But despite his initial disillusionment, he couldn't bring himself to do that. And when he went out to the house a couple of afternoons later, with the sun shining and the lilacs that bloomed so profusely around the place showing touches of lavender and purple and pink and white, Alan felt a fresh rush of hope. That weekend, he took some sheets and soap and towels out to the house, stopped on the way to buy a few staples and, in effect, moved in.

By the time the Memorial Day weekend was approaching, he'd mapped out a game plan, had talked to some carpenters, painters, wallpaperers and plumbers and was lining up a contingent of reputable workers who'd shortly be taking some positive action.

He had no illusions about getting the place ready in time for the Fourth of July weekend, and made up his mind that what he was going to do on that weekend was to fly to Savannah and surprise Kay.

Then, by God, he'd take her over to the riverfront and sit her down on one of those benches and, with privacy from hotel employees and the telephone, they'd *talk*.

Meanwhile, he'd been asked to be the principal speaker at the Memorial Day observance in Mansfield, which was scheduled for Sunday afternoon on the obelisk-centered village green. There were men in town who were Second World War veterans, and he wondered why one of them hadn't been asked. Then it occurred to him that people were more and more trying to show their support for the men who'd fought in Vietnam, and this was the town's way of giving them an added endorsement.

It made him uncomfortable to think about speaking about Nam, though, and by Saturday afternoon he still didn't know what he was going to say.

In the late afternoon, he wandered out onto the front veranda, a cold beer in hand. The weather finally had turned warm, the lilacs were in bloom and their sweet scent perfumed the spring air.

Alan sat down on a rickety old rocking chair, propped his feet up on the porch railing and tried to collect his thoughts. But all he could coherently think about was Kay; his preoccupation with her seemed to be troubling him more and more as time went on.

Lately he'd been wondering if maybe he should ditch everything and go try to find a job in or near Savannah. He couldn't imagine there would be a teaching post open in his field, though—sometimes he wished he hadn't opted for quite such a specialized area—and he honestly didn't know what else he was qualified for.

Still, there should be something. For that matter, he didn't have to work. But he couldn't imagine lounging around and living on inherited money the rest of his life, nor could he imagine joining up with Kay in the inn business. She didn't need him, anyway. She had Homer, who was becoming more valuable to her with every passing day.

Also, much as he liked Savannah, he couldn't quite imagine living there on a year-round basis. There was so much of Vermont in him. On the other hand, he was coming to the conclusion that living in Vermont without Kay would be like living in perpetual winter. . . .

Rocking back and forth as he sipped his beer and tried to force Kay out of his mind and to put together some thoughts that would make sense for a speech tomorrow, Alan saw a car coming down the road toward his property and then turning into his driveway.

The car rocked to a stop, stirring up a cloud of dust, and he noticed there was only one person in it. Then, he saw the silhouette of a head behind the wheel that even from this distance looked familiar, and his pulse began to throb erratically. When Kay got out, facing him across the scrubby lawn, he felt as if he was about to go into cardiac arrest.

Kay was wearing a bright red cotton dress and slim white sandals, and a big white straw hat, tilted back at an angle, rode atop her glossy dark hair. She was also wearing sunglasses, which made it impossible to read her expression. So when she faced him, arms akimbo, and said, "Well, when a person's about to move somewhere else he might tell a person so, wouldn't you say?" he couldn't tell from her soft Southern voice whether she was really angry, merely annoyed or, possibly, amused.

He pushed back the rocker, put aside the beer can and carefully made his way down the front steps. He stood a few paces away from Kay, regarding her warily, as if he was afraid he was disbelieving his own vision.

Kay let her eyes fill themselves with the sight of him. He'd been working around the grounds as much as he could these past couple of weeks, trying to make some order out of chaos, and he'd acquired the basis of a good tan. He was wearing faded jeans that hugged his taut hips and thighs. His white, short-sleeved knit shirt was open at the throat, revealing gold strands that curled tantalizingly. His hair, as usual, needed a good combing. To Kay, he looked like the most lovable, sexiest and totally desirable man on the face of the earth.

She saw him frown and heard him say, "Look, I did intend to tell you I'd moved."

"When?" she demanded.

"Well . . . maybe tomorrow," Alan hedged.

"Hmm," Kay said skeptically. "It's a good thing that when I went to your apartment your house-keeper was there, and she gave me directions out here. Otherwise I might have gone back to Savannah without ever catching up to you."

That, of course, was a patent lie, she thought, and had to suppress a smile. Because she was in danger of throwing her arms around Alan, devouring him with her kisses, she forced her eyes away from the face she found more fascinating than any face she'd ever seen and let them rove over the house.

"Well," she said, "you have rented yourself quite a place, haven't you? Thinking of adopting a Boy Scout troop?"

"Er," Alan said, then tried again. "Kay," he admitted, "I didn't rent this place. I bought it."

Kay whipped off the sunglasses, moved a foot or so closer and scrutinized him. "I take it," she said, "this was your grandmother's house? This is the place you talked about in Savannah, isn't it?''

"Yes." He nodded.

"And you've *bought* it?"

"Yes."

"Why, Alan? It would seem," she observed, "that you must be thinking of settling down on a rather large scale."

Alan moistened lips suddenly gone dry, and said, "I'd forgotten how big the damned place is. The day I got the key and came out here I thought..."

Kay waited, and when he didn't finish his sentence she said, "So? What did you think?"

"We can go into that later," Alan muttered uncomfortably.

She smiled at him, and he would have sworn he could feel his temperature rise. "Well," she said, "*later*'s a word with a nice sound to it."

"What do you mean?"

"There's a kind of promise to *later*," Kay said. "It means there's going to be something."

Alan looked at her and knew that whatever he had to do, wherever he had to do it, he was never going to let her go again.

He said huskily, "With us...there's going to be a lot of something."

Her mouth trembled. "That's what I was hoping you'd say," she admitted.

Neither of them could have said which one took the next step forward. They went into each other's arms and became wrapped together in a lilac-scented world and said with their lips all the things they hadn't yet put into words.

Alan felt as if it had been forever since he'd held her last, and his love and need for her became twin, irresistible forces. He cupped her face between his hands and could manage only to whisper, "You don't know how much I want to make love to you. I want to make love to you so enormously much I can't wait. Kay..."

Kay chuckled. "Is there a bed on these premises?" she asked him.

"Not much of a bed, darling."

"If it's your bed," said Kay, "then it's good enough for me."

The afternoon waned, sunset swept over the mountains and the hills and the streams and the valleys, to be nudged away by a star-filled darkness. And Alan and Kay made love.

Much later, they trailed out onto the side porch, and Alan found another rickety rocking chair for Kay to sit on. They talked, but still not about themselves.

Kay told him that Gary had found a buyer for her shares of Dillard and Abernathy; in fact, the man was probably going to take over the whole firm. It seemed certain Bill Abernathy would agree to the sale.

"And," she added, "I have some real news for you. Homer proposed to Francey and she said yes. And not just because she wants to have an on-the-scene father for her child, either. I think Francey's coming to love Homer more with every passing day. So things are working out."

She took a sip of the tall, iced drink Alan had fixed for her, then said, "Oh, there's another thing. The Creightons are going to buy my house on Oglethorpe Square."

Her lovely face was outlined by moonlight, but try though he did Alan couldn't see her expression clearly.

On the other hand, there was no trace of sadness in her voice.

"That's what you really want to do?" he asked nevertheless.

"Definitely," she said. "I'd never move back there. My place at the inn is enough of a Savannah residence, anyway."

There was something in the way she spoke that alerted him. He took a deep breath, then said, "I don't know how you're going to react to what I'm about to say. Feel free to say you think I've flipped, if you do. But..."

He paused, and after a moment Kay urged, "Come on, Alan. This curiosity is driving me crazy."

"Well...that day I came out here, the day I got the keys, I realized how big this place is and I thought to myself, 'It isn't a house, it's a hotel.' That thought, inevitably, led to other thoughts." He groaned. "Hell, Kay," he protested, "help me out on this, will you?"

"No," she said serenely. "This is one you're going to have to go alone."

He grinned wryly. "I've never been a good salesman," he confessed, "but this is a pitch I'd dearly love to put over with you. You see...there are a lot of winter sports around here. And the place is right next to Mansfield, which, after all, is a college town. Visiting parents are always looking for places to stay, and as it happens, there aren't very many of them in this particular area. So I got to thinking that this place could, maybe, be converted into an inn. There's a tenant house that could be fixed up as an annex. Even the barns could be made into dining rooms, a recreational hall, I've seen that done elsewhere and the effect can have a lot of charm. In other words, the place could become..."

"Yes?"

"A real Yankee inn," Alan finished.

Kay was silent for so long that he thought she was going to veto his whole concept, nor could he blame her. When he thought about it rationally, it *was* pretty far-out.

But then he heard her chuckle softly, and she said, "A *Yankee* inn, eh? Tell me...might there be a job opening for a Southern innkeeper?"

A couple of stars fell out of the sky and lit Alan's eyes. He managed, "Oh, God, Kay, would you? I mean, could you? I mean..."

"Why do you think I'm here?" Kay asked softly, and spoke the magic words she'd never said before. "I love you so much. Too much to spend my life in Savannah with you up here. That doesn't make sense, as I came up here to tell you. I was afraid if I waited for an invitation we'd both be old and gray...."

She went on before he could protest that. "True, I didn't know you had a potential inn ready for me to refurbish. But just looking at the surface of this place, I'm already itching to get started. The doing is the challenge, and that's the best of all. Half the fun went out of the Randolph House for me once I had it just the way it should be."

Alan said slowly, "I want to be very sure I understand exactly what you're saying."

"That's the cautious college professor in you," Kay teased.

"One more statement like that and I'll show you how cautious I am...not," he growled.

"That's something you've already shown me, my dearest," Kay said. "Not that I won't welcome future demonstrations. But right now...if you want to be sure you understand exactly what I'm saying...what I'm saying is that romance is great—and we've got plenty of that, thankfully—but when you get into the serious 'us' stage, compromise has to come into the picture. I don't think either of us has been *unwilling* to compromise, Alan, I think we just couldn't figure out how to get started. You here. Me there. So many invisible obstacles in the way. Well, you see, darling, that's the thing with invisible obstacles. We imagine some of them to be a lot bigger than they actually are. When I took a close look at ours, I knew something Francey said that first time I phoned you up here was true. We're living in an age where transportation and communications are easy, very easy, compared to anything they've ever been before. All we need is to take advantage of what's there for us to take advantage of. Are you following me?"

"Keep going," Alan instructed.

"Well, it seems to me you and I have the chance to have the best of two worlds. You can spend your vacations in Savannah—except when you go off to Egypt—and a lot of the rest of the time I'll be up here, especially now that I'm going to have a 'Yankee' inn to run. Homer can handle the Randolph House for me beautifully, most of the time, and there's always a phone at his elbow if he needs advice."

Kay paused and looked across at Alan. "You know," she said, "I'm beginning to feel awfully much as if I've been proposing to you."

"Have you?" Alan asked huskily.

"I might answer that question...if you'd return the favor," she said, her voice just a little on the shaky side.

She heard Alan's low chuckle. "Would you believe it," he told her, "I'd been thinking about chucking this whole scene and making my way South?"

Before Kay could answer that, he got up and spanned the distance between them. He tugged her out of her rocking chair and enfolded her in his arms. He put a whole vocabulary into the kiss he gave her, and she came back with an entire unspoken language of her own.

Vermont moonlight splashed the two of them, and when it silvered her hair Alan could imagine how she was going to look years from now, out here on this same porch. Beautiful. Desirable as ever. And even more his—as he would be even more hers—with every passing year.

Six exciting series for you every month... from Harlequin

Harlequin Romance·
The series that started it all

Tender, captivating and heartwarming...
love stories that sweep you off to faraway places
and delight you with the magic of love.

◆

Harlequin Presents·
Powerful contemporary love stories...as individual as the women who read them

The No. 1 romance series...
exciting love stories for you, the woman of today...
a rare blend of passion and dramatic realism.

◆

Harlequin Superromance®
It's more than romance...
it's Harlequin Superromance

A sophisticated, contemporary romance-fiction
series, providing you with a longer,
more involving read...a richer mix of complex plots,
realism and adventure.

Harlequin
American Romance™
Harlequin celebrates the American woman...

...by offering you romance stories written about American women, by American women for American women. This series offers you contemporary romances uniquely North American in flavor and appeal.

◆

Harlequin Temptation™
Passionate stories for today's woman

An exciting series of sensual, mature stories of love...dilemmas, choices, resolutions... all contemporary issues dealt with in a true-to-life fashion by some of your favorite authors.

◆

Harlequin Intrigue™
Because romance can be quite an adventure

Harlequin Intrigue, an innovative series that blends the romance you expect... with the unexpected. Each story has an added element of intrigue that provides a new twist to the Harlequin tradition of romance excellence.

Harlequin Books®

PROD-A-2

What the press says about Harlequin romance fiction...

"When it comes to romantic novels...
Harlequin is the indisputable king."
— *New York Times*

"...always with an upbeat, happy ending."
— *San Francisco Chronicle*

"Women have come to trust these
stories about contemporary people,
set in exciting foreign places."
— *Best Sellers,* New York

"The most popular reading matter of
American women today."
— *Detroit News*

"...a work of art."
— *Globe & Mail* Toronto